"I'll give you the privilege of becoming my vassal! ...Here ya go. A ceremony to bind master and servant."

LUNA ARTUR

A girl who attends Camelot International High School. She's the scum student president who sold her own Excalibur and stole exam answers.

LAST ROUND Arthurs

SCUM ARTHUR
&
HERETIC MERLIN

1

MORGAN LE FEY

The world's oldest, most terrifying sorceress, who invited Rintarou to the King Arthur Succession Battle.

"Please keep up your strength for the battle to come."

CONTENTS

LAST ROUND Arthurs

1

Taro Hitsuji

ILLUSTRATION BY
Kiyotaka Haimura

YEN ON
NEW YORK

LAST ROUND ARTHURS SCUM ARTHUR & HERETIC MERLIN

Taro Hitsuji   VOLUME 1

Translation by Jan Cash
Cover art by Kiyotaka Haimura

LAST ROUND • ARTHURS KUZUARTHUR TO GEDOU MERLIN Vol. 1
©Taro Hitsuji, Kiyotaka Haimura 2018
First published in Japan in 2018 by KADOKAWA CORPORATION, Tokyo.
English translation rights arranged with KADOKAWA CORPORATION, Tokyo through
TUTTLE-MORI AGENCY, INC., Tokyo.

English translation © 2019 by Yen Press, LLC

Yen On
150 West 30th Street, 19th Floor
New York, NY 10001

Visit us at yenpress.com
facebook.com/yenpress
twitter.com/yenpress
yenpress.tumblr.com
instagram.com/yenpress

First Yen On Edition: July 2019

Yen On is an imprint of Yen Press, LLC.
The Yen On name and logo are trademarks of Yen Press, LLC.

The publisher is not responsible for websites (or their content) that are not owned by the publisher.

Library of Congress Cataloging-in-Publication Data
Names: Hitsuji, Taro, author. | Haimura, Kiyotaka, 1973– illustrator. | Cash, Jan Mitsuko, translator.
Haimura, Kiyotaka, 1973– cover artist.
Title: Scum Arthur & Heretic Merlin / Taro Hitsuji ; illustration by Kiyotaka Haimura ; translation by
Jan Cash ; cover art by Kiyotaka Haimura.
Description: First Yen On edition. | New York, NY : Yen On, 2019. | Series: Last Round Arthurs ; Volume 1
Identifiers: LCCN 2019015603 | ISBN 9781975357504 (pbk.)
Subjects: CYAC: Gifted children—Fiction. | Contests—Fiction. | Inheritance and succession—Fiction. |
Arthur, King—Fiction.
Classification: LCC PZ7.1.H59 Sc 2019 | DDC [Fic]—dc23
LC record available at https://lccn.loc.gov/2019015603

ISBNs: 978-1-9753-5750-4 (paperback)
978-1-9753-5751-1 (ebook)

10 9 8 7 6 5 4 3 2 1

LSC-C

Printed in the United States of America

Over there is yesterday in all its radiance. Here is today,
    faded and colorless.
And tomorrow is bound in ashes.

We reached the dismal end of the play, of our dreams.
I watched it as the cold wind blew.

Yes, he was there among the Knights of the Round Table.
Together with the one they called strong, noble—the once
    and future king.

Be that as it may, their swords etched him into stone,
    disappearing into sand and verse.
Like a dream at dusk, like a mirage of a fleeting night.

I watched everything as I slumbered.
Watched as the cold wind blew.

John Sheep

FROM LAST ROUND ARTHUR

⑭pening the Stage Curtains

"…'Now, boy. Our young king. On this most holy day of our Lord and Savior, you must pull this sword from the stone,' said Merlin."

There was something unusual about this night.

Surveying the scene, one could see the countless skyscrapers towering over like gravestones and feel the dry wind weaving through darkened silhouettes. The white moon gleamed in the sky like a skull. The bone-chilling air drifted past, sometimes seemingly holding its breath, as though it, too, dreaded something sinister.

"'With all due respect, Lord Merlin,' began Sir Kay. 'It is by the will of God that whoso pulleth this sword shall not be but the rightwise king of this realm,'" recited a Japanese boy, around sixteen or seventeen and wearing a school uniform.

He was of medium height and build with cropped black hair, a straight, shapely nose, and intense almond-shaped eyes.

A bold, sarcastic smile played at the corners of his mouth.

"'Therefore, it is inconceivable that God would give it to my squire and stepbrother, Arthur.' At Sir Kay's words, 'Nay,' responded Merlin."

The boy held a worn book open in one hand.

It was a copy of *Last Round Arthur*, a first-edition book, published by Cornaliver Press—written in 1884 by John Sheep, a scholar on English folklore.

He continued to balance it in one hand as he dramatically recited its contents to himself.

"'*Ye there, Sir Ector, must understand this already. This boy had been born to this world the rightwise king of Britain and ruler of the entire world.*'"

Not a single person was there to hear his performance, read like a true balladeer. That was because he stood on the roof of a skyscraper—on its ledge, to be exact.

"'*Ye lord, ye knight, bear witness. Christ, born onto this night, will show us a miracle to point at who the rightwise king of this realm is to be.*'"

Even with the whole city sprawling out below him, he didn't seem fearful as he stood alone, illuminated from behind by the silver moon.

"At Merlin's wishes, Arthur grasped the handle of the sword in the stone and pulled it out with ease, so all the people therewithal proclaimed in shock, '*We must make Arthur our king. It is God's will that he be king.*'"

Satisfied, he slammed the book closed.

"...Arthur became the true king of the nobles and common people, sworn to rule thenceforth with justice. Thus, the curtains drew open to the adventures and battles of Arthur—*rex quondam, rexque futuras*—the once and future king.'"

As he finished, the boy placed the book at his feet.

Then he glanced down with stony eyes and eyesight that far surpassed any normal man. Soon, he narrowed in on his target in the streets—inky in the night like the bottom of the sea... He smiled ever so slightly.

"Well…guess it's time to start…"

Then—he jumped.

From the roof of the skyscraper, he dived right into the darkness below.

At first glance, it looked like he was committing suicide.

But as he plummeted down, pulled by the force of gravity, there was no trace of sorrow or hopelessness that one might expect in the face of a person attempting to die.

"This is where the dream continues—the battle to become his successor!"

As he hurtled through the sky, his cacophonous laughter echoed and echoed through the night.

CHAPTER 1

Kings and Jacks and Jokers

Sharp and sprightly, a shower of silver streaks darted and danced around, tracing arcs in the air and rippling as they flew. Each time these flashes met one another, screeching metallic clangs echoed and cut through the night, as sparks burst forth and flickered.

Darkness settled deeply in a valley between the skyscrapers.

Under the moonlight, two girls clashed against each other fiercely with their blades. One girl's weapon of choice was a bastard sword. The other's was a rapier. Their weapons were old-fashioned for this day and age, as if they were in the wrong era.

"HYAAAAAAAAAAH!"

"UUUUUUUGH?!"

If their weapons seemed out of place, the girls were even stranger. To summarize their uncanniness, the two were moving at a speed *far beyond what could be considered human.*

They'd travel a dozen yards in one step. With a leap, they'd launch themselves high into the air, and in a single breath, their swords glinted countless times as they slashed rapidly at each other. As they whipped their weapons around, the sheer force of the attacks created a vacuum, splitting the hard asphalt like paper. Even the best athletes in the world were no match for their agility.

There was something extraordinary about them.

Their frenzied fight progressed under the stars without anyone else's knowledge. The moonlight bounced and twinkled off the swords, and more flares of light came from their gritting blades. But to the eyes of a normal person, the pair would've only registered as flickers in the darkness.

If anyone could see the two, they'd quickly realize the girl with the bastard sword was at an obvious disadvantage.

"Oh-ho-ho-ho! Is that all you can muster, Luna Artur?!"

The girl with the rapier flipped around and thrust three times in succession. She moved at lightning speed, going for the forehead, the stomach, the chest—with three glimmers of silver light, she meteorically assaulted the bastard-sword girl.

"—UUUUUUGH?!"

The bastard sword nimbly met the sudden lunging attacks that pressed her. She knocked one strike aside, thrust another away—and the third blow met her blade.

SHLIIIIING! The air vibrated with the ear-piercing sound as they collided in an extravagant blast of sparkling lights.

"GAAAH?!"

The impact sent the bastard-sword girl flying, tilting backward as she tried to regain her balance.

Based on appearance alone, the rapier seemed thinner, lighter, and weaker compared to its large counterpart, but in truth, it was overwhelmingly superior in combat.

"—Gah?!" Keeping her distance from the rapier girl, she took two, three steps back. "Hah…hah…hah…," she panted, steadying her breath as she readied both arms again.

She looked fifteen, maybe sixteen, a polished young girl of

mixed Japanese and English descent, wearing the uniform of a neighboring school. Bathed in the white moonlight, her blond hair gave off a faint glow, gleaming like gold and drawing her out of the shadows. It framed her face like a halo.

Her dignified eyes were large with shining iolite irises—almost feline in nature. Sheer will and determination beamed out of them, flashing like blue flames and piercing through the darkness. They seemed to bore into the soul of those who stood before her.

Her skin was whiter than snow, her face deeply chiseled and defined with a delicate little chin. Though her curves were elegant and feminine, her limbs carried a youthful vigor… It was as if her features were pulled together by divine will, inspired by a sculpture of a goddess carved from the finest marble in the world.

She might have been hidden under the veil of night, but her presence and mystique couldn't be concealed. It didn't matter if someone had seen her a million times before—she'd still be breath-takingly captivating with each and every look.

Unfortunately, her sword was extraordinarily…ordinary. It was a plain and rugged bastard sword—incredibly commonplace in medieval times. Compared to her, the weapon was mediocre at best.

"Hmph…you think you could beat me with such a shabby sword?" sneered the rapier girl as she rammed its tip at her.

This girl from Northern Ireland wore a black dress coat and also looked about fifteen or sixteen years old with silver hair that instantly brought to mind shooting stars soaring across a winter night's sky. In pigtails, she was like a white rabbit racing against a snowy backdrop. With her sharp emerald eyes, pointed face, and porcelain skin as smooth as a bisque doll, her appearance was reminiscent of an elf from a Tolkienesque legend.

And the sword in her hand was worth a mention—or two.

It was a rapier, but obviously not just any normal one. Its blade was forged from a curious metal that had a peculiar luster, neither gold nor silver, and its guard and hilt were adorned with glittering decorations. The sword was clearly not man-made—it was too fiendish and holy.

"Don't you dare underestimate me, Luna Artur," she spat, turning the point of her rapier at her opponent—Luna. "I won't let you mock me any further," she warned. "Using *that* kind of sword on a fellow candidate hoping to succeed King Arthur! How indecent of you... Now draw your Excalibur."

Her hunger for battle and intimidating demeanor assailed Luna, nearly knocking her out.

"If you don't fight with everything you're worth—if you won't face a fellow King with your Excalibur, then this isn't a true battle!" she cried out. "Now draw your King's sword...your Excalibur!"

Her rapier—her so-called Excalibur—sparkled divinely in the night.

For a while, Luna stared straight at her opponent and her visible hostility, practically radiating out of her entire body. She allowed herself to be ridiculed for a little while longer before opening her mouth to respond...

"Why, my dear old (ex)-friend Felicia, I'm afraid that's impossible," she announced.

"What do you mean?"

"Like I said. I can't fight you with my Excalibur."

"What? Unbelievable! Are you dare implying you're unwilling to hurt me because we were once friends—*now* of all times?!" Rapier in hand, Felicia narrowed her eyes in indignation. "You belittle me! I've already *prepared* myself to enter the King Arthur Succession Battle! I can't stand that you're feigning kindness when it's actually contempt!"

In a rage, Felicia channeled her untamable passion into a roar at her opponent.

"Well, that's because...I sold it...," Luna started to admit.

Her (ex)-friend froze like a statue.

"...Because I sold my Excalibur...for money."

"..."

"That's why I don't have my Excalibur right now. So...it's im-poss-ible!"

Heh. The corners of her mouth loosened slightly into a gentle smile.

"WHAAAAAAAAAAAAAAAAAAAAAAAAAAAAAAT?!" Felicia screeched hysterically, blinking in disbelief. "No way!! You sold it?! Why would you do such a thing?!"

"Heh. I had a teeeeny bit of trouble getting together some money... But wow!" she merrily recounted. "That thing was super-old, but I guess it's still the legendary sword Excalibur! I made a killing off it, so—"

"Why you FOOLISH GIIIIIIIIIIIIIIIIIIIIIIIIIIIIIIIIIIIIIIIRL!" Felicia's voice rose by an octave. "D-do you understand *anything*, Luna?! The Excalibur is essential! It's a King's main weapon, and you need it as a participant in the King Arthur Succession Battle! What are you going to do after losing it this early on?!"

"It's okay! I'll save up and buy it back sometime!" she said placatingly in an easy-breezy tone. "Anyway, let's put a pin in this for today..."

She tried to leave.

"Like I'd allow THAAAAAAAAAAAAAAAAAAAAAAAT?!"

"UWHAAAAAAAAAAAAAAAAAAAAAAAAAAAAAGH?!"

With merciless zephyrean speed, Felicia slashed at Luna's back, an attack that she barely managed to block by a paper-thin margin.

"Whaddaya think you're doing, Felicia?! You're taking this joke too far!"

"Joke be damned! You think I'd let this slide?! I'll make you drop out of the battle here and now! Prepare yourself!" she exploded, her voice shattering the night as she ranted without pause.

"O-okay...um, how much money do you want?! Ha-ha-ha...," Luna chuckled, forming a coin-shaped circle with her pointer finger and thumb.

"It's not about money! Do you take me for an idiot?!" She callously plunged her sword.

"EEEEEEEEK?! Wai—wait a second! I—I got it, okay! Let's settle this with the Jacks! With the knights!" she blustered in a single breath as she took her distance in a fluster. "I mean, the true King will stand at the pinnacle of humanity as the ruler of the world, right? And, um, a King's worth is reflected in the knights that swear their allegiance to them. We're Kings! In that case, shouldn't we leave our fates in the hands of the Jacks?! We should, right?!"

"Hmph. Well...there might be some merit in that," Felicia agreed, sheathing her sword and thrusting out a hand. "Your claims are in-line with the goals of the succession battle. In that case, we'll have a fight between our Jacks... Challenge accepted!"

Her arm was adorned by a gleaming silver bracelet, decorated with a stone fragment with the inscription VIII.

"*Keter Chokhmah Binah Chesed Gevurah Tiphereth Netzach Hod Yesod Malkuth. —Mana, disperse and circulate through my Sefirot to my Da'at!*" Felicia recited. A phosphorescent light rose out of her body.

This was her Aura, her astral light—the source of life, the sublimation of her mana, and a power fueled by miracles.

"*My Aura, guide my knight. The eighth seat of the Round Table, heed my call!*"

With that, her Aura burst into several streaks of purple light, electrifying the air, as they ran and danced through the surroundings. After becoming intricately tangled together, they created a magic circle that transformed into a Gate.

This Gate summoned and materialized a *knight* into the world. The figure was muscular and youthful, probably around twenty. His hair was cropped and blond like a lion's mane, his eyes a vivid green, and his masculine face was well put together. He was a young knight, full of majesty, who carried a gleaming sword and wore white armor on his tall, big-boned, gaunt form.

This was the secret ritual of the Dame du Lac—the *Knight Summoning*. This miracle would call forth a knight from King Arthur's Round Table to serve as a vassal, a Jack. This magic could only be performed by a King—a candidate competing to succeed Arthur's throne.

"I have humbly arrived on your command…my liege," he announced as he came to stand next to Felicia, his armor clattering all the while.

This knight was nothing to scoff at. First, there was his understated valor, which made modern weapons seem like nothing but playthings. He had a powerful and overwhelming presence that shook people's souls.

He was beyond human—the phrase described him so perfectly that it was impossible they would fit anyone else better.

"Hmm? That looks like a pretty strong Jack. I don't have any complaints about having him as an opponent!" Luna boasted coolly even while facing him.

"Hmph. Hurry and call your Jack."

"Well, don't get ahead of yourself. I'll call mine right now."

With a collected expression, she glanced at Felicia, who snorted unhappily, and without skipping a beat, Luna grabbed the stone pendant on her neck with the inscription III.

"Here I go... *Keter Chokhmah Binah Chesed Gevurah Tiphereth Netzach Hod Yesod Malkuth— Mana, disperse and circulate through my Sefirot to my Da'at!*"

As she recited the words, a blinding glow emanated from her body, too.

"*My Aura, guide my knight. The third seat of the Round Table, heed my call!*"

In midair, a Gate opened to summon a knight from the Round Table as the stars seemed to waltz and cut through the darkness. From that fantastical scene, a girl dropped down to stand next to Luna.

She was beautiful. Under the faint moonlight, she was unimaginably beautiful—almost ethereal to the point she nearly glittered. She seemed barely older than the girl who summoned her.

Her vibrant hair could only be described as glacial-blue flames— with piercing blue eyes to match. She was like ice incarnate. And as if her beauty wasn't already beyond human comprehension, her whole body also gave off a dauntless air, making her seem unapproachable.

It only took one glance to see that she possessed power far beyond the reach of any ordinary human...meaning she was the same type of being as the male knight before her.

"Hah... How's that? What do you think of my Jack?"

With this girl next to her, Luna proudly puffed up her chest.

"Whaaat?!" Felicia shouted.

"Wh-what...is this...?! This is absurd...!" her knight stuttered.

Their eyes widened in astonishment as they looked at the Jack.

"Wh-what is wrong with that Jack...?! Luna...why would you do this?!" Felicia squeezed out, gulping and breaking into a cold sweat as she lost her cool.

She was perturbed by the state of this poor Jack.

Her elegant curves were emphasized by a leotard and fishnet tights—not of her own volition, of course—and she wore a bunny-eared headband… No matter how anyone looked at her, she was a bunny girl, plain and simple.

"…Huh?" Luna scowled upon realizing her Jack's condition.

"Sniffle, sniffle…" The bunny girl in question hugged her own body in embarrassment and scrunched herself up in an attempt to keep their eyes off her. Her face turned beet red, and her entire body shook and trembled.

"Wha—what's with you?! What's with that ridiculous, skimpy costume?! Where's your sword?! Your armor?! What in the world happened?! Are you even taking this seriously?! Are you an idiot?!" Luna hounded, causing her knight to sniffle even harder.

"Uh… Y-you were the one who forced me to take that sketchy escorting job because you needed money! Even after I told you I didn't want to do it—!"

"Oh yeah! I completely forgot! Tee-hee. ★" Luna stuck out her tongue adorably and bopped her own head.

"H-how could you…? How can you treat a knight of the Round Table like this…? This is too much for me…" The knight whimpered, overcome with tears as she slumped over.

"S-sorry! I shouldn't have made you do that, Sir Kay! I said sorry!" Luna pleaded, quickly trying to comfort Sir Kay, the crying bunny girl.

Felicia and her Jack stared at the unfolding farce with unimpressed eyes for a while.

"…Clean them up," she ordered expressionlessly.

"…Understood." The young knight readied his sword like a mechanical doll.

"Wait?! W-w-w-wait a second! W-we should talk it out first, shouldn't we?! Right?! Violence doesn't solve anything!"

"Silence! Your words mean nothing!" she yelled, brushing aside Luna, who was pitifully tenacious. "You pretty much sold your precious Excalibur for spare change! You made your Jack work for money! You're absolutely unacceptable! There's no way you're fit to serve as King! I cast my judgment upon you!"

"Don't you think you're being kind of unreasonable?!"

"Act now, my Jack! Please beat this idiot within an inch of her life!"

"As you wish!"

Brandishing his sword, he stormed toward Luna at a terrifying speed, tearing through the space between them. Compared to his seraphic moves, Felicia and Luna seemed to move at a snail-like pace.

"Ugh—! Now! Get down, Luna!" Sir Kay rose to defend Luna with her weapon, but—

"RAAAAAHHHHH—!!"

In the same moment, he closed in on them with the feral ferocity of a lion and swung his weapon to rend them in two.

The two Jacks' swords crashed against each other—clanging and making the air ring.

"UUUUUGH—?!"

On the receiving end of a magnificent blow, Sir Kay flew through the air like a baseball, blasting through the glass-paned wall of a nearby building.

"Wha—?! He's strong—!" Luna yelped as she witnessed this and held her breath.

Felicia's knight didn't waste another moment and turned his attention to Luna. "Prepare yourself!" he blared, closing in and swinging his sword down on her.

Or at least, that's what was supposed to happen—but something else got in his way.

"—Gngh?!" The young knight must have noticed something suddenly, as his sword stopped in its tracks before pivoting and finally sweeping over his head.

At the same time, a loud screech of metal tore through the air and echoed around them once again. He'd raised his blade to meet the sword of *someone else.*

In a flash, that *someone* twisted skillfully in midair, and their second sword flickered and twirled in a fantastical display, like lightning. While still upside down, whoever the newcomer was, they aimed for the young knight's torso.

"Tch!" Attempting to defend himself with his sword, the knight braced for impact, and their blades thundered. The force of the blow was great enough to knock him far back despite his stature, causing the soles of his feet to cut a path of sparks into the asphalt for several yards.

"You coward! Reveal yourself!" His eyes attempted to locate the tactless intruder, who'd spinelessly assaulted him from above.

But this third party was gone—without a trace.

"Heh… Where do you think you're looking? I'm over here."

This voice bounced and bounded off the walls, making anyone who listened stop in their tracks. That was all one could do.

At some point, the newcomer had moved behind Felicia…and held a bare blade to the base of her neck.

"No way…" With the chilling sensation of cold metal brushing against her skin, she was completely dumbfounded…

"Wha—?! Impossible?! When did you—?!" The knight's eyes were open wide, practically about to split at the corners. He could only stand there, burning the image of his own lord driven into a corner into his retinas.

"Oh, don't even think about trying anything funny, all right? Yeah, you, the Jack over there," warned the intruder sporting a

thin, ghastly smile, bringing the blade closer to Felicia's neck while he spoke. "Pull any tricks, and I'll slice this girl's head clean off without blinking an eye."

The third party was a boy about sixteen or seventeen, Japanese, and wearing the uniform of a nearby school. With the exception of the swords he held in his hands, he looked relatively ordinary.

But the tenor of his threat suggested he'd really kill her if he wanted to... There was something inexplicably dreadful about him—enough to make a person's skin crawl.

It was obvious he wasn't any ordinary person.

At this astonishingly unexpected turn of events, the four—Luna, Felicia, the young knight, and Sir Kay, poking her head out from a gap in the broken wall—were completely stupefied and stunned.

This was a group of beings with supernatural strength, capable of dashing across the sky in a single leap and splitting open the earth with their swords. But even they were overwhelmed by the figure before them.

"What—? Who *are* you?" croaked Felicia, voice quivering as the stranger continued to press a sword against her neck from behind. "You couldn't be…another participant in the King Arthur Succession Battle…could you?"

"Well, I guess I am. Not like I got an official invitation from the Dame du Lac."

"Th-then…you're a King? Or are you a Jack?"

Bam! Instead of an answer, he kicked Felicia in the back, launching her into the air.

"Ahhh?!"

"M-my liege!" Felicia's knight moved fast as lightning to catch her in his arms.

"Pfft!" The boy laughed. In that moment, his figure blurred sideways, disappearing in a mist.

"—Huh?!"

He appeared suddenly in front of Luna, shielding her.

It was almost as though he'd teleported.

"Well, *I* couldn't care less if I cut her head off here and now, but...well, where's the fun in that? I'll let you slide for today— Get lost!" shouted the boy, smiling boldly at Felicia and the young knight. "What? The King Arthur Succession Battle has just begun. We've got tons of time to play around. Let's call today a friendly introduction and leave it at that. How does that sound?"

His laughter was absolutely radiant, like a kid who'd gotten his hands on a new toy... At the same time, something about him seemed insane.

"Grr...!!" The defeated pair glared at the calm, composed boy. "What in the world...?"

Unable to understand the current state of affairs, Luna and Sir Kay could only blink in response.

For a while, this tension and anxiety hung in the air and the silence.

"...Very well. As you request, I shall withdraw for today...," Felicia eventually declared, returning her Excalibur to its sheath.

"My King, are you sure?"

"I don't mind. I hardly intend to lose to this boy in a fair fight, but...if he'd felt like it, I could have been slain a few moments earlier. If I don't repay this debt, I'd be violating the code of chivalry. We'll leave it at this for tonight."

"As you wish...," her knight solemnly replied to her decision.

"You there...may I have your name?"

"It's Rintarou—Rintarou Magami." The boy snickered with a savage grin.

"Rintarou...Magami...?" Until that moment, Luna had been completely silent but now responded, befuddled.

"...I'll remember this, Mr. Magami." No sooner had she heard his name than Felicia glared at the boy—at Rintarou—with rage. "I won't forget this insolence! Prepare yourself for when we meet again! I swear on my pride and sword that I, Felicia Ferald, will strike you down!"

"Sure, I'd like to see you try. Not that I think you've got the skills for it anyway."

Ignoring his taunts as he shrugged shoulders, Felicia turned to Luna. "Lastly, this is a warning. You'd do well to withdraw from the King Arthur Succession Battle."

"Huh?! Why?! There's no way I'd do that! I wanna become King, too!" She stamped her feet like a spoiled little brat.

"I'm telling you, you can't do it," Felicia muttered in a low voice. "Before the battle started, the management arm of the Dame du Lac evaluated you. Do you even know what they said?" She looked coolly and pitifully at her. "You've got the weakest Jack, you drew the weakest Excalibur, and you're the worst candidate for King Arthur... Everyone thinks you're a laughingstock."

"...!" Luna was silent.

"The rumors were true: Your Jack's unbelievably weak. In that case, your Excalibur must not amount to much, either... I suppose it doesn't matter, even if you did sell it." After denouncing her mercilessly, Felicia turned away. "By crossing swords with you today, I'm now confident you deserve your title as the weakest candidate. Even if you take part in the battle, you'll only end up dying in vain. Luna, I advise you to withdraw. I'm warning you as your former friend. If you won't listen...then you leave me no course but to force you out."

At the end, there was something left unsaid, a sort of steadfast resolve, but Felicia didn't explain and left her opponent with those words as she and her knight launched themselves off the ground and flew high into the sky—weaving and disappearing between the skyscrapers.

"They're finally gone..." After confirming they'd completely left the scene, Rintarou sheathed his swords.

Then he turned to Luna, standing behind him still confused.

"Now then...you didn't get hurt, right? ...Your Highness."

"Huh? No, well...I didn't. But what's up with you?"

"Heh, you'll know soon enough," he nihilistically spat, leaving the question unanswered and turning his back to Luna. "Well, that's that... Today's the opening act. Peace out, Your Highness!"

Then he started running at a terrific speed and, in the next moment, vanished into the twilight streets like the wind.

"Ah...seriously, what's with that guy...?" Luna, now standing alone, could only sigh.

"I can't fathom who he might be." Finally getting back up, Sir Kay had come to stand by her side. "...But I doubt he's up to any good. Please make sure you stay on guard, Luna."

With that comment, the knight stared with the sharp, alert eyes of a warrior, piercing through the darkness after Rintarou... in her bunny girl costume.

"Well, the King Arthur Succession Battle has finally started... It's going to be a long road from here on out." But despite her words, Luna had a slight smile forming on her lips. "Hmm...Rintarou Magami...huh? ...Ha-ha-ha..."

At that moment, another scene was playing out in a back alley between some buildings.

"What a blunder... He completely spoiled my start."

There, concealing herself, was Felicia bitterly cursing Rintarou.

"I was supposed to force Luna Artur out tonight... If only that guy…if only that Rintarou Magami hadn't intervened! Who in the world is he?!"

"Felicia…" Standing beside her as she seethed was her young knight, reserved and quiet.

…At that moment, another voice spoke out to them.

"Oh my, what a disappointment, Felicia…or should I call you Lord Ferald?"

Though she was boiling in this alley with anger and resentment, it was instantly brought down to a simmer by this frosty voice—as if doused in ice water. From the deep shadows of the alley, these words suddenly intermingled and tied themselves tautly to the pair.

It didn't seem to carry any human warmth—ceaselessly ruthless and cold.

"'I'll handle the King Arthur succession candidate Luna Artur myself and force her to drop out…' You were so enthusiastic, so eager, but the state you're in now… Why, as an ally, I find you deplorable."

Two figures, one big and one small, approached them.

It was the larger shadow who'd ridiculed Felicia. "You're from one of the many old noble houses carrying King Arthur's bloodline in modern times. As the head of the house of Duke Ferald, aren't you embarrassed? Lord Ferald…"

"L-Lord Gloria?!" Felicia yelped, not even attempting to hide her surprise and suspicion. "Why are you here?! What business could you possibly have?!"

"Oh… No need to be so on guard. We've joined forces in the King Arthur Succession Battle—in order to be the last ones standing… Aren't we basically comrades?" The shadow—Lord Gloria—sneered in considerable glee.

It was difficult to make out the figure under the dark veil of night in the alleyway.

"When a comrade's in distress, you'd like to help them out... Isn't that natural?" Lord Gloria dragged forward, inching closer... and suddenly drew a sword out from the murky abyss.

It was as long as a person was tall—a two-hander. The blade was pitch-black and thick, the hilt cast in a sinister shape. The very sight of it was soul wrenching, as though grating on one's sanity... That was the kind of ominous aura the sword unleashed in the space between them.

This was bad. That sword was bad news.

There was something about the sword that evoked an instinctual fight-or-flight response.

"Yes... With my Excalibur's powers, we could handle those small fry..."

"Please wait!" Felicia called out sharply, while internally reprimanding herself for cowering in response to his frigid suggestion. "There's no room for you to step in here, Lord Gloria! This isn't your time!"

With that, she yanked out her own Excalibur and turned it on Lord Gloria. The tip of it trembled slightly.

"By the name of my household, I, Felicia Ferald, swear to force Luna Artur to drop out by my hand! She's *my* prey. If you interfere, you'll be violating the code of chivalry! And if you choose to oppose me, then our alliance is over!"

"—?!" Next to her, the knight's eyes flung open in surprise.

You're doing this, my liege? Are you really starting this here? With this man?

As he picked up on Felicia's desperate, steadfast resolve, he wordlessly readied himself to protect Felicia. Suddenly, the two were assailed by an intense premonition of death, coiling around them as if it were a poisonous snake.

Gazing upon them, Lord Gloria seemed amused as the two shrank back from him...

"Ah-ha-ha, I'm only kidding, Lord Ferald. I won't do anything to harm your precious friend," he teased, thrusting his sinister sword back into the darkness from whence it came. "I'm counting on the elven blood that runs thick in your veins. When Dame du Lac announces the quest for the four treasures, your powers are bound to come in handy. We've formed an alliance, after all... Besides, we're Kings, one and the same. Let's be a little more friendly with each other, shall we?"

"...!" Felicia watched Lord Gloria with extreme caution and slowly put her rapier back in its scabbard without breaking focus. Her fingers were still faintly quivering.

"Well, if that's settled...what about that Rintarou Magami? Was that his name? He's sort of a nuisance," Lord Gloria cursed, without any concern for her wretched state. "What in the world is he? It doesn't seem like he's a King from King Arthur's bloodline, and he's not a Knight of the Round Table...so not a Jack, much less a Queen who grants us our quests..."

In that case...

"Ha-ha-ha... Then maybe we can take him at face value to be a Joker?" stipulated the smaller shadow, nestling closely to Lord Gloria.

In no way did the shadow look like a Jack, as the figure was cloaked from head to toe in a hooded pitch-black robe. But based on voice and build alone, the silhouette seemed somehow feminine, womanly.

"Oh? Do you know anything about him?"

"...No." After a moment of silence, the woman in the hood quietly shook her head. "But I know he's an aberration. The organization running this King Arthur Succession Battle, Dame du Lac, does not approve of these uninvited players... Yes, I believe he's like *me*."

Then, as if something was funny, she chuckled to herself. "I see, a Joker. How fitting. Ha-ha-ha... Regardless, this is a one-sided game, a guaranteed win. Well...I'll chalk it up as entertainment."

In genuine delight, Lord Gloria also let out a guffaw. "Now then, let's get back to our conversation, Lord Ferald. Just as promised, Luna Artur is your prey. I won't interfere... Is that fine with you?"

"...As long as you promise, I have no complaints."

"But...if I see you can't handle someone the likes of Luna... well, you understand what will happen, don't you?" Lord Gloria gave her a composed grin.

Was there any other person in the world who could cause such terror and fear with a simple smile?

"Ngh?!"

Beyond this masked smile was ill will and intimidating malice—bottomless in depth. Felicia felt as though she were nothing more than a child.

"I expect...results from this coming battle." With these parting words, the man turned on his heel and disappeared into the back of the alleyway.

The hooded woman followed after him like a shadow.

"...Luna...I..."

Felicia could only watch the pair leave as a distraught expression marred her face.

CHAPTER 2

Rintarou Magami

The scene was the international city of Avalonia.

In the coastal waters of the archipelago of Japan, this futuristic city was built on the vast man-made island of New Avalon.

This artificial island had originally been built as a foothold to reach new forms of energy reserves, lying in vast amounts at the bottom of the waters nearby.

But thanks to its location, New Avalon encouraged the rapid accumulation of foreign currencies and served as a convenient place to make deals and distribute goods, which caused companies from countries around the world to set up shop and invest in the city. This further expanded the need for other businesses and marketplaces, accelerating the upward spiral of supply and demand. As a result, people of all races and cultures mingled and mixed together there—aptly earning it the label of an international city.

If Adam Smith were still alive, his eyes would have sprung out of his head had he seen the pervasive effect of these energy reserves on the economy. He might have even fainted.

The more money was poured into the city, the more it profited... It was a modern-day gold rush, or so sang the choir. With dreams of getting rich quick, the endless stream of young businesspeople and investors never petered out.

It was the hottest city in the world, an island made of fantasies—where dreams could become reality.

It was the gathering place for the vigor and energy of people around the globe.

Let us raise the curtain in this international city of Avalonia.

"Phew! Yesterday's demonstration went perfectly!"

It was morning in Area Three of Avalonia.

Rintarou Magami was in an upbeat mood as he walked along a large road, littered with a handful of pedestrians.

He was dressed in a new school uniform—a blazer, leather shoes, and a bag. These were issued by Camelot International High School, where he was transferring that day.

He'd gone as far as to move and transfer from mainland Japan to this island to participate in the King Arthur Succession Battle, held by a collective of part-human, part-fairy women called the Dame du Lac.

"Hmph, well…the King Arthur Succession Battle, huh?"

It was the same King Arthur who'd spearheaded the knights of the Round Table in the fight for his people and the world. This legend was not a folktale but an irrefutable historical fact. After reaching his end, exhausted from battle, King Arthur's soul continued to slumber in the legendary Avalon Island… It's said someday in the future, when the human world falls into chaos, he will wake from his sleep to save the world once again.

The King Arthur Succession Battle was a magical ceremony to revive King Arthur.

"Eleven people from the bloodline of King Arthur, the Kings, will participate with eleven knights of the Round Table, their respective Jacks, in a fierce, all-out battle to succeed the King.

"The four Queens will sequentially announce four quests, which the participants need to complete to collect King Arthur's four treasures… In other words, the holy sword known as the Treasure of the Spade, the holy grail known as the Treasure of the Heart, the holy lance known as the Treasure of the Club, and the holy stone known as the Treasure of the Diamond. The King with all four will be named King Arthur's successor—the Last Round Arthur.

"They'll inherit his soul to become the second King Arthur, holding the entire world in the palm of their hands and earning the honor of becoming the rightful King of all… What an exciting prospect. It'd be a waste not to stick my head into this fun."

As he muttered to himself, Rintarou let out a contained chuckle.

"Anyway, I'm not a King carrying his bloodline or a Jack summoned from Camlann Hill. In order to get my teeth in this fight, I need to join forces with one of the Kings, but…"

In that case, which of the eleven Kings would he serve?

"Hmph…that much is obvious. Yeah, Luna Artur… I've decided she's my king."

That's why he'd made contact with her the previous night—to flaunt his power.

It went without saying that Rintarou Magami wasn't a normal person. To tell you the truth, he'd been born with unimaginable power beyond any human being.

In layman's terms, he was what one could call a reincarnation. And he had enough power to cheat the system.

He'd use his powers in this peaceful world to get even with those blasted Dame du Lac jerks. He'd have his fun with them… That was his ulterior motive.

That's right... I'm not good or bad... I'm a Joker.

Rintarou grinned and raised his head.

Spread out in front of him were plain buildings inspired by Western aesthetics. In the distance, he could see the gate to Camelot International High School, enclosed by a wrought iron fence. Based off Western castles and noble estates, the school buildings towered over the campus in pride.

For some reason, during the early planning stages for Avalonia, the European—particularly English—corporations placed the majority of their bids to lobby for a distinctly European cityscape.

Anyone who entered this castle-esque campus would feel as though they were wandering straight into a novel.

"Now then...Luna Artur was in Class 2-C, wasn't she?"

Of course, Rintarou was a natural. He didn't miss a beat. He'd already laid the groundwork by falsifying his documents to guarantee he'd transfer into the same class as Luna. This was a piece of cake for Rintarou. After all, life was rigged in his favor.

"Heh-heh-heh... I bet she'll be surprised when she sees me, huh? I wonder how dumb her face is gonna look. I'm *so* looking forward to it."

As he chuckled to himself, he calmly stepped onto the school grounds.

Right as Rintarou passed through the school gate and entered the front yard, he saw something before him.

"What the hell is thiiiiiiiiiiiiiiiiiiiiiiiiiiiiiiiiiiiiiiiiiiiiiiiiiiiiiiiiiis—?!"

Rintarou was taken aback, and a dumb look came over his face.

It was hard to believe the sight in front of him: A giant stage had been constructed in the middle of that yard, and a large crowd of students—chiefly boys—was pushing toward the stage.

On top of it was a familiar girl.

"Hey, everyone! ★ WHOO-HOO! ♪ Thanks for coming so early in the morning—!"

Those flaming-blue eyes and hair were unmistakable—it was the girl who'd been dressed in a bunny suit the night before: Luna's Jack, Sir Kay.

Well, she wasn't in a bunny girl outfit now but a sparkly, frilly, cutesy costume fit for an idol. Of course, the boys were incredibly receptive to it.

Coupled with her nonpareil good looks, she gave off the illusion that she was a real-life idol who'd come to campus to perform.

"YAAAH! ♪ How are you all doing today?! ★" Sir Kay energetically yelled in a flirtatious voice with the mic in one hand while she waved the other.

The students surrounding the stage each lifted a fist into the air and went into a frenzy.

"""""YEAHHHHHHHHHHHHHHHHHHHHHHHHHHHH!"""""
"""""Li'l Kay!"""""
"""""Li'l Kay!"""""
"""""We L-O-V-E you, li'l Kay!"""""
"""""YEAHHHHHHHHHHHHHHHHHHHHHHHHHHHH!"""""

They were filled with fantastic passion and consumed by zeal. In fact, their enthusiasm was enough to rival the live performances of a certain idol group in Japan. With bloodshot eyes and excitement cranked up to the maximum, the audience and their over-the-top delirium...to put it mildly, they were terrifying.

"Ah-ha! ♪ Yeah! You're a great crowd, and you make me so happy! I can really feel your energy! ★" Facing chaos and reckless passion, Sir Kay turned around on the stage, her skirt flaring up, to make way for her signature pose... "*Sniffle*... Why am I, a proud knight, doing...this...?"

Upon closer examination, her face was red from embarrassment, seemingly on the brink of tears, and her whole body shook. No matter how anyone looked at it, she was apparently pushing herself to her limits.

Despite that...

"""""YEAHHHHHHHHHHHHHHHHHHHHHHHHHHHH!"""""

"I love when you act like you don't want to do this! It's HOTTTTTTTTTT!"

"Like, it makes me want to be even meaner! You're GREEEEEEEEEEEEEEEEEEEEEEEAAAAAAAAAAAAAAAT!"

"""""Li'l Kay! Keep it going! Keep it up!"""""

"""""YEAHHHHHHHHHHHHHHHHHHHHHHHHHHHH!"""""

It seemed the students didn't mind at all.

"Ugh...th-then I'm gonna do it! You make my heart throb... and I'm gonna make sure to spread it to the ends of the earth! Here's a new song! 'The Knight of My Love'!" With that, a pop song came on the speakers, and Sir Kay despairingly started to sing.

"""""YEAHHHHHHHHHHHHHHHHHHHHHHHHHHHH!"""""

The whole courtyard was dominated by a roar of excited cheering.

Well, they couldn't even catch the lyrics of the song, much less hear it, as their earth-shattering screams surged through the campus.

"...What the hell is this?" Rintarou was flabbergasted by the uproar threatening to rupture his eardrums.

"Huh...? You've really done it this time, President Luna."

"...Yeah. Another big hit."

He noticed a booth set up a little ways from him in a tent labeled STUDENT COUNCIL EXECUTIVE COMMITTEE. It was probably the managers of the curious live performance. Or rather, the several students on standby were the ones pulling the invisible strings behind this whole operation.

In the middle of the group was a certain girl. As if a king on his throne, she was cockily lounging in a plastic folding chair with her legs crossed, drinking from a wineglass filled with a deep crimson beverage (probably grape juice). That was unmistakably Luna Artur.

"So anyway... How were the ticket sales?" she asked, sipping out of her wineglass.

"We sold out, of course!"

"We were pretty aggressive about the price this time around. But it made the tickets go even faster, never mind hurt ticket sales!" joyfully reported one of the henchmen (an officer of the student council) around her.

"Heh... Next time, let's make VIP seats three times the price!"

"Yes, that'd definitely work! We could even price them five times, no, ten times higher!"

"I'm sure fans of Kay will be scrambling for them no matter what the price!"

"Ah-ha-ha-ha-ha-ha-haaa! Just as I thought! Kay's a money tree! Felicia hasn't got an eye for *anything* if she thinks my talented Jack was the short straw!"

"Huh? What's a Jack? What are you talking about?"

"Just talking to myself! Don't worry about it, ah-ha-ha-ha-ha-ha-ha-ha-ha-haaaa!" Luna laughed loudly, basking in comfort and luxury. "At the end of the show, Kay will push me as a candidate for the next student council election, and I'll have the votes of all these pigs. The presidency is as good as mine... Mwa-ha-ha, it's the perfect plan!"

"Yes, perfect. Plus, the current student council Executive Committee is the only reason these people can even see Kay's live performances. And we can only do this because *you* lead the committee, President Luna... Hee-hee-hee..."

Luna and her flunkies emitted incredibly evil cackles.

"By the way, President Luna... The soccer club asked if they could borrow Kay for a day to serve as their manager and boost morale. They basically groveled... How would you like to proceed?"

"Hmph. Ask them to figure out how many votes that would get us. And research how many votes we got last month when we gave her over as a cheerleader for the basketball club."

"Roger that! Then I'll get to it right away—"

They're all corrupt... I hate this school already...

Rintarou grimaced as he watched their exchange, running thick with the dark side of politics and entertainment, and he found himself unimpressed.

"Hmm?"

"Oh."

Rintarou's and Luna's eyes met.

"You're that guy from yesterday!" exclaimed Luna, who'd been slurping her grape juice.

Under the collective gaze of the student council members trying to grasp the situation, Luna approached Rintarou. "What?! Rintarou Magami! You go to my school?!"

"Starting today. I'm a transfer student."

"I see. That makes sense... What a surprise!"

"I'm the one who's surprised. About all this stuff." He glanced at the stage with a half-vacant expression.

"Hey, everyone! How did you like the new song? ★"

""""It was AMAAAAAAAAAAAAAAAAAAAAAAAAZING!"""""

"Then make sure you've got my manager's back! Luna's running again for president, so make sure to V-O-T-E, okay?"

""""Leave it to UUUUUUUUUUSSSSSSSSSSSSSSSSSSSSS!"""""

"Ugh... *Sniff*... This level of embarrassment... My self-respect as a knight, long gone... K-kill me."

"""""SO KYUUUUUUUUUUUUUUUUUUUUUUUTE!"""""
Rintarou plugged his ears and winced. "What kind of place is this? What are you trying to do to this school?"

"God, you're so annoying. I'm the student council president... In other words, I'm the king of this school. Basically, this school belongs to me. What I do with what's mine is my own business, isn't it?" declared Luna, unremorseful and practically glowing with smugness as she puffed out her chest.

Wow, this girl's scum... Not that I should be the one talking.

Rintarou's head was starting to hurt. "Well, whatever. Doesn't matter to me what goes on here." Changing gears, he stared straight at her. "Now then, how 'bout we have a little discussion about *my* business."

"Oh!" Her expression sharpened slightly in response to his cold, small smile.

"Do you know the reason why I transferred and came to this school...the reason I appeared in front of you, a King?"

"Yeah, of course I do, Rintarou Magami!" Luna nodded vigorously, putting the pieces together, and boldly looked over Rintarou.

"Heh... Saves me time." He smirked, an icy little grin of someone who'd walked the underside of the world. "I want to become your—," he started sharply.

"You came here to become my vassal, didn't you?!" she pridefully interjected, puffing out her chest grandly with full self-confidence.

"Huh? ...Wha—?" He hadn't caught on. He blinked.

"Oh, it must be because I'm overflowing with charisma, right?! One look at me, and you wanted to dedicate your body and soul to me as my manservant— I get it! God! It's hard being so charismatic sometimes!" Luna continued rambling nonsensically.

She dragged the folding chair over and set it up in front of him, parking herself right into it, crossing her legs, and finally leaned back into the seat.

"A ceremony to bind master and servant. Go on. Lick it."

With an arrogant look, she thrust her shoe at Rintarou.

"..."

"Heh, what's wrong? I just told you I'll let you become my vassal. Now, Rintarou... Kneel before me and lick it—"

"ARGHHHHHHHHHHHHHHHHHHHH!"

With all his might, Rintarou clocked Luna in the face with his bag.

With leftover momentum, she fell backward and rolled over.

"That hurt! Wh-what do you think you're doing?! You rude lout!"

"SHUDDUP—!! You think I'm the one who's rude?! Are you just *naturally* condescending?! What kind of idiot acts like this?! Are you crazy?!"

Luna and Rintarou were going head-to-head, glaring at each other in close quarters.

"I couldn't have said it better myself, Mr. Transfer Student!"

Following this lively voice, a group of students surrounded Rintarou and Luna.

At the group's forefront stood a beautiful girl, both incredibly serious and fit. She wore an armband that read ETHICS COMMITTEE.

"Luna Artur is an evildoer who brings chaos and disorder to our school! You can't serve her! Now, let us join forces, Mr. Transfer Student!"

"Gah?! Tsugumi Mimori?! I've got to deal with you now, too?!"

Anger flashed in Tsugumi's eyes as she pointed straight at her target. "Luna! What *is* that?! What is with that shady show wreaking havoc on our public moral?!"

"Huh? It's just my political campaign. Isn't that obvious? The student council presidential election is coming up."

"Hooooow is that a political campaign?! How much money

did you make from this show?! That's obviously a violation of the school rules—"

"Ah-ha-ha-ha-ha-haaa! Tsugumi, you fool! I *am* the rules!"

"Ugh! Just because you've got a grip on the administration's weak spot and no one opposes you! Did you really think I'd simply stand by and allow this to happen?! I definitely won't accept this! Ever!"

"Oh. This is totally a battle between the evil dictator versus the noble uprising," narrated Rintarou, totally exasperated.

"Too late! Conversation over! I'm going to have you in cuffs this time! You'll be in the guidance counseling room writing up reflection essays on all the crimes you've committed up until now!"

"What?! Like I'd ever do that! It's practically the same as giving up my presidency! A student with a record can't become president!"

"That's the goal! King Airhead! I'll force you out of the presidency and bring order back to this school!"

"Heh, you really are an idiot! Don't you get it?! I, Luna Artur, am the one and only King of this school! Now and forever!"

"There's no use arguing with her! Everyone, follow after meeeeeeeeeee!"

"""""YEAAAAAAAAHHHH! DOWN WITH THE TYRAAAA-AAAAANT!"""""

"""""FOR FREEEEEEEEDOOOOOOOOOOOOOOOOOOM!"""""

With Tsugumi at the head, the revolutionaries—er, students— rushed Luna all at once.

"EVERYONE! ENGAGE, ENGAAAAAAAAAAAAAAAAGE!"

"""""COME ON, YOU LOT! PROTECT OUR KIIIIIIIIIIII-ING!"""""

"""""GET RID OF THAT TREASONOUS REBELLLLLLLLLL!"""""

With Luna leading the raging student council officers, they started a scuffle.

"""""WE SUPPORT PRESIDENT LUUUUUNAAAAAA!"""""

"""""WE'LL DO ANYTHING FOR LI'L KAAAAAAAAA-
AAY!"""""

At that point, Sir Kay's biggest fans joined in as well, and the courtyard turned into pandemonium all at once—bursting gales, crashing waves, bloodcurdling screams, pained cries. It was like a scene straight from hell.

"What is *with* this school…?" Rintarou muttered, sobering up in the face of this over-the-top spectacle.

"Ah-ha-ha. I guess this is the…natural state of school?" offered someone from behind.

When Rintarou turned around, he caught sight of a female student standing there. "Nice to meet you… Uhhh, you're…Rintarou Magami, right?"

When she tilted her head as she greeted him, he felt his soul was captivated for a split second.

She had a gentle face like a doll's, but her meek smile made it exceedingly clear that she was living and breathing. Softly held back by a hairband, her glossy long hair was the color of a glistening crow's wing, and her dark eyes were like large drops of black diamonds. All around her delicate and willowy body, her skin was smooth as porcelain, and the nape of her neck peeked out of her shirt—a dangerous, coy allure.

Judging from her facial features, it seemed she had some European blood flowing through her veins… It wouldn't be wrong to say she embodied the ideal of a perfect Japanese woman: refined, collected, and unspeakably beautiful.

"Uhhh…and who are you?"

"Nayuki… Nayuki Fuyuse—*yuki* as in 'snow' and *fuyu* as in 'winter.' I'm the secretary of the student council." She smiled at Rintarou and bowed.

Though her name was icy, her movements almost seemed to invite a spring breeze to blow around her.

"Rintarou, you're a transfer student from mainland Japan, right? …Were you surprised?"

"Yeah, I was… I was hoping to do the surprising, though," he muttered, half watching the endless brawl continuing in front of his eyes.

"You were trying to surprise someone?"

"Yeah, well, sorry. Don't mind me." He shook his head. "Anyway, what's up with this school? I can't believe they'd let people get away with all this violence."

"Ah-ha-ha. That's because… Well, long story short, all the students support her."

"Support her? Like that? …You're kidding, right?"

"Nope. Sure, there's a faction resisting Luna, but if you ask around the whole school, there are a lot of people who support her."

"…Is everyone okay? There's something off about this school."

"Luna does outstandingly well in school and sports. When all is said and done, she has all the skills to be the student council president… Like, she improved the unpopular menu at the cafeteria, stood up to a teacher who'd harassed female students before throwing him out of the school, and planned all kinds of fun events," Nayuki relayed nostalgically, enjoying and reminiscing about something in the past.

"Of course, it's not like she did those things for everyone else's benefit. She just wanted better food, she personally didn't like the teacher in question, and she wanted to have fun. But if we let Luna do whatever she wants, however she wants, for her own interests and desires, everyone ends up happier as a result… That's just the kind of enigmatic person she is."

"…" For some reason, he suddenly went silent.

"Huh, Rintarou? Did I…say something that upset you?"

"Not really. It's nothing." He shook his head back and forth and changed the subject: "But anyway, looks like you're pretty taken by Luna, huh? …Though not as much as that bunch."

""""""AHHHHHHHH! WE'RE LUNA'S SHIEEEEEEEELD!"""""""

He took a cursory glance at the students who'd offered up their bodies for Luna's sake.

"Well, that… Ha-ha, that's because Luna is our savior."

"…?" When he turned his attention to Nayuki, he saw she was gazing with gentle eyes at Luna, rampaging around.

What happened? Trying to remain natural, Rintarou wanted to ask her a question.

"Rintarou, I leave Luna in your hands from now on, okay?" mused Nayuki cryptically.

"Huh? Why? Excuse me, but I just met her."

"Well, it's just… It seems like Luna has taken a liking to you, Rintarou."

"Huh? To me?"

"Yeah. That's actually really rare. She never says she wants someone to become her vassal. She's generally not the kind of person who'd force someone to serve her."

"Hmm?"

Well, she must've thought I had some value, too…

That was his conclusion. It must have been thanks to his demonstration the night before.

Well, that's fine. It kinda got off to a rough start, but what I'm going to do won't change. But at this rate, I'll need to put off that conversation with her until after school…

A sly smile secretly wormed its way onto his face.

Later, Rintarou absentmindedly finished his transfer paperwork at the school's administrative office. And just as he planned, they had him go to class 2-C immediately.

"Okay, we have a new student joining the class starting today, Rintarou Magami here... All of you better get along with him, got it? Okay, Rintarou. Go ahead and introduce yourself."

Rintarou was urged on by the homeroom teacher from 2-C, Mr. Kujou, a slim, tall, bespectacled man.

He stood up on the teacher's podium. "Uh, I'm Rintarou Magami. Nice to meet you. My hometown is ——. My hobbies are ——."

As he went through the standard procedures, his eyes scanned around the classroom.

Wouldn't expect anything else from an international school... Looks like half the class's Japanese and the other half foreigners...

He inattentively breezed through his scrappy introduction.

"Ah?!"

Just as he expected, Luna was at the back of the classroom. For some reason, as soon as their gazes met, her eyes sparkled like a kid who'd spied her favorite toy.

"...?!"

Upon closer inspection, he noticed Sir Kay was among the class in a school uniform. It was likely Luna used magic to trick others into thinking Sir Kay was a student, too. That way, she could remain close to Luna and guard her.

With everything that happened the day before, Sir Kay was obviously cautious of Rintarou. But he ignored her glare as he examined the other faces.

Then he saw something.

...Oh?

An unexpected face. Nayuki Fuyuse was also in the class.

When their eyes met, she smiled serenely and gave him a small nod.

Well, it doesn't really matter. I don't care about anyone except Luna anyway.

Just as he thought that, he had reached the end of his introduction.

"—Yup, I hope to get to know you from here on out."

To tie everything together, he bobbed into a bow to keep up appearances.

With that, a smattering of applause started up in the classroom.

"I feel for you, Rintarou... You've transferred into a pretty terrible place...," Mr. Kujou sympathized as he patted Rintarou's shoulder. "You might already know, but...this is a problem class that's home to the biggest problem child of them all. We always end up the epicenter of trouble."

"What?! Mr. Kujou, who in the world could that be?!"

"It's you! *You!* How many ulcers do you think you've given me?!" Mr. Kujou yelled with an exasperated look at Luna, who'd shamelessly raised her hand and burst out with the interjection. "Well, it's not just Luna. For some reason, this school has a ton of people with a whole lot of problems..."

"Ah... Does it really?" Rintarou didn't really care at all, but he gave a praiseworthy attempt to respond to his teacher's warning.

"Yeah. As a newcomer, you'll find a lot of things will be pretty confusing from here on out. If anything happens, don't hesitate to come to me for advice. I'll try to help you out the best I can."

"Ah-ha-ha-ha-ha-ha-haaaa! Oh, Mr. Kujou, you're such a push-over!" taunted Luna. Her laughter was contagious, and after a while, all the students were chuckling, too.

"I can't believe all of you... Well, it doesn't matter. Anyway, make sure to get along with Rintarou."

It was probably an ideal class.

Including Luna, it seemed that the entire class trusted the homeroom teacher—within reason. And though Kujou referred to them as problem children, he seemed to be a softy who looked after his students.

If I were a normal transfer student, I might do well here... This would be the part where I'd feel relieved, but none of that matters to me.

Though he was looking at the class before his very eyes, it was as though this scene was transpiring in a world far removed from him. That's when Rintarou suddenly recalled the path his life had taken until that moment.

—Don't screw with me... What the hell are you?

—N-no way... Soccer was all I had...!

—But I studied so hard... How could I lose to a guy who's no work and all play...?

—If we're both human, how can there be such a difference between us?!

—You monster. You're not the same as us. You're not human.

—Ugh... What have we been doing with our lives up until now...?

—I... I should have never given birth to you...!

As he trudged through life alone, he'd always just watched these happy, lively cliques from the outside, unable to join in.

Hmph... I don't expect anything anymore from the world on this side. *"The right place..." "The right people..." I've been betrayed too many times by them.*

He shook his head to push the revolting memories to the back of his mind.

I don't care about this side. *The moment I get a little serious, they always treat me like a monster and an outcast... I don't care anymore...*

As he absentmindedly contemplated those chafing thoughts, Rintarou headed to the seat that'd been assigned to him.

...

It seemed Luna Artur was quite popular. She was the center of attention by every definition: People were always around her everywhere she went.

Rintarou had wanted to find somewhere he could speak alone with Luna about the succession battle. Instead, he was stuck exchanging pleasantries with other students curious about the new transfer student. He had to play it safe and indifferently attended his boring classes, pretending to work hard.

During these moments, Rintarou was being good. He did his best not to attract attention. He stifled his true self, enduring this figurative suffocation somewhat desperately. He acted the part of the uninteresting, unremarkable, unskilled, unthreatening, and unextraordinary student.

He wouldn't try his hardest at anything. He would do his best to go easy on everything.

Eventually, the students lost their interest in Rintarou, because he was so good at pretending to be someone with no characteristics or traits that stood out... After a while, he melted into the background of the class.

That was fine. If no one had any interest in him, that'd actually put him at ease.

However—

The next incident happened during fourth period.

On that day, the fourth period was math.

Standing at the podium was Takashi Sudou, the math teacher,

a middle-aged man who'd started to bald slightly. "Uh, okay, well, everyone, let's get this class started right away!"

Though his word choice and appearance were friendly enough, Sudou started the class in a tone that hid an underlying fussiness or punctiliousness.

And sure enough, the further the class progressed, the more the classroom filled with dread.

"Wow, you guys are insanely low-level. Come on. Can no one solve this problem?" Dripping with contempt, his words reverberated throughout the quiet classroom.

The lesson plan was undoubtedly malicious, and Sudou continued forward with zeal. That's because he didn't actually intend for the students to understand anything.

On top of that, his questions were nasty, constantly full of tricks and false answers. The students wouldn't learn anything, even if they were able to solve them. It was obvious his goal was to simply bully the students with his trick questions.

"Did any of you actually study? You didn't, did you? You know, back in my day, I took my schooling quite seriously. Kids these days just aren't like that anymore."

His words were overfamiliar—almost friendly—but there was a bottomless unpleasantness mixed into them, seeping out.

"Dammit... What is it with that question...?"

"I just don't get it... It looked so easy at first glance..."

But an unsolvable problem was naturally unsolvable, so the students could only curse him under their breath.

All the while, Sudou tastelessly gloated as he looked over his students.

I see. This school has a ton of people with a whole lot of problems, right...

Rintarou snorted at his curious conclusion as he inattentively listened in on the class, letting Sudou's lecture go in one ear and out the other.

"Mr. Sudou is, well... He recently started at the school and moved here... He was originally trying to become a mathematician, but his dreams were crushed, and he ended up becoming a teacher," whispered Nayuki, who sat to Rintarou's left. "It's like he's mean to students out of spite, so Luna beat him to a pulp in a math competition the other day... But ever since, Mr. Sudou has been holding a grudge against the class—because she's here."

"...Geez, what a petty guy." He could only sigh.

Mr. Sudou wrote one math problem after another in rapid succession on the blackboard with the sole goal of shaming Luna in any way possible. He'd probably scrambled to put together these problems for that very purpose.

Well, in a way...those are foul play.

In one cursory glance, Rintarou saw through the malicious intent behind the teacher's math problems. But he didn't really care what happened: He didn't have any interest in that class or the lesson plan.

As Rintarou closed his eyes to drift into a nap...

"Now, Miss Luna Artur... How about you answer this next question?"

He went right for the main dish: Mr. Sudou thrust at the problem on the blackboard with a piece of chalk, then pointed at Luna, who sat one seat in front of Rintarou.

"..." She'd gone silent, stood up, and stared at the math problem. She just stared at it and didn't try to offer up an answer.

...Well, yeah... No matter how smart she is, it's not like she'd be able to solve that.

"Hwah—" Rintarou cut off a yawn in his tedium.

"Please wait, Master Sudou!" Unable to stand by idly any longer,

Sir Kay stood up and started to cover for Luna. "I—I…have trouble understanding math in this day and age, but is that really a valid problem?! It seems unreasonable and spiteful to me…!"

"Wha—? How could you say that? How rude. Don't blame me for being too dumb to figure it out. This is why your generation… What kind of education did your parents give you?"

"What?! How dare you insult…my father Ector?!"

If she had a sword, she probably would have unsheathed it and gone on a rampage. That was how angry Sir Kay was.

"Kay… Stand down. Stand down."

"Ugh…" Sir Kay bitterly withdrew at Luna's words.

"Now then, Mr. Sudou." Luna turned right around to face him. With a bold, arrogant grin, she launched off into a tirade. "I'm so disappointed… This couldn't have been the best problem you could come up with, could it? I'd have thought you would have been smarter if you're a teacher at the world's most famous international school? We're cutting-edge, you know."

"What?!"

With Mr. Sudou at the forefront, everyone in the classroom was in an uproar and turned their eyes toward Luna.

"G-gotta hand it to Luna! I guess she can solve a problem this difficult…?"

"No, wait! Even Luna can't solve that!"

"B-but if anyone could, maybe Luna…"

The classroom fluttered with unease and expectation.

Hmm…it must be a bluff, Rintarou thought as he rubbed at his sleepy eyes.

It was impossible for a high school student to solve that problem. Based on his research on Luna, it seemed she really did excel in her studies—but of course, only at the level of a high school student.

This was something Mr. Sudou probably knew, too.

"W-well, you can talk the talk, but…," he coolly replied to her taunts as he rubbed at his temples.

To be clear, Mr. Sudou seemed like the type to have a short temper to begin with. But seeing that he hadn't already flown off the handle, he was probably confident she wouldn't be able to solve this question.

However—

"Oh, I'll solve it for you, all right! With elegance and grace. You're nothing but a pathetic lowlife whose hopes and dreams were crushed. You can't acknowledge when you've lost, and you don't know when to give up. You're a coward with pitiful, feeble thoughts and ideas. You get enjoyment out of bullying those you think are beneath you, because you're despicable and desperate to make a fool out of others. You crave approval and want only to fulfill your own selfish desires, but you end up only inflating your own meaningless ego. You think you're superior to everyone else. But that brain of yours is totally devoid of anything important. Sure, I'll solve this problem. I'm sure you racked your brain to come up with it. I'll prove right now that the problem isn't hard at all, just another low-level task—a waste for you to have devoted your precious time and life to—"

Her smug grin would make anyone want to sink their fist into it. She kept blabbing on and on. It went without saying that Mr. Sudou's veins seemed like they were on the very verge of bursting.

"—is what Rintarou Magami said from behind me, Mr. Sudou," she alleged matter-of-factly, pointing at him as she returned to her seat. "Ugh, he's been whispering under his breath this whole time! It's honestly so annoying… Mr. Sudou, please do something about him!"

"…Huh?" Rintarou was taken aback, garnering stares from the entire class.

They started to whisper among themselves.

"A-are you serious...?"

"No way... Could he actually just solve it...? Really...?"

"Wh-what's with that transfer student...?"

"Wh-whoa, wait a second... I...," Rintarou sputtered, flustered by this unexpected turn of events.

He suddenly found himself at the center of attention. But when he noticed Luna had turned around very slightly to glance at Rintarou with a grin, it suddenly dawned on him.

U-unbelievable... This girl's using me as a scapegoat...?!

Luna was worse than scum, outstripping his imagination so badly that it made him dizzy.

"Huh, wow. It seems the transfer student is quite the overachiever..." Mr. Sudou's words dripped sarcasm—blue veins straining against his temple and a glare locked onto Rintarou.

Wait, really? He's just going to let her off the hook and take out his anger on me?! How stupid is he?!

Now... How would he proceed?

Rintarou felt this would end up being nothing but trouble, so he scratched at his head and sighed, just when he heard a whisper coming from behind him.

"You can solve it, right?" asked Luna in a hushed tone with her hands behind her head, totally relaxed.

"Hunh?"

"I can't do it, but I know...*you* can, right?"

Rintarou was cornered into silence.

"As a King, I command you to...solve it in my place."

She was either provoking him or confident in his abilities. Either way, he didn't know why she'd passed the problem along to him—or say that to him.

He didn't know why, but—

Ah, well. In order to enter into the King Arthur Succession Battle, I need to get on her good side. To do that, I guess I can't make myself look bad in front of her.

With his top priority in mind, he decided to go along with her challenge.

"Yeah, that small fry of a problem is a piece of cake," he announced, sluggishly standing up, as though he couldn't be bothered.

"Really? Well then, I'll have you solve it right away. Hurry up—come to the blackboard! Come on!"

Rintarou ignored Mr. Sudou's smile, a mixture of contempt and irritation seeping through, as he thought.

Ah, well, I really don't like revealing my true strength and standing out, but… That's because—

—Don't screw with me… What the hell are you?

—N-no way… Soccer was all I had…!

—But I studied so hard… How could I lose to a guy who's no work and all play…?

—If we're both human, how can there be such a difference between us?!

—You monster. You're not the same as us. You're not human.

—Ugh… What have we been doing with our lives up until now…?

—I… I should have never given birth to you…!

He forcefully pushed aside those unpleasant memories, gnawing at his life up until now.

That's because—I'm just too good. Nothing good has ever come from me going all out.

Rintarou answered right where he stood. "There are two extrema. At (1, -1), point α is one minima, and its minimum value is negative two, while point β at (3, 2) is the other minima—with a minimum value of one. Then, if you use the Mahler expansion theorem, you can find one more extrema, but...I think the answer you wanted was probably just those two... Am I wrong?"

"Oh, should I give you a hint? First, you take this formula... Wait, what?" As Mr. Sudou gleefully started writing something on the blackboard, he froze, gradually comprehending the words Rintarou had spat out. His face paled.

Though the class didn't understand a lick of Rintarou's rapid-fire answer, they could gather it was correct from the look on Mr. Sudou's face.

"Mr. Sudou. That problem contains functional determinants from multivariable calculus. At first glance, you might be able to pass it off as a high school math problem, but it's obviously advanced college-level math. Besides, you'd need to know how to use a Rassem matrix, which was only recently publicized in an academic journal. Without that fundamental knowledge, you'd never be able to solve it. I can't believe you'd give this problem to us. I mean, that's just juvenile."

"Wh-wh-wha-wha...?" For a while, Sudou was overcome by shock, leaving him trembling. "H-how? Even if you knew advanced math...how did you solve this problem so easily...at first glance... without even using an equation?!"

"Beats me." Rintarou sat back down, done with this conversation.

But Mr. Sudou was far from finished. He couldn't save face anymore: Those hopes were completely squashed. "Ah-ah-ha-ha... Rintarou. It seems you're quite good at math. In that case, how about I test just how good you are?"

Though he was calm, his smile contained no joy at all.

"Ugh... We're still doing this? Give me a break..."

From there, Mr. Sudou wrote one math problem after another on the blackboard, quizzing Rintarou. Every last one was unpleasant and dirty. After all, Mr. Sudou had racked his brain, planning to grill Luna and force her into submission. In fact, he was no longer trying to keep up appearances: His problems became remorselessly difficult and diverged further and further from high school math.

However—

"Using linear algebra, it's clear the approximated limit for that partial differential equation is 3n."

"What?!?"

Rintarou breezed through them all.

Doing the calculations in his mind, he didn't even pretend to write the equations down or take time to think for show.

The problems were continuing to increase in difficulty, but that still didn't stop him.

"I… I—I thought of these problems all night long… How could you solve them so easily…?"

Left and right, Rintarou effortlessly solved equations, giving better answers and methods to solving them—completely outstripping Mr. Sudou's expectations. As they continued, this teacher was forced to keenly realize something, whether he wanted to or not: When it came to mathematical expertise, he and Rintarou were miles apart.

Back when Mr. Sudou aspired to be a mathematician, there was an impenetrable wall of actual geniuses who stood in his way…but this boy was a different story. He was the highest wall of them all.

The students simply stared emptily at Rintarou as they watched what he was doing.

In his various attempts, Mr. Sudou had put what little pride he had left on the line. He tried to corner Rintarou, but in the end, his efforts came to nothing.

It was close to the end of the period.

"—which means, when the three Euclidean dimensions are separated into sets, i, ii, and iii fulfill the requirements, which they are equivalent to... That's your proof," spat Rintarou, looking terribly bored.

"Th-this is absurd..." Mr. Sudou collapsed to his knees on the spot, soundly beaten.

"Hmm? Is that enough? Aren't these just graduate school problems? If you were trying to become a mathematician, this couldn't have been all you learned, right?"

With this careless remark, the class heard Mr. Sudou's heart break.

"*J-just* graduate level...? All I've learned...?"

At that moment, the bell rang, saving him from further suffering.

"Ugh...ah...ahhh...," Mr. Sudou groaned, staggering out of the classroom like a sleepwalker.

Even after the bell finished ringing, the classroom remained... hushed, noiseless.

"""""" """""
......

It was hard to even breathe under the oppressive silence that had seized the class while everyone stared at Rintarou.

Without any context, it might have seemed like a thrilling scene: A student had shown up a hated teacher... It should've felt triumphant. They should've been relieved.

But of course...

"...Wh-what's with that guy...?"

"A-amazing...! That was really cool, but..."

"Yeah, wasn't that kind of weird...? Is he *really* a high schooler...?"

"No... Maybe he's one of those prodigies?"

"In other words, he was hiding his gifts until now...?"

There was surprise, there was praise...and there was a thick air of confusion, hidden under their words, in the gazes that gathered on Rintarou.

This *confusion* always irritated him.

That's because he was well aware: Lurking behind acclaim and admiration, this confusion would eventually and inevitably transform into jealousy mixed with fear. When that happened, they'd treat him like a monster and begin to shun him. He already knew that all too well.

Dammit. I've done it again... He internally clicked his tongue in disapproval.

That's right. Upon reflection, that was always the case with Rintarou Magami.

It wasn't merely math. In any subject, sport, and specialty, he could always win—just like that.

Due to a certain set of circumstances, he'd been born with talents and gifts that far surpassed the ability of any human. It was almost excessive. He could leave others behind in the dust, even those desperate to succeed, and when it came to anything and everything, he could be the best—without any work or hardship on his part. In fact, Rintarou could easily break through the limits of a normal genius, prodigy, or prophet.

Thanks to that, he'd been treated as an outcast and monstrosity by those around him since childhood. Even his birth parents had distanced themselves from Rintarou out of fear and left home.

Only characters in light novels admired and lionized those

who cheated through life and surpassed the human domain. In real life, they'd be expelled like a foreign object: That was the reality of the situation.

Ah, well... I need to focus on performing my ordinary student act again for a while.

Hiding in plain view with bated breath, Rintarou would try his best to hide his natural-born powers and stifle himself, slinking back into his constraining, claustrophobic life—back to genuine suffocation.

This world was so dull. He was going to lose his sanity from boredom.

But well, it doesn't matter anymore.

Yes. He no longer expected anything from the world on *this* side.

What he wanted was *that* world. That's the real reason he'd made his way to this artificial island—to enter the King Arthur Succession Battle.

He'd transferred to this school as a cover to get close to Luna... It wasn't as though he was trying to enjoy life as a happy-go-lucky student or anything. There was no way for a wolf to live hidden among a flock of sheep.

"Ah, well," he muttered, collapsing onto his desk and trying to nap as an escape from their ogling eyes.

"Bwa...ha-ha..." In the seat in front of him, Luna's shoulders started to shake. "Ahhh-ha-ha-ha-ha-ha-ha-ha-ha-ha-ha-ha-ha-ha-haaaaaaa!" Suddenly, she stood up and dissolved into laughter as if she couldn't contain it for a moment longer.

As expected, the students in the class, Rintarou included, were overcome by surprise and gawked at Luna. Then, laughing all by herself, she turned on her heel to face him.

"That went great! Didn't it, Rintarou?!" she exclaimed, giving him an energetic thumbs-up and smiling with the warmth of a midsummer sun.

"Huh?" Bewildered, Rintarou and the surrounding students gaped.

"Listen up, everyone! I'd actually..." She pulled out a stack of paper from her desk drawer and threw it above her head. The bundle of...printer paper hung in the air for a moment before fluttering down throughout the classroom.

They were all blank. Without a doubt, none of those papers had anything written on them.

Or that should have been the case, but—

"What's this...?"

"...Hmm? Th-this is..."

As they gathered those pieces of paper and looked at them, their eyes filled with surprise for no apparent reason.

"Hey, Luna, is this...?"

"Yup! It's Mr. Sudou's question-and-answer sheet for his problems in class!" she proclaimed with an arrogant grin. "We got intel from the student council that Mr. Sudou was preparing hard questions in order to get revenge on me! We stole the problems from his computer beforehand and copied them!"

Is this girl—?! Is she doing what I think she's doing?! Rintarou scowled and groaned internally. *She must've used magic, the* Sleight *spell!*

By magic, he meant incantations, chants that brought things into existence and altered reality to make dreams or wishes come true.

It wasn't a particularly special power: *If you think about something hard enough, it'll come true...* The truth was that before science and civilization, everyone could tap into this power. In fact, a few centuries ago, magic users were a dime a dozen.

However, with modern human knowledge in hand, people were held captive by the Curtain of Consciousness, causing the number of magic users to dwindle. Though a child or two would occasionally display a peculiar power or have a strange experience, that was about the extent of it. Everyone accepted there was no such thing as magic anymore and stopped chasing dreams concerning it.

Well, one such use of magic was *Sleight*, which altered people's knowledge.

On the *other* side, it was an incredibly popular type of magic. Rintarou happened to be using it at that very moment to conceal the swords hanging at his hip... It was the most rudimentary of rudimentary magical feats.

In this case, Luna used *Sleight* to give the students the illusion that Sudou's problems and answers were printed on the blank papers.

I mean, of course, basic stuff like Sleight *wouldn't work on people from the other side like Sir Kay and me...*

"J-just as we'd expect, Luna! I can't believe you'd actually taken countermeasures like this! How admirable! What shrewdness!"

"Uh-huh, go on, praise me more, Kay!"

...I mean, of course, basic stuff like Sleight *wouldn't work on people from the other side like me.........*

Strangely expressionless, Rintarou looked around at the other students surrounding him.

"So in other words... Rintarou was able to solve the problems so easily because..."

"Right, he was Luna's accomplice all along! Of course!"

The spell was highly effective on the students of *this* world.

It was all thanks to Luna that Rintarou was able to solve those problems... No one doubted the hoax.

In the middle of it all...Luna suddenly stood beside him and wrapped an arm around his shoulders. "To tell you the truth, we're totally childhood friends! It's like we were destined to meet again at this school, right?"

"Huh?! What are you say—? Mgh?!"

His eyes swam around in confusion. *What's she saying?!*

But to keep him quiet, Luna had brought her hand around to cover his mouth and turned to the students to continue blabbing.

"Oh yeah, when we were little, we were always up to no good… When I was planning on giving it to Mr. Sudou, he was all, like, 'Sounds fun, why don't you let me in on it?!' Right? Rintarou?!" She grinned as she waited for him to give the affirmative.

But he had no idea what she was aiming for, so he chose to remain silent.

"Ha-ha-ha, so you guys were friends! A class clown on your first day, huh?"

"Huh, childhood friends… So that's how they're on the same page."

"Phew, Sudou's dumb face… Now that was a real masterpiece! Good job, Rintarou!"

Without particularly doubting her, they accepted her slapdash explanation.

"Wow, Luna, you're so sly."

"Yeah, just what we'd expect from you! We've got a lot of weird teachers at this school, after all… We gotta have a hotshot like Luna as student president, right?!"

Of course, as soon as she picked up on their conversation, Luna used the conversation to sell herself even further.

"I know, right?! I'm always on the side of the students! I take from the rich and give to the poor, the president of justice! Please vote for Luna Artur for student council president!"

"Ah-ha-ha-ha-ha! Don't worry—leave it to us!"

"Yeah, you get my vote for the next election!"

A scene was unfolding before Rintarou: the bustling class with Luna at its center.

Th-this girl... She's making all this out to be her doing?! She's turning it into good publicity for herself! What scum!

Wasn't this a little extreme—to take things this far? Even Rintarou couldn't help but shudder, when suddenly Luna whispered: "Rintarou... I need to talk to you."

"Huh?!"

"Meet me on the roof after school... That's a promise. Got it?"

She had her say and left in high spirits.

"Ah?! W-wait for me please, Luna! What do you mean you're childhood friends with Rintarou Magami—?" stuttered Sir Kay, trailing after her like a faithful dog.

Then several more students followed after Luna, as if pulled by gravitational force.

"Hmph...," he snorted as he watched her take her leave.

It was more than convenient for him if she was making contact first.

Regardless...I'm trying to get on the good side of...an armful of a girl.

He'd thought she'd be an ingenue from the noble house of Artur in the English countryside...but he was solely mistaken. It seemed she was a headstrong girl—unrelentingly so.

Damn. She completely upstaged me...

Thinking back to it now, Luna might have been weaving the *Suggestion* spell to shift the brunt of Mr. Sudou's anger over to Rintarou. His actions were unnatural enough to raise suspicion. Either way, it was the first time someone had Rintarou wrapped around their finger.

When it came to skill and talent, there was no doubt Luna was inferior to Rintarou.

But she'd done an amazing job using that to her advantage.

With what had just happened, the class probably thought Luna was the puppet master—with no bounds or limitations. On the other hand, they saw Rintarou as an assistant, dancing on the palm of her hand.

Hmph, I don't like this... I don't like that she's taking the wheel.

But... Rintarou realized people were directing a different type of stare at him now.

"Hey, Rintarou. We're expecting a lot from you as her accomplice, okay?"

"Ha-ha-ha, I imagine being her babysitter's going to suck! But you're childhood friends, so you're stuck with her, I guess!"

If he purely looked at the outcome, he could kind of see how Luna had covered for him after he'd gone overboard... But that only held true if he ignored everything else.

"But if we let Luna do whatever she wants, however she wants, for her own interests and desires, everyone ends up happier as a result... That's just the kind of enigmatic person she is."

He recalled Nayuki's words that morning.

"Hmm, you don't say... It's not like she's *that person*...," he muttered to himself, leaving his seat.

After everything that happened...the end of the school day was finally here.

On the wide expanse of Camelot International's roof, Rintarou leaned back on its wrought iron fence and looked up at the sky as he waited for Luna.

Just how long did he wait?

He was still quietly gazing into the sky when he heard the creak of something rusty echo softly. The door to the roof opened, and on the other side was Luna.

"Heh... Sorry I made you wait!" She barged through, making her way to stand in front of Rintarou. As soon as she stood there, she boldly thrust out her chest. "Oh! I'm so pleased you've arrived before your King, as is fitting! Now then, time's a ticking, so let's cut to the chase... Huh? What's wrong, Rintarou?"

With a start, she noticed he was acting very strangely.

Trembling and quivering, his hand holding on to the iron fence was shaking something fierce.

"Rintarou, what's wrong? Are you sick? Y-you should hurry and see a doctor—," stuttered Luna.

"...How...long...?" he muttered.

"Hmm? What? I can't hear yooou."

"Just how long were you going to make me wait, you IDIO-OOOOOOOOOOOOOOOOT?! *Gah!*" He let out a gut-wrenching yell, and on the verge of tears, Rintarou grabbed her lapel.

Upon closer inspection, the sun had set long ago, and it was... indeed, the sky was pitch-dark... It was already the middle of the night.

"Oh, sorry! Sorry! I had a teeny-tiny delay when I was preparing something! So yeah, maybe I ended up just a *tad* late! Tee-hee. ★"

"This isn't a 'tad' late?! I've gotten used to getting the cold shoulder from society, but even I can't stand someone standing me up, YOU ASSHOLE!"

"What? I came like I promised, didn't I? Hmph... You're such a petty guy."

"You're! Freaking! Late!!"

More than fashionably late, Luna wasn't even bashful, much less remorseful. To be exact, she was being impudent.

Up till that point, Rintarou had all kinds of people in his pocket, making them work at his leisure, but with this girl, he was starting to feel like he was losing his touch.

"W-well, it doesn't matter now! Anyway, you! You said you had something you wanted to talk to me about?!"

"Yeah, basically."

"What a coincidence! I do, too!"

"...Hmm? ...I see." Luna smiled coldly, looking like a know-it-all.

"Yeah, after all we've been through yesterday and today, I imagine we're on the same page, right?"

"Right. There's only one thing we'd want to talk about...at a time like this."

They turned fierce, restrained smiles at each other. Then Rintarou made the first move, getting right into it. "Luna. As a participant in the King Arthur Succession Battle, would you—?"

Let me join in? Rintarou started to say, but—

"As you wish! I'll give you the privilege of becoming my vassal!"

"Let me... Huh?" He was cut off mid-line by Luna with her out-of-the-blue remark, delivered with absolute conviction. He couldn't make a retort or a sound. He stared blankly back at her.

"I see it. I see where you're coming from, Rintarou!" she gushed, leaving him in the dust. "You want to become my vassal since I'm the true King, right?! But you're kinda shy, so you didn't take me up on it before, but now you're really regretting it, right?! It's fine! I totally understand! It's basically part of a King's job to figure out a commoner's true feelings, especially if they're emotionally stunted—"

Luna pulled a folding chair out of nowhere and positioned it eagerly in front of Rintarou. She plopped right into it, crossed her legs, and leaned far back.

"That's that. Here ya go. A ceremony to bind master and servant. Lick it," she commanded. With an arrogant grin, she stretched out one of her legs and thrust her shoe in front of Rintarou.

"GAAAAAAAAAAAAAAAAAAAH!" he screamed, lunging forward to grab a leg of her folding chair and mercilessly flipping it upside down—with Luna in the seat.

"AHHHHHHhhhhhhhhhhhhhhhhhhhhhhhhhhhhhhhhhh?!" From the impact, she rolled away. "Hey! Th-that hurt?! Seriously, what do you think you're doing?! You're a dummy! A real dummy!"

"What do you take me for?! Hey! You! How would you come to this conclusion with all that happened yesterday?! This isn't even *close* to what I wanted to talk about!"

"Huh?! This isn't what you wanted?! No waaaay..." Luna's eyes went wide in disbelief. "Geez. This was so boring. Hmph. Fine, like I care. I'm sure you'll come crawling back and beg to be my vassal. I'll see to it." Then, finished with her business, Luna turned on her heel and headed to the door.

"D-don't leave! Please actually listen to what I have to say! I'm begging you!" He grabbed Luna's shoulder in a panic.

Oh, of course. From beginning to end, he was at her beck and call.

"It's obvious I want to talk about the King Arthur Succession Battle! Give me a piece of the action by letting me join your side!"

Luna stopped right in her tracks even as she was about to leave.

"The King Arthur Succession Battle is a competition between eleven Kings trying to find King Arthur's four treasures on this man-made island! The rules are simple: The first to gather the four treasures wins!

"But the rules allow Kings to kill each other in combat and steal treasures from other candidates! In other words, the second half of the battle will definitely be a clash between the Kings, especially once the treasures are revealed!

"You get it, right? A King like you needs some firepower!"

"..."

"Luna, let me fight on your side. If you do...I'll make sure you win," Rintarou arrogantly proclaimed to Luna, who was silent.

Suddenly, a dignified voice echoed around them.

"Please wait, my King!"

It was at that moment that the jewel pendant hanging at Luna's neck started to glow. Responding to this light, a Gate opened in midair, letting through Luna's Jack, Sir Kay. With her long blue hair fluttering, she gallantly came to stand protectively next to Luna...

...in an incredibly revealing nurse costume.

"What's that?"

"Well, the school regulations allow the students to work part-time, and I gotta say it's a total lifesaver. We're really making progress on our war chest," raved Luna in pride.

Rintarou was at a total loss for words and faced her with a blank look. "Hey, what kind of work are you even forcing your Jack to do?"

"Luna! Y-you can't trust him!" Sir Kay desperately implored, trying to hide her embarrassment with enthusiasm.

"...So that's a Round Fragment, huh...?" he muttered as he glanced at the pendant on Luna's neck.

The Kings each had their own jewels, Round Fragments. They were pieces of the very table that seated King Arthur and twelve of his highest-ranking knights. With their Round Fragments, all the Kings from his bloodline could summon their Jacks—the knights of the Round Table, slumbering in Camlann Hill. The Jacks served as their defense and offense, a necessity for the Kings to find victory in the succession battle.

Excluding King Arthur's first seat and the thirteenth Seat of Danger, there were Round Fragments corresponding to the second to twelfth seats.

"That's right. The one in the third seat of the Round Table, Sir Kay—King Arthur's foster sister. That's your Jack, isn't she, Luna?"

Rintarou gazed at Sir Kay with an inexplicable look of nostalgia as she writhed in embarrassment and suspiciously glared back at him with hostility in her eyes.

"You were brave enough to face Master Felicia and her knight— I see you're no ordinary person. But that's exactly what makes you suspicious! For what reason would you approach us?!"

"Well, sure. I guess any normal person would wonder why I'd purposefully come to the *weakest* King Arthur succession candidate... Right?" he jeered.

Sir Kay's eyes burned sharply with rage.

"Hey, hey, don't get angry, okay? I'm not the one who said it. Those damn Dame du Lac were the ones who told everybody that. But well...you guys already know why they call you the weakest, don't you?" Rintarou shrugged. "In this succession battle, victory is determined by the strength of each King's Excalibur...and of that King's servant Jack."

By Excalibur, he was referring to the generic term for the sword wielded by the former King Arthur. It was shorthand for the King's sword.

The participating Kings each had been granted an Excalibur by the Dame du Lac. This sword could shape-shift to reflect the condition of each King's soul.

"But you're basically worthless and talentless, which means you had a shit Excalibur—which you sold off. To top it all off, your Jack is Sir Kay... Welp, I'm sorry to say this, but she was King Arthur's weakest knight."

"Y-you dare call me the weakest knight?! You dare make a mockery of me?! I was stronger than Sir Dagonet! Take it back!"

"Sir Dagonet was the jester in the royal court, wasn't he...? Is that really the brand of chivalry you espouse?" he asked, unimpressed as he looked at Sir Kay, who was bitterly quivering and close to tears. "Whatever. Anyway, let me tell you... I'm *strong*." He suddenly grinned. "If I back you up, your potential will skyrocket. You'll actually have a chance at the battle. What do you think? Would you let me join your side? I'll make sure you win, Luna."

"Huh. Okay? So *who* are you...actually?" she asked quietly. With that, Luna narrowed her eyes slightly. "I don't know how, but it seems like you even know about my Excalibur."

"Does it really matter who I am? The reason I know about your Excalibur is... Well, let's just say I have an in with those Dame du Lac guys."

"What's your goal? Why me? I'm the one with the most disadvantages, right? I don't know what you're plotting, but if you want to win, shouldn't you choose someone else?"

Rintarou grinned gruesomely.

"It's 'cause it'll be fun." He didn't try to make up appearances as he answered. "Whosever side I'm on will win anyway. So why not take the largest stakes...? The weakest underdog is the most fun to support... Am I wrong?"

"Wha—?" Sir Kay was at a loss.

Rintarou Magami was a walking, talking embodiment of arrogance and narcissism, greater than any being in heaven or on earth. He was a false deity who feared no god.

"I'm bored of this world."

Suddenly, Rintarou unsheathed his sword.

"Look, there are a lot of stories about people who get powers that basically cheat the system, right? That's what I've got...and it's boring as hell. There's no reason for living. You don't even get a sense of accomplishment. Living is as good as being dead."

He held the same two swords from the night before: The left was a sword cane, and the right was a long sword. They both glinted sinisterly in the moonlight.

"But...I might still be able to enjoy *this side* of the world a little...right?"

As he lowered his swords lazily, Rintarou swelled with an intimidating demeanor and overwhelming bloodlust.

That made Luna's and Sir Kay's skin prickle. It was electric.

"I'll ask you again. Luna. Let me join your side. Let me dedicate my life to you. If you won't, I'll make you agree by force..."

"Guh... You've shown your true colors now, you scum...?!"

At that moment, Sir Kay was enveloped by a sharp burst of light, coiling around her to form a sword, armor, and a surcoat. By sublimating her mana, she materialized her Aura into a knight's armaments.

"As though we would let a boor like you defile our sacred battle!" She'd transformed into a knight, gallantly confronting Rintarou by turning her sword at him.

"Oh? You want to have a go? ...Fine by me. It'll be great for demonstrating how strong I am." He remained calm as he savagely smirked.

They'd reached a volatile situation: A clash between them was inevitable.

As the situation reached its boiling point, Luna strutted over to him without a care in the world.

"...Huh?"

The combatants were so taken aback by Luna, defenselessly entering the path of their swords, that they couldn't move.

She clapped a hand on Rintarou's back. "You're hired," she said unceremoniously.

Doubting his ears, he blinked in response.

"Seriously, Rintarou! You're just so obtuse sometimes!" She happily smiled.

He was still in the dark.

"In other words, it's basically the same thing, right?! What this all comes down to is you want to become my vassal, right?! I totally understand!"

"......Yeah?"

"All right, I'll hire you! Rintarou, I'll let you become my vassal! I was just thinking I wanted you to become my vassal, too! Well, let's hurry up and get the ceremony out of the way!"

She was in high spirits as she pulled a folding chair out of thin air.

"THAT'S NOT WHAT I MEAAAAAAAAAAAAAAAAANT!!"

"WAAAAAAAAAAAAAAAAAAIIIIIIIIIIIIIIIIIIIIIIIIIIIIIIIIIIIIT!"

Rintarou and Sir Kay were up in arms as they pressed into Luna at close range.

"Why does it always come down to this?! Is there something wrong with your head?!"

"You can't, Luna! This guy's already suspicious enough as it is! He's probably up to no good. How can you make this good-for-nothing edgelord your vassal?! You're like a little sister to me, and I absolutely can't allow this!"

The two closed in on her.

"What? But, Rintarou... You want to fight for me, right? You want to help me win, right? You want to make me the true King, right? And you said you'd risk your life for me, right?"

"Y-yeah, but..."

"Then you're basically my vassal—and a super-loyal one, at that."

"...Yeah? I—I guess? Maybe I actually wanted to become

your vassal to begin with? Huh? I don't know what's happening anymore..."

"And Sir Kay. At first glance, you're right: He's a try-hard. But...it seems he might really be strong. And most importantly, this is more fun!"

"...F-fun...?"

"Because Rintarou's serious about this, right? He said he seriously thinks this'll be *fun*, so he wants to join this fight, right? Isn't that *fun*, in and of itself?!"

"W-well...um, Luna? Aren't you basically saying he's just insane?"

"Ha-ha! I'll take this talented loose cannon and use him to my advantage! That's what a King does...right?! Well, as the true King, my heart's big enough to welcome him in!" she announced proudly with a smug little grin and her puffed-out chest.

Faced with Luna's overtly childish naïveté, Rintarou and Sir Kay let go of their hostility in spite of themselves.

"Damn, and here I was thinking of scaring you and taking control of the situation. But things realllly aren't working in my favor. Well, who cares. I don't mind if I'm a vassal or whatever as long as I can fight on your side."

"Ahhh, I don't even know what to say... Luna, you're so similar to *that kid*...always gathering up weirdos and oddballs just because it'd be 'fun.'"

Rintarou and Sir Kay sighed deeply, finally finding common ground: They were exasperated by Luna.

Then Sir Kay looked straight at her again and chose her words carefully.

"Luna. This is your battle. If that's what you wish...then I will raise no further objections. As a knight under your service, I defer to you."

"Sir Kay…"

"…I was truly a worthless knight. In the end, I couldn't protect my younger brother…Arthur. Even on that day where everything started, when he pulled the sword from the stone…when the Round Table crumbled…when Camlann Hill was faced with devastation…"

"…"

"That's why *this time* I'll protect you. That's the reason I answered your call at Camlann Hill so earnestly… Though you might've drawn the short straw because of that." Then she once again turned back to Rintarou. "Listen up, Rintarou Magami. Regardless of your reasons, if you do wrong by Luna, mark my words: I swear on my life to strike you down, even if my strength is no match to yours… Remember that."

"Yeah, I'll keep it in mind. Especially if it's a warning coming from you."

"I-is that so…?" Truth be told, she hadn't expected Rintarou to nod and agree without putting up a fight.

With that, Sir Kay suddenly melted into particles of light and disappeared into the night. She dissolved and returned to her original place—to her part-time job.

After he sent Sir Kay off into the night, he turned to Luna. "Now, my King. The King Arthur Succession Battle started yesterday night…but they haven't even announced a single one of the quests yet. We don't even know when they'll be announced."

"Yeah. Right now, we gotta investigate, be on the lookout to see how each King moves…or who the Queens are…"

"Then what's your move?" he asked Luna in a slightly low tone. "We've still got a lot to do, even before they announce the quest or before the real scramble for the treasure begins. We can investigate what the other Kings are doing. We can find someone to make a temporary alliance with. We can review and strengthen our defenses. On the other hand, in order to increase our chances, we could go on the offensive and attack the other Kings to get them to fold. In that case…we could even assassinate them."

"…"

"Now, Luna, what would you like to do? Just tell me the course you want to take… No matter what it is, I'll do everything I can to help you become the victor."

Her eyes were unusually serious as she looked straight at him. "You're right. After all, there *is* something important I must do… in order to win this battle."

"Oh?" The corners of his mouth scrunched up.

"Rintarou. We'll start right away…right now." Her gaze was even more dignified and sharp than usual—the air of a King.

"Great, I love that you're being assertive… So? Give me some details."

"You're an outsider, so you probably don't know yet, but—" She lowered her voice to confide in Rintarou. He was giddy with joy.

"We absolutely must get our hands on some *very important information* for the King Arthur Succession Battle. We're going to do that tonight… Are you ready?"

"Oh? I didn't realize that was the case… Fine by me. Let's make it happen."

Luna pointed the way for their next plan of action.

And Rintarou was genuinely delighted as he grinned and grinned and grinned—

CHAPTER 3

The Lonely Demon and the Midnight Sun

Luna's proposed mission was to infiltrate a certain establishment.

The aforementioned information was apparently hidden in this building.

Somehow, Luna had prepared intelligence and a map of the location in advance for their plan to break and enter, and they had a detailed meeting right before they started their work.

Using the sewer pipes, they entered the establishment from below and crawled carefully forward on their hands and knees in a ventilated air duct that snaked along the ceiling. Eventually, they removed a vent cover and stealthily dropped down onto the floor.

Once they investigated their surroundings, they found they were in an endless corridor, continuing before and behind them. Here and there, dim emergency lights along the corridor indistinctly lit up the darkness. They turned to each other and nodded, then started running soundlessly.

They checked the time on their clocks and compared that to the scheduled rounds of the facility guards in their minds. From there, they chose a route where they were sure they wouldn't come across any guards and quickly sprinted through the building.

After some time, they arrived at the door of a certain room—their objective.

That door had a card reader.

It could only be opened by running a key card over it.

"Hmph, easy-peasy." Luna pulled out a key card—she'd gotten her hands on it from heavens knows where—and ran it by the card reader.

Beep. With that small electronic sound, the red light on the reader turned green, and the door lock clicked open.

"...You sure are prepared." Rintarou immediately opened the door and slipped into the room.

There were countless desks, chairs, computers, printers, and shredders lined up in the room. It must've been an office.

At the very back of the room was a heavy safe.

"Rintarou. That's the one."

With an incredibly retro-looking dial, the object in question was out of place for the modern office. Unlike an electronic safe, it served as a simple physical defense mechanism, incapable of being cracked using hacks or other backhanded tricks...normally, at least.

"Unfortunately, I couldn't get the combination to this safe even when I used my information network to its fullest extent. Can you do it?"

"Ha... Who do you think you're talking to?" Rintarou smiled faintly and put his ear next to the safe's dial. Then he noisily started turning the dial to the right and left, listening for subtle changes to deduce its combination.

Two, three times, he spun the dial quickly, turning it right and left to the indicator, until he eventually heard a *clink* of a small bell—and the safe was open.

He'd taken fifteen seconds, if that.

"Wowza…"

As he felt Luna's wide eyes gape at him from behind, he grabbed the lever of the safe and pulled it open with a *clunk*. The only thing inside the giant safe was a manila folder secured by a string and two grommets.

"We did it!" She eagerly pulled the envelope out and checked its contents.

There was no mistaking it: That was the incredibly important information Luna needed.

"Yeah! This battle's as good as ours! It's all thanks to you, Rintarou!" She shivered from intense emotion and excitement.

"Are you gonna tell me what you're using that for now…?" he asked in a hushed voice as he folded his arms.

It seemed he was starting to regret what he'd gotten into—that or he might have just been scared. He was unusually shaky, breaking out into a cold sweat, and an oily sheen seeped out of his pores.

"Hee-hee. You haven't…lost your nerve, have you?" she snickered, her mouth forming a thin, cold, crimson line in the darkness. "I guess I didn't expect you to be such a coward? Was that bravado just for show?"

He clicked his tongue in annoyance. "I said to tell me what you're using that—"

With that, Luna beamed as she pointed to the bundle of documents and yelled, "You mean—with the questions for our midterms?!"

When she said that, the air faintly trembled as her words reverberated throughout their surroundings.

"…"

"…"

For a while, heavy silence settled over Rintarou and Luna.

Yes, they'd just infiltrated...their very own school, Camelot International's faculty building—as though they were on an espionage mission in another country. Indeed, this room was simply a regular office.

"Well, you see... My approval rating as president has been dwindling, just a tiny bit... It's all thanks to that annoying resistance movement and their smear campaign," she started, giving Rintarou a staccato explanation.

"I still don't understand why people even support you in the first place... Anyway, how are these related?"

"Well, I was thinking I'd take a shot at boosting my approval ratings in one go."

"Uh-huh."

"Basically, I'll take these test problems and float them by the students close to flunking out and the sports teams, so they can focus on their matches. That way, I can swing some more votes."

"..."

"In other words! This solidifies my victory in the next presidential campaign—"

Slaaaaap!

The noise coldly echoed around them. Rintarou had expressionlessly hit Luna across the head with a notebook.

"That hurt?! Wh-what do you think you're doing to your King?! You brute!"

"What do you think *you're* doing?! What part of this is supposed to help you 'win the King Arthur Succession Battle'? How is this 'important information' that you absolutely had to get your hands on? You idiot!"

"Wh-what?! It's important, isn't it?! As the true King, I also hold the throne of student president... If I lose my throne as the King of this school, I'd be too anxious and depressed to fight in the King Arthur Succession Battle!"

"Who cares about that stuff?!"

"You dummy! How can I be King Arthur and rule the world if I can't even be King of this school?!" she declared in all seriousness.

"Okay, that's a decent point, but there's something really wrong with your reasoning!" Rintarou yelled, pulling at his hair.

As he did that, Luna had a scummy grin as she gave him an order. "Look, Rintarou, we're going to take pictures of the problems, then hurry up and get out of here, okay? Heh-heh-heh..."

"I...might've made a mistake by deciding to side with you..."

With a sigh, Rintarou pulled out his smartphone...

Beep, beep, beep, beep, beep, beep, beep!

Unexpectedly tearing through the silence in that dark room, an alarm started to blare loudly.

"Huh?! What?! What *is* this?!" she exclaimed, confused, as they heard sounds of a large crowd pushing toward them from the corridor.

Eventually, the door of the office was flung open, and countless shadowy figures surged in like an avalanche.

The person at the front of the group was—

"Aha! You fell right into my trap, Luna!"

With an armband that read ETHICS COMMITTEE—it was Tsugumi Mimori.

"T-Tsugumi?! Why are *you* here?!"

"This was all a trap to catch you!" she declared, chest confidently puffed out in victory. "I knew you were sniffing around the staff room trying to steal the test questions! We twisted that around on you. The Ethics Committee used everything it had to execute this plan!"

"Wh-what?! You're treating me like some sort of villain?!"

"You're clearly a villain!" yelled Tsugumi.

"You're obviously a villain!" shouted Rintarou.

"Ugh?! I thought getting that key card was way too easy... I can't believe myself!"

"Heh! We caught you red-handed with some super-small security cameras we just installed! Now that's what they'd call 'conclusive evidence'!"

Uh-oh, sorry, Miss Ethics Committee. I already hacked all those cameras and killed them in advance. I don't think you got any footage. If I knew what I know now, I wouldn't have bothered.

In his mind, he raised his hands together in silent atonement.

"All that's left is to catch you here, and victory is ours! We'll free this school from the tyrant's reign!"

Please try your best. I'm praying for victory and glory to the noble uprising against this oppressive regime.

This time, he raised his hands together in silent prayer.

"Rest assured, Mr. Transfer Student! I'm sure Luna coerced you into helping her, right?! Yes, we already know!"

"Oh, right. Yeah, sure, that's the truth. Please save me—"

With Tsugumi throwing him a metaphorical lifejacket, Rintarou was more than ready to throw Luna under the bus.

"Now, how to get out of this predicament?! Any ideas, my faithful vassal, Rintarou?! Hey, what are we gonna do?! My right hand, Rintarou, the one who helped me with this plan! You swore you'd devote your life to me, Rintarou—my faithful partner! We're thick as thieves and bound by the same fate, right, Rintarou?!"

Th-this freaking girl...!

With her blabbering on and on about their friendship, Luna effectively closed off all possible escape routes. His veins popped out on his temple, straining under his skin.

"Huh? Mr. Transfer Student? A-are you really an accomplice…?"

As Tsugumi trembled in astonishment, Luna smirked nastily and coiled her arm around Rintarou's.

"Of course!" she grandly declared. "I'm a King, he's a vassal, and we're of one body and heart! He'd faithfully offer up his life for me, and I'll fight with my life on the line in exchange! There's nothing stronger than the two of—"

"Ahhhh—! That's enough! Okay, okay, fine! I'm on the dark side with you! I'm on the dark side, too!"

He wanted to punch her.

Oh, how he wanted to punch Luna and her skeevy little smile, playing across her face beside him.

Meanwhile, Tsugumi had finally come back to her senses and raised her voice expressionlessly. "Ugh! Whatever! Everyone! Restrain them both!"

""""ROGER THAAAAAATTTTTTTTT!!"""" the committee members belted in unison, leaping at them.

"Let's go, Rintarou!"

"Ugh?! Like we'd let you catch ussssssssssss?!"

As the students tried to grab them, Luna and Rintarou threw them aside, obstructing them with body checks, nimbly tripping them up with their feet, cutting through the rest, pushing their way out of the crowd—

"We're through!" The pair escaped the mob and rolled into the corridor at the same time.

Then they used their momentum to bound to their feet and run for dear life.

"Th-they got away, Tsugumi!"

"It's okay! We have tons of people deployed all around the faculty building! We'll catch them for sure! Now, everyone, move as planned!"

At her command, they gathered into one, running after Rintarou and Luna with all their might.

"Hey! Yo! Luna! Just how many enemies do you have at this school?!" He dared to glance behind him as they booked it through the corridors.

""""STOPPPPPPPPPPPPPPPPPPPPPPPPPPPPP!"""" roared the committee members. Like a tsunami, a sea of students rushed over to them.

"Ughhh! Those disrespectful jerks! How dare they go against their King!"

"You're more like the King of the underworld! Which makes them the heroes by association!"

Their comic timing was perfect, even though they'd only recently met.

"Ugh, I don't see their leader—that Tsugumi chick! They're definitely trying to circle ahead! Even if we keep running, they're going to eventually corner us!"

"Ugh, well played, Tsugumi..."

"What do you want to do? Do you want to just use *Mana Acceleration* to force our way through?"

Those from the *other* side could awaken a skill called *Mana Acceleration*. It was a special way of breathing, which sent mana down the path that connected the sefira in their bodies. That allowed them to push their bodies' senses and abilities beyond human limits.

In the East, it was known as qigong or alchemy. In the East and West, now and in the past, those who unconsciously tapped into this power usually became one of the few heroes displaying extraordinary bravery.

"I mean, it'd be a chore trying to get out of this by relying on our normal human abilities without *Mana Acceleration.* Especially considering that there's so many of 'em."

"But I don't want to roughhouse them when they have no idea what they're getting into."

The two were struggling to decide on a course of action...when suddenly, they heard a high-pitched noise that rang in their ears. Their surroundings transformed.

Almost instantly, it was as though the world was enveloped in an uncanny feeling, as if painted over with ink.

"—Huh?!"

"What was that just now—?!"

The two of them automatically stopped in their tracks.

It might have been midnight, but the world was still as delicate as always, held together by human movements and interactions. That's why they felt the presence of a large crowd, even when they were far from earshot—and then the sudden sensation like it'd gone far away.

This was different from their unremarkably normal day-to-day life, fogged over by an inexplicable *something*... It felt eerie, as though they'd been pulled into...another world.

When they came to, they found themselves in a place that was their school but also wasn't their school.

At the same time, the other students had hardened up like statues.

"Wh-what is this? I can't really put what it is into words, but this strange feeling..." Luna batted her eyes in confusion and looked over the scene in front of them.

He clicked his tongue. "It's the *Netherworld Transformation* spell."

"*Netherworld?*"

"Yeah. It's a type of barrier that temporarily screws up the

Curtain of Consciousness, which separates the real world and the illusory world. By someone else's hand, we've been brought over to the underside of the real world...an illusion, a projection of the space in front of us. We've been pulled into a place called Never-where." Rintarou gave a perfunctory glance at the frozen students. "Because of the Curtain of Consciousness, the people of the real world can't perceive the illusory world. That's why time stops for them when they're thrown into another world."

"Who would do something like this...?" she asked, tilting her head.

He grinned in amusement. "That's obvious, isn't it? It's a setup...by your enemy."

"What?!"

"Did you forget? The King Arthur Succession Battle has already started. There's no need to wait for the four treasures to be announced. You can defeat your rivals before that."

At the same moment, they heard the wind howl.

One of the frozen committee members suddenly started moving and lunged at Luna, pouncing toward her.

Their speed was beyond human ability, as fast as a discharged bullet.

"—Huh?!" Her reflexes were slow, and she watched the student's arm savagely lash out at her in silence.

But the arm swiped through thin air.

"Whoa there!" Rintarou had quickly swept Luna under his arm and jumped backward.

As he began to kick at the wall to leap farther away, the corridor seemed to fall behind them and flow away like a torrent. As he bounded from wall to wall, he turned over upside down to kick the roof and jumped even farther back—

—to make a spectacular landing. They skidded across the hallway another dozen yards.

"Th-thank you...," Luna stammered.

"That's the *Puppet* spell. If they can control this many people at once...our enemy must be a pretty strong sorcerer, huh?" He let Luna down and looked forward.

When he did, the frozen students started coming to life one after another.

The students had an ominous, yellow glow around them, looking at Luna with empty, spiritless eyes, and slowly approached them exactly like zombies.

"But if they're involving bystanders to get you...they're willing to use some pretty dirty tricks!" he shouted as he yanked Luna into a nearby classroom, where he closed the door and wrote the words KEEP OUT in archaic Celtic Ogham letters.

It was a *Confinement* spell. He'd locked the door using magic.

Before long, the students gathering outside the closed door were vigorously starting to bang on it. As the shrill sounds filled the classroom, the door started to creak and groan under the weight of their balled fists.

"Tch... It won't last long." He looked outside the classroom window.

Because of the *Netherworld Transformation*, the world outside the window was strangely wriggly and warped. An other-dimensional space spread out ahead of them.

If they fell into that space, they wouldn't get out alive. There would be no escape through the window.

Even with this revelation, Rintarou wasn't flustered or shaken. He was simply analyzing the situation calmly.

Someone is magically controlling those guys and increasing their

*abilities. At someone's command, they're super-eager to kill Luna...
and trying to reason with them is impossible. Making a getaway is
also impossible... Hmm.*

In that case, there was only one answer.

"Guess we've gotta kill 'em," he concluded mercilessly, pulling
out his sword.

In his left hand, a sword cane. In his right, a long sword.

Their frosty blades glinted, bloodthirsty like their handler.

"Heh, no hard feelings, okay? You just got unlucky getting
drawn into this fight," he scoffed casually with a smirk—morally
broken, cold-blooded, and matchless.

He readied himself for the door's inevitable collapse and the
flow of students that would come barging through as he shamelessly overflowed with murderous glee.

But when he did that, someone grasped his shoulder.

It was Luna.

"...What?" He gloomily turned to Luna.

Her eyes bored deep into Rintarou with complete seriousness,
almost frighteningly so. For a moment, he was at a loss for words
before her vividly beautiful eyes.

"Rintarou. That's one thing I won't allow," she stated with dig-
nity and a stern will, which seeped into his ears and soul.

He realized Luna was acting completely different. She wasn't
her usual jokester self, instead bearing an air of majesty and roy-
alty. It made him almost unconsciously submit to her.

"H-huh...?" To be honest, he was kind of annoyed at himself
for being overawed by this brat. "Hey, do you understand the situation we're in right now? They're all under the control of an enemy
hiding who knows where. You think we can get out of this without killing them? If you get caught, they'll rip you to shreds," he
retorted.

"It doesn't matter what's going on!" she asserted. "I won't allow you to lay a hand on those kids! That's the only thing I won't allow! Ever!"

Tch... He clicked his tongue. *Eh, she's a girl after all...* Discouragement colored his face.

"You're soft. Do you really think you can become King—?"

"I do this because I *am* a King!" She boldly brushed off his contempt and ridicule.

"—Ngh?!" He couldn't stop his eyes as they flung open.

Like a flash of light, her voice cast away the darkness.

"Sure, those kids are part of an insolent uprising against me, but they're students under my rule all the same! In other words, they're my vassals and subjects! I won't allow a sword to be turned on them! A King's duty is to protect her kingdom, and if you ignore such a basic rule and lay a hand on them... Rintarou, as King, I *will* pass judgment on you!"

Her sword sang as she unsheathed it and held it in both hands like a cane, as her gaze blazed with sincerity and continued to stab away at Rintarou.

Is this really the same irresponsible dunce who tried to steal the test questions?

Almost doubting his vision, Rintarou couldn't do anything but be perplexed at her presence. This confident stance made Rintarou recall the memory of facing a certain person.

He remembered a distant and nostalgic scene in a grand grassy field of old Britain.

There was a pair of blazing blue eyes, hardened by witnessing countless battles, and a gentle smile that never disappeared. In this memory, the figure's golden hair moved with the wind, the armor sparkled and gleamed brilliantly, and the cape was majestic.

He remembered the treasured sword, the Excalibur, imparting a blinding glitter—neither gold nor silver. It'd been carried in the hand of a young King—*that guy*. With confidence and pride filling his face, he'd always say to his waiting vassal by his side—

"■■■■. This is a King's command…"

"Rintarou! This is a King's command!"

At the sound of her voice, his consciousness stopped wandering in his old memories and snapped back to the present.

Chanting something, Luna gripped her pendant at her chest, and a Gate opened out of thin air. With the sound of mana bursting forth, Sir Kay was summoned.

This time, she wasn't in any sort of cosplay. She was fully in her knight form.

"I'll distract those kids! You work with Sir Kay to find the person putting up this attack and cut them down!"

Unconsciously, he found himself looking at Luna's hand.

What she held was not an Excalibur, shining in all its brilliance.

There was nothing extraordinary about it. It was just some rugged bastard sword. It was obviously inferior compared to her capabilities.

If that'd been the real Excalibur, then—

That's too bad. He didn't notice this moment of pity passing through his brain.

"H-hmph… You're placing a tall order on yourself, considering you don't even have your Excalibur. You really think you can keep it up long enough for me to crush the puppeteer?"

"Hey! If I can't, it just means I was never fit to be King!"

"Damn, don't be a hero when you don't need to be… You're exactly like *him*."

"…Him?"

"Tch… Seems like the King I'm serving is a handful."

Ignoring Luna and her quizzical look, he quickly returned his swords to their scabbards.

"Okay, I've got it. GOOOOOO!"

As Rintarou yelled desperately—

—*Bam!* The students ripped through the door and rushed into the room.

"AHHHHHHH!"

"HAAAAAAAAAAAAAAAH!"

Rintarou and Luna moved into position. With the waves of students pushing toward them, the two slammed into the mob, delivering a blow with the force of their bodies, pushed the students back, and forced a path through the sea. With that, they jumped out of the classroom.

They should have expected that when they got out, the students would go after them in droves.

"Whaaat?! L-Luna?! What's going on?!" shouted Sir Kay, following after them with no real understanding of what was happening.

Luna yelled back, "Sir Kay! Follow Rintarou!"

"Well, but—"

"Hey, let's get a move on! C'mon, you amateur knight!" He grabbed onto her cape and left Luna behind as they furiously sprinted away.

"AHHHHHHHHHHHHHHHHHHHHHHHHHHHHHHHH?!"

As she was pulled along by her arm, Sir Kay's shrieks were immediately swallowed by the dark depths of the hallway.

"Don't you dare die until I get this done! You unreliable King!" he yelled.

"Rintarou!" Luna blurted, hurling her words at him. *"I believe in you!"*

"!" Unintentionally, he'd stopped in his tracks for a moment. "Hmph…" He sighed, snorting and picking up his pace.

As expected, it seemed whoever had set this up was after Luna.

The students didn't even cast a glance at Rintarou and Sir Kay escaping, instead choosing to flood around Luna.

"Heh, be patient! My vassal will release you from this despicable grip on your souls!" she declared.

Even though she was clearly targeted, Luna was wearing her usual fearless, smug grin. Jumping onto her, countless students swarmed in on Luna, unarmed. Under the control of magic, their movements were agile and fierce, predatory. Their speed and power couldn't be compared to any normal human.

However, she was flexible and energetic even when the students viciously closed in on her.

"Hah!"

She sidestepped a student trying to grab her from the front.

She stopped the fist of a student trying to punch her from the right and launched them overhead in a masterful hip throw.

She jumped over a student trying to body-slam her from the left.

She did a somersault off the shoulders of a student advancing on her and landed perfectly.

On top of the crowd, she nimbly leaped from shoulder to shoulder of the students beneath her, until she eventually jumped clear of the crowd to run in the opposite direction of Rintarou and Sir Kay.

The turbulent wave of manipulated students followed closely after her.

...So she believes in me...huh?

As Rintarou ran down the hall and explained the situation to Sir Kay, he was deep in thought.

What an idiot. What if I abandoned her? Or if I was actually part of an enemy group? Isn't she suspicious or paranoid? ...Yeah, she probably won't live for long...

His mouth sarcastically contorted at the thought of Luna's carelessness.

But... It's the first time anyone in this era has ever said that to me.

Well, it didn't really matter. They were just words, after all. They didn't hold any real value.

Rintarou shook his head back and forth and pulled himself back together.

"I—I see. Okay, I understand what's happening now!" shouted Sir Kay, sprinting behind Rintarou down the corridor, as wild and fast as a tempest. "In that case, I think one of us really should've stayed behind in order to protect Luna!"

"Hey, hey, Sir Kay... You're as overprotective as always, huh?" His smile was steeped in sarcasm.

"Huh? What do you mean by...'as always'?"

"You got a direct order from the King, right? She told us to butcher the puppeteer... Shouldn't you follow her command and believe in your King as her vassal?

"Well, not that I'm her vassal or anything," he added, grumbling in a low voice.

"Rintarou... Could it be that you have some ties to King Arthur's time?" she asked, as if she'd noticed something about him. "It seems extremely odd to ask you when you are a person of *this* era, but...did you and I perhaps serve the same King?"

"The enemy is controlling a ton of students and sicking them on Luna in the netherworld. On top of that, whoever it is has strengthened the students by supplying them mana," he explained, all the while ignoring her original question. "Of course, magic has an inverse relation to distance. To use a spell this strong, the caster has to be close by. It'd be impossible for the culprit to control that many students and make them that strong from outside the netherworld, even for a wizard from Arthur's time."

"...You mean to say the puppet master has to be somewhere in this space?"

It might have been because the situation was so tense, but Sir Kay didn't press him any further and went along with his explanation.

"That's right. We need to blot them out."

"B-but... Just where could this person be hiding?!" With a vaguely impatient expression, Sir Kay looked around the vicinity.

Though the floors, ceilings, and walls were configured like a normal school building, the corridors were like a maze going forward, backward, left, and right into one another. The floor plan had obviously gone bonkers.

"The *Netherworld Transformation* probably distorted the space. If this keeps up, we'll be stuck here forever! We need to find the person who set up the trap fast, or Luna will—"

"—Wait!"

Rintarou stopped in his tracks.

As he squinted ahead of them in the corridor...he saw a palm-sized girl with wings on her back scattering glittery dust from her scales as she drifted along.

"Is that a Messenger Pixie?" he asked uncertainly.

The pixie noticed them approaching, her eyes meeting with Rintarou's, and nodded. Then she flitted away, turning to the right at the T-shaped corridor ahead.

It was as though she was telling them to follow her.

"I see. It's an invitation from the puppet master," he concluded with a smirk.

"...Could it be a trap?" Sir Kay asked apprehensively.

"Well, that's unlikely. They already went through the trouble of using *Netherworld Transformation* here, after all. What would be the point of luring us into a trap here...? If it were me, I'd keep quiet and let my unsuspecting victims drop in the pitfall on their own. Besides," Rintarou continued, "even if it was a trap...I'd just crush it."

"*Sigh...* Wow, so dependable. Who are you, really?"

It went without saying that Rintarou didn't reply to her exasperated question.

"C'mon, let's go, Sir Kay. The mastermind behind all this is waiting."

He darted after the flying pixie without hesitation.

Following the pixie through the corridors and going right at a crossing, they went through a classroom to a window. It extended into another corridor, where they climbed one stairwell after another.

"Ugh... What *is* this place? It makes me feel kind of sick," Sir Kay lamented.

Rintarou let her complaints wash over him as they continued to earnestly climb the stairs that seemed to go on and on and on and on.

Based on the number of stairs they'd climbed, they'd already far surpassed the height of the school building.

But finally, at the end of the staircase, they caught sight of a door.

The pixie was floating beside the door as though waiting for them.

"…It's the exit."

The door clunked as Rintarou turned the handle and pushed through. They stepped out…

"!"

The vast courtyard of Camelot International spread before them, filling their field of vision. When he turned around, he saw the door was the main entryway to the first floor.

"…I don't like this one bit. This is why I dislike magic. I can't tell what's going on." Sir Kay groaned, her head hurting from the curious phenomena in front of her. She closed her eyes halfway, fed up with the whole thing.

He paid Sir Kay no mind as he continued to stride forward.

In the middle of the courtyard were two shadows waiting for them.

"I see. So you were the ones who set this up…"

Waiting there were the familiar faces of a certain boy and girl. That was because he'd just met them the night before.

"You finally made it… You're late, you know?"

It was one of the Kings participating in the King Arthur Succession Battle—Felicia. Attending her was her Jack, the young knight. The two had been waiting for them to come, completely ready to wage war.

The pixie that'd guided the two flew to Felicia with a twirl and circled around her before disappearing like a mirage.

"Good grief… You don't look the type, but you sure use shifty tricks, don't you?"

"Hmph, were you surprised? I have ancient elven blood running through me, and I'm pretty much the best with magic. Unlike you, Luna, who's brawns over brains… Hey, wait!"

Huh? Felicia tilted her head.

"Wh-where did Luna go? …Oh?! Did she send you so she could lean back and watch? Ugh, she always takes me for an idiot…!"

"What are you ranting on about? We split up just like you wanted. Let's hurry up and get this fight started," he stated, smiling fiercely as he drew his swords and readied himself.

"Now, we'll have you pay back your debt from last night, Rintarou Magami," replied Felicia's Jack, standing in Rintarou's way and preparing his sword.

"Ha! Like you could. You don't know your own place," Rintarou spat at him.

"Y-you're the one who doesn't know your place!" shouted a voice.

"Whoa?!"

Sir Kay wrestled Rintarou from behind and pinned his arms behind his back.

"Hey, what do you think you're doing?! Let me go?!"

"Be quiet! You don't know anything about that knight! You can't strong-arm him!" She flipped Rintarou around and threw him behind her. "I didn't think you and your knight would have appeared here, Master Felicia. Ugh, there's not much I can do now! Though I have my flaws, as someone who also lived through King Arthur's reign, I will have to be the one to fight you!" she swore under great distress, pulling out her weapon. "Rintarou Magami, I'll buy you some time. But make sure to beat Master Felicia," she ordered, stiff from the tension.

"Hmph…Sir Kay," said the Jack. "Come to think of it, quite some time has passed since our swords last met like this."

"…Ugh?!"

"But do you…actually believe you can stop me?" The Jack maintained his composure as he leisurely readied his sword.

"AHHHHHHHHHHHHHHHHHHHHHHHHHHH!" With no room for argument, Sir Kay leaped into action, giving a spirited scream as she bolted toward the Jack.

In an instant, the earsplitting clash of metal tore through the night.

"Hmph, you never change. This is all you can muster?"

"—Guh?!"

Her desperate attack was fended off by his sword, easily pushing it back to defend himself.

"You're the weakest of the knights of the Round Table. Sir Kay, you should do well to remember the reasons why you were ridiculed."

"Ugh, uhhh… AHHHHHHHHHHHHHHHHHHHHHHHHHH?!" Roaring in frustration, Sir Kay quickly struck him from every angle.

Her blows danced like flashes of lightning, faster than any normal human would be able to achieve in their lifetime. But Felicia's Jack could easily see through all her moves and handled them one after another while barely moving himself.

It was obvious one was more talented than the other. He handled Sir Kay with ease.

Their swords crossed fiercely a dozen more times before the Jack finally made his move.

"Hah—"

"—Ngh?!"

The battle was over. It happened in an instant.

In a single moment, Felicia's Jack had suddenly slashed at her with seraphic speed, as though a whirlwind or storm. As for Sir Kay, she narrowly met the strike with her own sword—

—but she wasn't able to stop the blow, and the tip of the Jack's sword grazed her, cutting through her armor like paper.

There was a spray of crimson, rising upward. In an instant, Sir Kay's body went limp, and the Jack landed a brutal reverse roundhouse kick in her stomach the moment she dropped to the ground.

"AGHHHHHH?!" Blown away by the impact, she rolled to Rintarou's feet. "Guh! Hah... Hah... H-he's strong!" She coughed, hacking up blood as she tried to get up.

Though her body trembled under pain and injury, she staggered to her feet using her sword as a cane.

"Ha-ha-ha, as excepted of you and your valor, *Sir Gawain!*" called out Felicia with pride upon witnessing the events unfold in front of her.

"...Do you get it now? Rintarou, do you see what I mean?" Sir Kay bitterly squeezed out. "That's right. That Jack is...Sir Gawain. He's the eighth seat of the Round Table and chosen by the armor-smiting blade Galatine. The heir of fearless King Lot from the Orkney Islands and like a son to King Arthur, who ruled all of Britain in his greatness—"

"Yes, that's exactly right!" Felicia continued, crowing triumphantly already. "My Jack, Sir Gawain, is famous as the strongest of the Round Table! His bravery outstrips all! He's noble, upright, and trusted by King Arthur—a knight among knights!"

"Ah, my liege. To declare I'm the strongest of the Round Table and a knight among knights... Why, you know how the truth embarrasses me."

But Sir Gawain was not at all bashful: In fact, his smile was prideful and hubristic.

"On the other hand, that Jack over there is well-known for being the weakest knight of the table—Sir Kay! She was given the third seat, out of King Arthur's pity, and is a dismal knight! You didn't stand a chance against us from the outset! Oh-ho-ho-ho-ho!" Felicia laughed loud and hard.

"Exactly. Would you please stop dragging the Round Table's reputation with you... Stop cheapening King Arthur," cursed Sir Gawain, mixing pity with contempt.

"—Grgh!" Sir Kay leaned on her sword, hanging her head, as she gritted her teeth.

There was no retort. Even in modern legends of King Arthur, it was still widely accepted that she was the weakest at the Round Table.

In her defense, Sir Kay was not weak in the slightest. But the others of the Round Table were too far beyond human potential in their ability.

"Damm...it! I—I... I..." In frustration, her face quivered and crumpled.

Rintarou gently rested a hand on her trembling head. "Don't worry about it, Sir Kay. I mean, in the first place, your role in the Round Table wasn't even to battle, right?"

"Wha—?!" Her eyes opened wide in astonishment and looked up at him.

"If you weren't there for that dude Arthur, his military rule would've easily been cut off halfway through."

"What're you saying, R-Rintarou...?"

"Well... Putting that aside for now, I guess it's time for the main show...," he remarked as he went front and center, followed by Sir Kay's shocked eyes.

"Mr. Magami... You want to fight? With Sir Gawain? ...Really? But you're a person of this era," Felicia said scornfully, eyebrows raised.

"I'll tell you this, but I won't allow any more blunders like last night, Rintarou Magami. That surprise attack was just a lucky hit, I'll have you know. And I won't let it happen...again." With that comment, Sir Gawain carefully readied his sword.

He seemed intimidating in a way he hadn't been until that moment, now completely serious and composed.

"Guh...it's no use...Rintarou. Challenging Sir Gawain head-on is..." Sir Kay made her appeal desperately while enduring the pain of her wounds. "I don't know...how you're so powerful in this day and age...but to put it bluntly, there's a fundamental difference between you and those from the era of King Arthur. With the passage of time, modern humans have lost their strength... They no longer have heroes. There's no way you could win head-to-head against a legendary hero . Unless...you have a trick up your sleeve?!"

"Huh? I haven't got any tricks," he replied casually.

"Ugh...of course you wouldn't...!" She gritted her teeth with regret.

"A trick is something someone of lower rank plays on someone of higher rank, right? That's why I don't need any tricks."

"...Huh?"

"What?"

"...Hah?!"

For a brief moment, everyone was taken aback by his strange word choice.

"That's inexcusable, Rintarou Magami," said Sir Gawain as irritation faintly appeared on his tough and stoic mask of a face. "To me, it sounds like... It's almost as if you're trying to say I'm inferior to you?"

"Yeah? You're a little slow. I'm not *trying* to say that, I'm saying you *are*," he jeered, smiling as he gestured and pretended to cut his own neck. "Gawain... You're not even worth calling my enemy."

"...Hah?!"

"Wha...?"

What's this guy saying? Is he an idiot? A fool? That or he just talks big.

Felicia, Sir Gawain, and Sir Kay were completely in agreement in their minds.

"Ah, well. Guess you're hell-bent on mocking me. You know the only way to atone for insulting a knight is death, right?"

"Th-that's right, Mr. Magami! You have no idea! You have no idea how strong Sir Gawain is! Just think! Think about how Sir Gawain is represented in games and manga and stuff nowadays! He's almost always set up as the strongest character and—" Felicia was running her mouth and started to spout ridiculous nonsense. With her prized Jack insulted, blood had come rushing to her head.

"Huh... A strong character? You mean Gawain?" Rintarou asked incredulously as he twirled and played around with his swords. "What a joke! If Arthur hadn't set things up for him, he wouldn't have been able to get anything done. You know, people call him a hack of a knight all the time."

"Wha—?" Sir Gawain's expression froze over.

"Huh?" said Felicia.

"Set things up for him? What did my brother do?"

Blinking back in confusion, Felicia and Sir Kay had no idea what he meant.

"Come on... Come at me, you little lackey. I'll show you how different we really are." After he finished his taunt, Rintarou suddenly stopped spinning his swords like a street performer and readied them.

In that instant, Sir Gawain made his move. His eyes burned with fury.

"RINTAROU MAGAMIIIIIIIIIIIIIIII!" He streaked toward him, faster than sound itself, as he broke through air.

"—Hah?!"

Emanating homicidal rage, Sir Gawain assaulted Rintarou's entire body like a gale.

"—Huh?!"

"Ha, that's fast—"

As the knight charged in a blur, Felicia and Sir Kay had lost track of his movements. He'd left behind the sound barrier and raised his sword, trying to hit Rintarou from above—it was lightning raining down from the heavens.

The move was a death blow Sir Gawain had tempered with blood and perfected in countless battlefields. It was a strike modern swordsmen wouldn't be able to defend themselves against, no matter how hard they trained—a method that ensured instant decapitation.

Even if the target attempted to evade the attack, they would be struck down faster than they could respond. If the target parried, their sword would break. That spoke to— No, that *was* the swordsmanship of a hero during the rule of King Arthur.

Those at the courtyard imagined, almost hallucinated, the image of poor Rintarou rolling over on the ground a second later, nothing more than a corpse.

But— *Clang!*

The sound of clamorous metal cut through the dark sky.

Upon closer inspection, yes, Rintarou had stopped the oncoming sword with his right blade, as though it were no large feat. He had held on to Sir Gawain's descending sword and stopped it in place.

He hadn't even used the blade. No, he was holding Galatine at bay with nothing more than the very tip of his sword.

"What's the meaning of this...?! What was that? It's like you're a street performer...?!"

"I-impossible...?!"

Witnessing this unbelievable scene from the sidelines, Felicia and Sir Kay froze in place. Even Sir Gawain was in disbelief at the sight before him.

"Heh—"

In the next moment, Rintarou slid the tip of his blade along the body of Sir Gawain's sword as he darted forward.

"AHHHHHHHHHHHHHHHHHHHHHHHHHHHHHHH!"

He passed by Sir Gawain, and his left sword shot at the knight's torso.

"GAAAAAH?!" Sir Gawain immediately went on the defensive and pulled back his sword.

Their swords clashed. The impact of each attack made the air tremble, violently sending sparks every which way.

With a powerful blow, Rintarou hit Sir Gawain and launched his body back in a fantastical display.

"NGHHHHH?!" Sir Gawain scraped the ground with the soles of his feet as he was pushed back a few dozen yards. Galatine, the famous armor-rending sword, creaked and groaned.

"How's that? You didn't expect that, right? I'm pretty awesome, huh?" he bragged, composed.

The rest were all taken aback with fear and shock slowly registering on their faces. They desperately wanted to believe the scene in front of their eyes—no, even going before that, they wanted to believe their very first encounter was from a dream.

"Hey, you ready?" It was Rintarou's turn.

Bam! The ground ruptured as he stomped on it, hard, and charged.

"—Huh?!"

Rintarou's swords formed an X as he bolted toward Sir Gawain, who stopped the attack with his own weapon gripped tightly with both hands.

Again, the swords rang out, the sound threatening to rupture the eardrums of those nearby— Pushing and rubbing against each other in a spiral, the two were beginning to stir up a hurricane with their movements.

"AHHHHHHHHHHHHHHHHHHHHHHHHHHHHHHHHHHHH-HHHHH!"

Then, with their swords still in place, Rintarou pushed Sir Gawain, who gouged deeper into the ground as he resisted.

"Don't get carried"—Sir Gawain defended himself and pushed away Rintarou's advances—"AWAAAAAAAAY!" Then he flipped around, pivoting on his foot to thrust at Rintarou's back.

"Heh!" Without even so much as a glance, Rintarou stopped the attack by swinging his left sword around behind him.

"RAAAAAAAAAAAAAAAAAAAAAAAAAA!"

When he turned around, he immediately hit Sir Gawain with his right sword.

"GUUUUUUUUUH?!" But he was extraordinarily fast as he reacted and countered.

Their swords clashed head-to-head several more times as the air and ground trembled under the impact of their might. Almost taking on a life of their own, their blades acted callously, rampaging, bringing forth showers of small sparks.

The force of their exchange blew the two of them in opposite directions, like balls bounding against each other.

"Why, you—"

"We're just getting started—!"

In the next moment, the two of them disappeared like mist and left a hollow of earth behind them as Rintarou and Sir Gawain collided in the middle.

Sword violently met sword over and over again.

"HAAAAAAAAAAH!"

"OAAAAAAAAAAAAAH!"

It was the advent of a terrific battle scene.

When Rintarou tripped the knight with his right sword, Sir Gawain leaped to avoid it and brought his own blade down. When Rintarou stopped that with his left sword and brought up his right sword, his opponent saw through the attack and pried himself away. When Rintarou quickly gave chase, Sir Gawain launched a counterattack. As the boy somersaulted to avoid it and aimed at his target's head, the knight countered. And so on and so forth.

It was both instantaneous and endless. As the fight raged onward, they met with one skilled technique after another.

Rintarou's two swords danced freely, skipped, twirled, and waltzed madly in the air.

Sir Gawain's sword swung straight, swiped, veered, and weaved all through the night.

Without exaggeration, each blow—one after another—was a death blow.

The darkness of the night was carved into countless pieces by the intricate, grotesque lines drawn by the swords.

Each time their weapons met, they'd parry even faster. Their speed kept increasing and increasing—it was as though there was no limit to stop at.

"Tch—!"

"What's wrong?! Hey! Weren't you gonna chop me up?!"

Clang! The sparks bloomed in a showy display, hanging in the air as the two swordsmen passed by each other in one moment, turning back in the next.

With an afterimage trailing behind them, they once again took aim and dashed forth, slashing savagely.

Again and again and again—

"Wh-what is...? What in the world is this...?!" stammered

Felicia, confused and overwhelmed by the transcendent combat that was occurring.

It was completely beyond her expectations. According to their little plan, Sir Gawain would stand before her, and Felicia would support him with magic—but with Rintarou and Sir Gawain, she could see no break or gap in which she could intervene.

"Mr. Magami… I can't believe you'd equal Sir Gawain in a match…?!"

"Equal him…? No, that's not right…," said Sir Kay.

He held the power to win against a battle with a dignified knight who had battled until the bitter end during King Arthur's rule.

Intently watching the battle, Sir Kay noticed the subtle change in the battlefield. "Rintarou is…gaining ground…?! No…he's… *becoming stronger!*"

From the start, Sir Kay had felt like something was slightly out of place—

It was true: Just as she'd discerned, the speed of his swords and attacks had been steadily increasing throughout the battle.

With each blow, his speed and power grew. It was like a dull, rusted sword becoming tempered and regaining its brilliance with each parry.

"Rintarou… You can't possibly be getting better *during* this battle, are you?!" Faced with surprise after yet another surprise, Sir Kay couldn't process any more information, leaving her on the verge of being overwhelmed.

"Ha-ha-ha-ha-ha-ha-haaaa?!" Rintarou laughed. "That's right! Good, keep that up! I've started to *remember*! Nothing beats a real battle for getting your intuition back!"

"Gruuuuuuuh?! What, impossible—?!"

Sir Gawain hadn't noticed when it happened.

But his rising torque had reached its limit while the speed of Rintarou's parries had surpassed already him, increasing more and more.

The battle between equals now leaned in one swordsman's favor. By this point, the knight had his hands full, barely stopping the successive attacks of his opponent's dual blades.

Rintarou had completely overwhelmed Sir Gawain.

"Take THAAAAAAAAAT?!"

"AGHHHHHHHHHH?!"

Rintarou swung his sword like he intended to bash his enemy with it. The blade ripped through the air, and Sir Gawain met it with his sword.

There was a clash—then the sound of an impact. The sparks flickered and wavered. The air itself trembled. The force and tension tore through the ground, searching for release.

The loser of the fight, the knight, was sent flying by the blast.

"GUUUH?!"

The fight was suddenly cut short when he tumbled to Felicia's feet.

"Sir Gawain?!"

"I-I'm fine, my liege…but…" He motioned Felicia to stop as she anxiously approached, and he finally got up.

From his forehead, sweat flowed freely in rivulets. He was the hero who'd fought each battle to the bitter end during King Arthur's rule. But at that moment, he struggled to breathe, on the brink of total exhaustion.

On the other hand…

"Heh, what do people say in these situations again? Right—I AM A GOD!" exclaimed Rintarou as he shouldered his swords with a smug grin.

There wasn't a drop of sweat on his forehead or a panting breath.

"Rintarou, you're amazing... I can't believe you did that to Sir Gawain... Just who are you...?"

"Sir Kay, it's dangerous. Keep back. I'm going to settle this here."

"O-okay..." *Huh? Wait, am I a useless side character?* Sir Kay inquired within herself.

Rintarou once again stood before Sir Gawain, who'd watched what was happening distantly and could only exhale in chagrin.

"I must acknowledge that Rintarou Magami...is strong... Even stronger than I am," the young knight concluded.

"...Huh?!" Felicia's face soured.

"It's certainly true he's arrogant, thinks he's essentially a god, and definitely has no friends—a true loner. He also has no manners or class and is scum among men...but he's not all talk, at least."

"...H-high praise, Sir Gawain."

"It's a different story with a King and an Excalibur, but for a modern human, it should be impossible for them to go up against a knight from the era of King Arthur, no matter how much they train. For example, had Sir Kay been born to this era, even she'd have made a name for herself as the strongest swordswoman."

"In that case...how is he...? How is Mr. Magami...?"

"I'm unsure. But the only ones who should be able to face a person from King Arthur's time would be someone who was also born in the same era. In that case, he must also have some sort of ties to the past."

As Sir Gawain and Felicia were going over that, Rintarou's patience started to wear thin. "Yo, just how long are you gonna spend talking in your little safe haven? You trying to buy yourself time?" He thumped the sword against his shoulder in agitation. "I'm in a hurry. While we're doing this, Luna's—"

Whoops, shouldn't say that. He'd almost said something that didn't suit his personality, causing him to unconsciously click his tongue.

"Hey, if you're gonna withdraw, hurry and do it already! If you're gonna fight, then fight! Now, which is it?!"

"Guh..."

Would they fight or retreat?

With hesitation spreading across her anxious face, Felicia ground her teeth.

"Let us prepare ourselves, my liege," suggested Sir Gawain, as if to console her, and once again went to the front. "We're out of options...are we not?"

"!"

"Let's use that...that *thing* you have."

"Y-yes, I understand..." Felicia nodded.

"Now, then... Rintarou Magami. Who are you?" quietly questioned the young knight. "We know you aren't some old, regular person born to this era. And your prowess as a warrior has overwhelmed me... What else resides within you?"

"Who knows."

"To speak of the dual wielders in the Round Table, I can only think of Balin le Savage or Galahad the immaculate paladin... But Sir Balin would be rougher and wilder with his technique, and Sir Galahad's technique is as elegant as a fine art. Your technique is wily enough to not apply to either... Though, actually, I think you're somewhat similar to Sir Balin."

"..."

"Now, what *are* you...Joker?"

"Tch... That doesn't matter." Rintarou evaded the question with visible irritation.

"You're right. It doesn't matter." The knight smiled. "There's no use in trying to pry into things when you're going to die anyway."

Rintarou faintly raised his eyebrows at this threat stated so matter-of-factly.

"...You won't be able to do it, Gawain. They've overestimated you in this era and raised you to the top ranks of the Round Table, but...your true strength at best is average... The table was packed with people much stronger than you."

"Wha—?!"

Sir Kay and Felicia were dumbfounded, while Sir Gawain lapsed into silence.

"Wh-what do you think you're saying, Rintarou! Sir Gawain?! Average?! That's idiotic! I saw it with my own eyes! Sir Gawain's strength was among the Round Table's—"

"Didn't I tell you? That was all because Arthur set him up for it," he responded indifferently.

"Hmph. So you really did know about that, Rintarou Magami..." Just about at the end of his rope, Sir Gawain's shoulders drooped. "The blood of the old Danann gods runs through me. They were the embodiment of the sun... I have the Sun's Blessing in my body. As long as the sun rises, my strength is thrice what it was... That's the kind of divine protection I have."

"Wha...? Th-thrice you say...?! What *is* that...?!"

"That's right. As long as the sun's rising... In other words, Gawain is only strong in the morning," explained Rintarou, nodding at the speechless Sir Kay. "Arthur knew that about his beloved little nephew and always made sure Gawain's matches were in the morning... That's all there was to it."

"I—I can't believe Sir Gawain had such an unfair advantage...," whispered Sir Kay, who, upon learning the astonishing truth, turned back to Sir Gawain in triumph. "Hmph! So that's all it was! So that's where all your bravery came from! If you weren't cheating, you wouldn't have been that—"

"Well, even without that, he's still stronger than you, Sir Kay," Rintarou retorted.

"MIND YA OWN BUSINESS!" she shouted, slumping over and on the verge of tears.

"Well, that's how it is. But the events of the King Arthur Succession Battle largely take place at night. Your pathetic skills won't see the light of day. In other words, you're three times as weak, Gawain," he provoked.

"I see... That's certainly the case." Sir Gawain remained mysteriously calm. "There's no use in hiding it. It's true my power is merely average among those who have a seat at the Round Table... To be honest, it's nothing to get excited about. But I wanted to rival Sir Lancelot and Sir Lamorak...so I used this ability to its greatest extent. I won't deny that."

"S-Sir Gawain..." Felicia anxiously gazed at her knight.

And in order to put her at ease, he showed her a small, fleeting smile.

"But I'll tell you this, Rintarou! As long as I'm with her...as long as I'm with Felicia, I'm the strongest knight at the table! I'll make sure Felicia is the true King in this battle, no matter what it takes! I came from Camlann Hill for this sole purpose!"

"Oh? Bold claim for a third-rate knight whose shitty divine gifts won't even work at nighttime... Do you still not get how different we are? Gweh-heh-heh-heh..." Rintarou chuckled in amusement and readied his swords. "Okay. How about you show me how you're the strongest? I'll crush you to a pulp!"

"Rintarou... Wow, this villain role really suits you. The way this is set up, you're making them look like they're the good guys," quipped Sir Kay.

Rintarou gloriously ignored her insults and sighs. "Okay, let's go!"

"Come at me! Rintarou Magami!"

Rintarou charged at him.

Sir Gawain readied his sword.

As he ran, Rintarou swung his swords in an X again while the young knight held his blade above his head to stop the attack. With residual force from the impact, Rintarou pushed him back. The soles of his feet dug deep into the ground in resistance and raised a cloud of dust.

"What's wrong, huh?! Weren't you the strongest knight of the Round Table (LOL)?!"

"GUUUUH—?!"

Of course, Rintarou was gaining the advantage again. His power completely surpassed Sir Gawain's, and the match was as good as done. It was just a matter of time—or so they thought.

Witnessing the drift of the battle, Sir Kay hollered confidently without thinking. "You won! This battle... It's our victory!"

"I wonder...if he really has?" said a familiar voice.

Felicia slowly pulled out her sword and brandished it above her head. It was the precious rapier sword—her Excalibur—proof she was worthy of being a King.

Then she yelled an incantation.

"'My sword, show my authority, show my sovereignty through your light!'"

Thump.

Felicia's mana blazed. The overwhelming, heavy Aura changed states and rose, gathering at Felicia's sword.

"Tch! I can't believe you'd use your Royal Road this early on!" Rintarou held Sir Gawain at bay as he gritted his teeth in annoyance.

A Royal Road. It unleashed the power from a King's Excalibur. Each Excalibur possessed latent power that could turn the course of a battle around in an instant. That was invoked through the Royal Road.

Of course, it was a King's trump card, something to conceal until a critical moment. It didn't bode well to introduce it so early in the battle.

That was because any power in the sword was halved as soon as it was used.

But Rintarou wouldn't have time to deduce Felicia's true intentions at the moment to understand why she was revealing the Royal Road now.

"What, you think that's gonna work? Sir Kay! Snuff that girl!"

"R-right!" Sir Kay charged at Felicia.

When all was said and done, Sir Kay was a knight from King Arthur's rule who'd fought her share of bitter battles. She moved swift as a tempest.

But her opponent's incantation was faster. "Royal Road— Excalibur the Radiant Steel Sword of Glory!"

In that moment, the sword in her hands released a blinding light, flooding the entire area with daylight and whiting out their vision.

"At that moment, King Lot, the King of the Hundred Knights, and King Carados set on King Arthur all at once.

"At their command, the three hundred knights and thirty thousand soldiers followed after them.

"But King Arthur drew the Excalibur. 'Know who you dare to challenge,' said the king.

"That sword glowed with the light of thirty torches, burning King Lot and his men blind.

"At that light, the enemies surrounding him—the kings and the knights and the soldiers—shuddered to think 'Oh, what have we done?' In that moment, they understood they were traitorous rebels and readied to flee—"

John Sheep,

LAST ROUND ARTHUR, THIRD VOLUME, NINTH CHAPTER

"Guuh—?!"

Showered in the light of Felicia's sword, Rintarou started to feel a little strange.

"Hmph!" In that instant, Sir Gawain pushed Rintarou back and rained down with sharp, heavy slashes on him.

Clash! There was the violent noise of scraping metal, as though it were crushing the air itself.

Using momentum from that impact, Rintarou barely leaped away, and his face contorted in frustration.

"Ugh, damn! My body feels *heavy!*"

He was close to coming to his knees and stuck his sword into the ground like a cane to support himself.

Yes, Rintarou's body felt abnormal, almost exactly as though it'd been turned into lead.

"How does that feel? What do you think of my sword's power?" boldly gloated Felicia, who continued to hold up her glowing sword. "The inscription on this sword is the Radiant Steel Sword of Glory, a sword that emits light to display the sovereign authority of the legitimate King. 'When bathed in this sword's light, enemies will feel their bodies become heavy and their powers wane.'"

Despite Felicia's words... "Ha!" Rintarou laughed.

As though to perk his body back up, he waved his sword around. "Heh. I feel a little sluggish, but this isn't that bad!"

"Oh? As expected. You can still move, huh?"

"Of course! If you're slowing down, you just have to use *Mana Acceleration* to make up for it! If you think a debuff is gonna do anything to someone on par with the Round Table knights, then—," he yelled bravely as he readied his sword again.

"I—I feel heavy... I can't move at all..."

"Sir Kay..." He turned a pitying eye to Sir Kay, fallen flat on the ground. "Tch... Well, I see how it is. You planned on cutting off my powers with your Excalibur and fighting me... But do you really think this cheap trick is enough to compensate for your lack of ability?" Even under limited power, Rintarou grinned fully through it all.

His expression indicated he still didn't doubt his victory in the slightest.

"That's right. It's true this light doesn't really work well on people of greater strength... In the past, King Lot didn't seem to even flinch in front of this light...but," Felicia started.

But she sharply looked over Rintarou and asserted, "This is a King's order, Sir Gawain! Slay the rebel Rintarou Magami right here, right now!"

"Understood!"

It was in that moment that Sir Gawain launched himself at Rintarou, and he swung his sword at the boy, putting the momentum from his dash behind the blow.

"Idiots always repeat their mistakes," Rintarou spat, hoisting his right sword up.

In an instant, blade violently met blade, battering the area with a ringing sound.

This was how Rintarou had fended him off, time after time, but—

"Wha—?!"

It was the first time his sword lost to Sir Gawain's blade, as it was sent flying back. And Rintarou found himself flung backward by the impact.

In this matchup, the victor was Sir Gawain.

"Wh-what? H-he suddenly got...?" Rintarou sputtered in bewilderment, and his eyes fluttered in confusion. He'd felt an incomparable power transmitted through Sir Gawain's sword for the first time in this battle.

"Now, Rintarou Magami. It's my turn. HAAAAAAAAAA-AAAA!"

With no regard or remorse for the perplexed boy, Sir Gawain's sword whistled as it came down.

"GUUUH?!"

Once again, swords met head-on as they fought and started to hit each other in a whirlwind. But this time, the fight progressed in exactly the opposite way it had before.

Each blow Sir Gawain struck was terrifyingly fast, heavy, and sharp. With a single stroke, he sent Rintarou soaring through the air and tossed him around as though he were nothing, ultimately making Rintarou retreat.

"R-Rintarou?! Why is this happening so suddenly?! What happened?!" asked Sir Kay, crawling onto the ground, still beaten down by the power of the Excalibur.

But he didn't even have a moment to reply as he held his opponent's sword, brought down like a flash of lightning, at bay over his head by meeting it with his two swords. But he was unable to hold his position, and his knee unintentionally hit the ground.

The knight's sword came ricocheting down, narrowly missing

Rintarou, who'd retreated farther back. In a flash, Sir Gawain pursued him with godly speed and thrust his weapon, which Rintarou tried to fend off with his right sword, but he was thrown back.

The Jack pursued him even farther in his weakened state.

"Dammit...!"

Sir Gawain's fierce attacks danced chaotically as he moved as freely as a bolt of lightning. And the Joker desperately stopped each one, continuing to fend them off.

The attacks were becoming more violent and came in rapid succession. The sheer force of it all was creating a vortex around them.

"Hah!" the knight shouted, and as though swinging a finishing blow, his sword blurred as it flashed.

"HAAAAH!" Rintarou narrowly stopped it with the swords he'd managed to pull back toward him, but— "GUAAAAAAH?!" Unable to stand up against his opponent's weight and impact, Rintarou was blown back and found himself rolling along the ground.

He used the momentum to hop on his feet again.

"Haaah...haaah...haaah...guh..." All signs of his previous easygoingness and boundless composure were gone... He started to pant. "What's going on? I feel like my body is heavy, but it's not just that..."

He thought over his unexpected disadvantage and gritted his teeth in annoyance.

"It's not as though my power is weaker from that light so much as...Gawain suddenly seems more powerful... But why...?"

He looked at the radiant sword and gasped, realizing something.

"I see, so that's what it is..."

"Oh? So you noticed? Couldn't expect less of you, Rintarou Magami."

"Yeah. That girl's Excalibur... That light is the same as the morning sun, isn't it?"

"Exactly. In other words, as long as my King has her sword, I can invoke the Sun's Blessing. With this, I can fight at three times my normal strength!" Sir Gawain pointed the tip of his sword at Rintarou. "You get it now, don't you?! Just as you said, as a knight of the Round Table, I might have been mediocre! But when I'm with Felicia, I'm the strongest knight of them all!"

Empowered by his words, Felicia also thrust out her chest. "It doesn't matter what kind of knight my Sir Gawain was before! He's my Jack! He walks beside me as I rule and is my finest knight!"

Then, next to Sir Gawain, she triumphantly poised her sword.

"......" Rintarou was silent. His face was turned down, and he didn't offer a response.

"Wh-what...? Then that's it—it's over. I never dreamed I wouldn't be able to keep up... This can't be anything but power creep... Power creep right from the start of the competition..." Sir Kay groaned from the ground, where she still couldn't raise a single finger.

"Now, let's settle this once and for all, Rintarou Magami! We'll beat you...and make Luna drop out!" shouted Sir Gawain.

"Yes. With this, we can devote ourselves to the succession battle without worry."

It seemed Felicia and her knight were sure of their victory.

"Yes, absolutely. Luna's always been meddlesome, even when we were young. She should know she can't win this battle... She'd know if she gave it some thought."

Rintarou let their conversation wash over him.

"In the first place...Luna doesn't have the character to be a proper King."

For just a moment, Felicia thought she could see Rintarou's shoulder twitch in response, but she continued anyway. "Luna always does everything out of her own self-interest. Doing whatever she pleases...and on top of all that, she even took a stranger as her ally in an attempt to win... Someone like her isn't fit to hold King Arthur's seat. If Luna becomes King, she'd put this world in chaos. No skills, no power... Luna is the archetype of a foolish ruler. Having her drop out is for her sake—and the world's."

"Ha-ha-ha. First, we have to deal with this Rintarou Magami. But...don't be careless, my liege. We don't know what that boy's true nature is."

"......" Rintarou was silent. Of course, he was silent.

He was letting their rambling go in one ear and out the other.

No one else in that place knew at that moment, but a certain phrase from Luna was ringing in his mind.

"Rintarou, I believe in you!"

"......"

"Oh, what's wrong, Mr. Magami? Do you always clam up the moment you're at a disadvantage? Maybe you're unexpectedly fragile?"

"Let's at least settle this fair and square as knights. Now, ready yourself, Rintarou Magami!"

"......" He still didn't make an effort to respond to their taunts.

...That was until he started to laugh in a low voice. "Heh-heh-heh..."

"Wh-what? Has he gone mad?" asked Sir Gawain suspiciously.

"No, you know what...? This is actually hilarious!" Rintarou snapped his head up to face them.

His expression overflowed with insuppressible delight, his eyes sparkling with the same excitement as a child's, his hands on a fun, new plaything.

"Huh…?" croaked Felicia, stunned in spite of herself, unable to comprehend how his expression was appearing—at that moment of all times.

"Holy shit, this is great! This feeling is indescribable—when you realize you can't wrangle something in without facing some resistance! That's right! This is it! This! This feeling! I've been waiting for this for so long!" he professed with glee. "You know what somebody with souped-up powers thinks about all the time? Everything's just too easy! My life up until now has been so boring!" He beamed. "So… This is a ton of fun… I'm glad I joined this battle."

A gruesome smile crept onto his face, with more than enough potential to send cold shivers down the spines of all those who saw it.

"Y-you're bluffing…"

"You cannot be flustered, my liege! We have the edge in this battle! Rintarou Magami may be a strong opponent, but as long as we maintain the power of your Excalibur and engage in an honest combat, victory is ours!" Sir Gawain proclaimed, biting back his slight discomposure as he stood to defend Felicia.

"Have the edge…victory is yours…huh?" Rintarou parroted back, his eyes locked on his target. "Well, I'm sure glad Luna isn't here…"

"What did you say?"

"I told her I'd actually get a *little* serious," he admitted, striking his right sword upright into the ground.

Then with his empty hand, he grabbed the blade of his other sword—then dragged it over the sharp edge.

"?!"

It went without saying that blood flowed out of his gaping wound.

He dragged his stained fingers on the back of his hands to

draw strange eye-shaped patterns, then muttered a spell under his breath.

In the next moment, the shapes burned bright crimson, glowing out of his skin.

Thump.

From inside his body, his mana ignited, restlessly restrained under his skin, kicking and writhing around.

"Wh-what is this...?!"

Thump, thump, thump... Shuddering, Felicia watched on as Rintarou's mana started to beat against his corporeal shell faster and faster, and Rintarou grew, becoming larger and larger.

ROAR!

Whirling and whipping around him, a black Aura rose up from within, sending shock waves in all directions, rushing out to find release. Facedown on the ground, Sir Kay was instantly blasted away by its impact, and Felicia's hair violently curled and lashed around under the hot air.

"GUUUH—?!" As Felicia lowered her arm from her eyes, she witnessed something she couldn't believe. "Wha...?"

There, in front of her—Rintarou had made a peculiar transformation.

His irises glistened gold, and his hair grew as long and white as the South Asian spirit Yaksha. All down his arms, a red fishnet pattern spread out from the backs of his palms. As his Aura ebbed and flowed, it surged out from his whole body, clinging to him to form a black robe.

And as if that wasn't enough, he emanated an insurmountable, colossal presence before them—as someone who was not human.

"Wha...? Wh-why does he look like that...?!" Felicia was captive to fear and withdrew by a step, then another.

"You can't be a Fomorian…?! Are you a descendant of…?!" the knight stammered, his eyes glued open in shock.

With white hair and magical, golden eyes—there was no doubt he was a Fomorian.

According to the Irish *Lebor Gabála Érenn* mythology, there were several divine families in existence. Among them were—the Fomorians. Until their eventual defeat at the hands of the Danann family, they'd been a wicked race, holding dominion over the world through their powers of darkness.

"Rintarou Magami… What in the world *are* you…?!"

"Time's up… Sucks for you, but I'm gonna need to clean this up right away, all right?"

Creak, creak… Menacingly, he stomped over to the King and her Jack, one intimidating, heavy step at a time.

It was the march of a demon king.

"GUUUUH—?!"

So be it, Sir Gawain seemed to think as he darted toward Rintarou—no longer dashing at a seraphic pace but a hellish one. Now three times as strong, he was three times as fast, too.

"AHHHHHHHHHHH!"

The sword he waved drew a terrific, silver whirlwind—and sliced through Rintarou's head with unexpected ease as it flew off his body.

"We did it—?!" he gushed in delight, colored by slight disappointment.

"Well, congrats."

Someone patted his back.

It was Rintarou, right behind Sir Gawain.

"…Huh?!" The knight only realized it then…that his headless body—right in front of his very eyes until this exact moment—had disappeared.

It was like a dream or an illusion.

"RAAAAAAAAAAAAAAAAAAAAAAAAAAAH!"

But Rintarou didn't give him time to understand the situation as he carelessly beat the knight's broad back with his sword.

"GUUUUUH?!" With great difficultly, he flipped back just in time to defend his body, but— "GUAAAAAAAAAAAAAAAAH?!"

His body sliced through the air upon impact with Rintarou's sword.

This power wasn't comparable to before. Had Sir Gawain's sword not been the famous Galatine, it would've been hacked in half, along with his body. This raw, savage force was out of this dimension.

"Guh— 'Dance, dance, nymphs of the flowers, dance and scatter as you bloom flowers of flames!'" recited Felicia, casting the fairy spell *Flower Fire Dance*.

As soon as she finished, Rintarou's surroundings became a storm of crimson petals, blanketed by the eddy of flowers until he wasn't visible any longer. Each one of the petals ignited, coiling around him to became one overwhelming hell of flames.

"What a joke!" he barked, waving his left arm.

Black volcanic flames erupted out of him, running amok and *burning out* Felicia's flowers.

"AHHHHH?!" she shrieked, flinching as she was hit with the backdraft from the clashing flames. "Was that the dark magic? *Black Flame*?!" She gulped, dumbfounded. "And...just now, did you just trick Sir Gawain with your dark magic, *Silhouette*?!"

To explain: Within the many forms of magic, there was something called *Family Magic*, special spells for certain illusory families.

Elven fairy magic manipulated the power of nature and the world.

Fomorian dark magic used the power of darkness, curses, and destruction.

Danann light magic controlled the power of light, blessings, and rebirth.

The blood and souls of these families allowed them to invoke *Family Magic*, meaning practitioners were only able to use the type of magic particular to their family line.

Going back, the reason Felicia could use fairy magic was because elven blood ran thick in her veins. In that case, the reason Rintarou could use dark magic was because...

"This is the power of the Fomorians. I can temporarily call on my ancestors."

"Call on your ancestors...?! Mr. Magami! So you're really a Fomorian...?!" she shouted, taking a good look at his white hair, golden eyes, the sinister pattern winding around his whole body, and the pitch-black Aura spurting out of him.

It was far from human, repulsive to look at, grotesque.

On top of that, his violent, overwhelming presence made it seem as though it could slaughter everything.

"W-we can't win..." Felicia sputtered in fear upon this realization.

It didn't matter whether she used her Excalibur at full force or if she used all the fairy magic she knew or even if Sir Gawain had the Sun's Blessing. In front of her very eyes, this boy was on a whole other level. This was beyond her.

It pained her soul to admit this to herself.

"Now, it's obvious I'll win, no questions asked, if I'm in this mood... But before that, you guys had some pretty interesting things to say, didn't ya?" Cutting to the chase, he eyed her threateningly. "You think Luna isn't fit to be King? You think she'll never be able to become King?"

"Ah...uh...," she faltered, cowering under those frosty golden eyes.

He roared, "You can't know till she becomes one, can you?! It's fine if you're hostile to her because of a battle, but don't go around dismissing people by your own random standards!"

"...Ngh?!"

"You know, that idiot Arthur, when he first started—"

Suddenly, Rintarou came to his senses.

What am I getting so worked up about? Everyone thinks King Airhead isn't the right ruler. I mean, come on, even I think that.

Anyway, this stupid battle is just supposed to be a game for me to kill some time. There isn't any reason for me to take it seriously. Like, I wouldn't respond this way if my character was mocked by someone in a game.

But then why am I acting this way?

"Tch... How about we end this soon?" he suggested, shaking his head slightly and brushing off his unwarranted irritation before readying his two swords.

Swirling up with the ferocity of a storm, his inky Aura roared out of his body. Even an amateur would've been able to see that his opponent was at an obvious disadvantage.

"Guh...?! Y-you monster! Beast...!" she accused in a trembling voice, slowly making her way backward.

Sir Gawain—and even Sir Kay—turned blue, their foreheads oily with dripping sweat. Anyone would be frightened. Absolute terror gripped the battlefield.

In fear and dread, all eyes were on Rintarou—a monster, a beast—in front of them.

"...My liege. We should retreat," proposed the knight bitterly, seeing the way things were heading. "I'm disappointed, but with him here, my Sun's Blessing amounts to nothing more than rubbish. Even if we choose to fight, we have no chance of winning."

"Th-that's..."

"It'll be fine. We are in your netherworld. If we focus on escaping, we might have a chance... I await your decision!"

"Ugh...uhhh...?!" she gritted in frustration for some time, holding her trembling sword.

Eventually, Felicia mumbled something.

Then they both slowly began to fade away. The world distorted, bending and wriggling around. The *Netherworld Transformation* over the school melted away.

"Ugh! Remember this, you monster! This isn't over!" she spat.

With this final line, Felicia and her knight fully disappeared from the distorting world.

...

"U-ughhh..."

"H-huh...?"

Lying facedown in a pile were the committee members as they finally began to open their eyes. Agonizingly slow, they got up one after another, though their consciousness was still clouded over and foggy.

When they looked around, they saw they were inside the school, which was coated black in the middle of the night.

"Why...are we lying around here...?"

"Weren't we...trying to catch Luna...?"

Gingerly, someone spoke to the students in their hazy state. "A-are you all okay?"

It was Tsugumi Mimori.

"Tsugumi...? Uhhh...why were we on the ground...?"

She shook her head helplessly at their concerns. "I—I don't know, either. I was also unconscious on the ground until a moment ago. I don't remember why I fell over, either..."

"You too...Tsugumi?"

Coming to their senses, they glanced at one another quizzically.

"Uh, I only remember up to running after Luna... Where is she?"

"Come to think of it, I don't see her around..."

"Where in the world could she have gotten to...?"

Back in the middle of the schoolyard, the *Netherworld Transformation* had faded away.

"Tch... It's been a while since I've been treated like a monster, *literally*," muttered Rintarou in resignation.

They were silent for a while.

"Uh, ah, so...Rintarou...?" Sir Kay whispered cautiously and warily, trembling at the sight of his grotesque figure. "Th-that was...something. I didn't think you had power...l-like that..."

Rintarou flipped around and glanced at Sir Kay.

"Eek—!" That was all she could muster, shoulders shaking, before she froze in place.

"..." A complex expression came over his face upon seeing her cower.

Then he muttered another incantation, and the swelling Aura vanished from his body, returning his eyes to their original color and his hair to its normal length. This colossal force wilted and deflated away to a normal person.

Before long, Rintarou was back to being human.

"Sir Kay, could you...not tell Luna what you saw just now?" he requested brusquely, returning his swords to their sheaths.

Her eyes went slightly wider at his request, and she was at a loss for words.

"Well, I'm used to people being scared like that. But the battle's just started, right? If she gets scared about every little thing, that'll be a problem when it comes to communicating or fighting later on..."

His explanation was out of character—no trace of his usual arrogance. It was almost as though he was making excuses.

"...Rintarou?" Without them noticing—Luna had come to stand a slight distance from them. "Hey, heeey, Rintarou. What was with that just now...? Why'd you look like that? What's with that power?" she asked, gazing at him in shock.

Was she here the entire time?! Damn... Did she see my Fomorian Transformation?!

He was shocked by his own carelessness.

It might've been because he was so aggravated by Felicia and Sir Gawain mocking Luna's abilities as a King. He'd been scatterbrained, not paying attention to his surroundings.

"Hey... What was that? Hey... Just what was that...?!" she questioned, quivering, eyes scared and serious.

Well, I guess anyone would react like that, he thought.

If anything, she'd seen her ally casually use some incredibly suspect powers. Being anxious and doubtful or overtaken with fear was natural. Of course she'd want to know about all the details and berate him.

"Hey, Rintarou, tell me... I'm listening?"

Just the other day, he'd planned to threaten Luna with his power, twist her arm, and force her to dance in the palm of his hand, if he had the chance... These cruel and diabolical thoughts came naturally to him, and if he still wanted to do it, he likely could.

But for some reason, Rintarou didn't have those intentions at that moment... With great uncertainty, he could only watch Luna as she fearfully approached him.

"Hey, what was that power? It seems really dangerous? Hey, tell me. Isn't that power—?"

It seemed it was unavoidable.

It was a short alliance. Ah, well.

Rintarou was deriding himself as he breathed out and turned away...

"—Isn't that power super-freakin' cool?"

"Hmm?"

That's strange. He must have heard her wrong. He tilted his head quizzically.

But as he looked over at Luna again, her eyes carried a child-like excitement as she brought her face up to his eyes and the tip of his nose.

"Whoa?!"

"Hey, hey, hey, hey, hey! Rintarou! What was that power just now?! What was it?! A transformation?! It couldn't have been a transformation, could it?! Your hair and eyes changed color and your hair got longer and you had weird clothes on and you even had these patterns all over you, and on top of that, you, like, powered up! Was that what you'd call a transformation?! Or was it an awakening?! It was, like, insanely cool! Hey, what kind of magic was that? Teach me! I want it, too! Wow! Wow! Woooow!"

Is this what it was like for a young child who'd met their hero?

Her face was flushed in incredible excitement.

"Whoa?! Calm down! You're too close! Get away! You're so annoying!"

His cheek twitched as he grabbed Luna's shoulders and yanked her away.

"Hey, hey! Just what was that?! I wanna do it, too! That's a King's order! Teach me!"

"Hey, calm down! That was a *Fomorian Transformation*! It's proprietary and mine—sucks for you! Only a few people can do that, even if they have connections with the Fomorians! Give it up!"

"What, really? Then I can't do it? Hmph... Fine." With puffed cheeks, she seemed genuinely dissatisfied, not putting on an act to be brave or anything at all.

But Rintarou couldn't help being suspicious about her behavior.

"What's wrong, Rintarou? Is there something on my face?"

"No... Are you really not scared? Of me?" he spat, somewhat offhandedly.

"Huh? Scared? Why?" Luna replied, unimpressed.

"Well, it's just... Isn't it obviously weird? It's not human."

"Well, I mean, I guess if you were a strange, unfamiliar monster or a hostile enemy, I *might* have been scared," she noted calmly, as though having to explain it was almost idiotic and a chore. "But you're Rintarou. You're my vassal."

At that nonchalant remark, he was at a loss for words.

What does she mean? I don't get it.

How could she say that to a boy she just met? Especially when she didn't know his true form?

"Ah-ha-ha-ha-ha-haaa! There's nothing more promising than having a vassal as strong as you! Heh, with an amazing vassal choosing to serve me, I really do have the capacity to be the true King... I'm close to conquering King Arthur's throne! Just you wait!"

"Huh...? I guess it's fine if it doesn't bother you, but...don't you at least want to ask about it? Don't you want to know why I have these damn powers...?"

"Huh? Did you wanna talk about it?"

"No...not really."

"Then not really, it's fine."

And that was that.

Ever since he'd met this girl, Rintarou felt like he was going insane, losing control of himself.

That was when Rintarou suddenly noticed something.

Bruises and cuts were all over Luna's body, scattered haphazardly, as she laughed loudly. Even more curiously, she didn't seem to have anyone else's blood on her. And on top of that, she seemed triumphant, no shadows of regret hiding behind her beaming face.

Did she...really get out of there without killing a single student...? Even as she got herself injured?

But how? How was she able to do that?

He knew the answer without even asking.

Luna had probably believed—in him.

She believed he'd do something about the situation. She believed in her vassal and stuck to her conviction. That definitely was her one and only rule.

"Huh? What's wrong, Rintarou? You don't look very happy." She cocked her head to the side and gazed into his face with a sassy expression.

To which, Rintarou stared back for a while, grumpy and unimpressed.

"Hey, Rinta—rogh?!" she gagged, as Rintarou gripped her throat with his claws.

"Shut up. Just keep quiet for a while," he warned in a low voice as he strengthened his grip on her throat.

"GUUUAAH?!"

"Rintarou?! Y-you—?!" shouted Sir Kay.

Her eyes darted around in confusion as her throat started to close, and Sir Kay readied her sword at Rintarou. But he didn't pay her any mind, focusing on muttering something under his breath. With that, the hand on her neck started to faintly glow, healing Luna's cuts and bruises before their very eyes.

"Rintarou...?"

When her injuries had more or less healed, he let go of Luna and turned his back on her. "Hmph. It's the *Healing* spell. If it were Danann light magic, it probably would've healed you better, but all I've got is dark magic. Well, those should heal up overnight anyway."

From the corner of his eyes, he saw Luna and Sir Kay blinking slowly as he started walking toward the school gate.

"Look, I'm going home now! ...Seriously, you made me steal those test questions and show my trump card right away. All that thankless work was a waste!"

Luna pattered over to him from behind. "Ha-ha, thanks, Rintarou! As a vassal, you've got a pretty good heart!" She slapped his back and walked next to him.

They simply walked side by side, making jabs and retorts, as they talked about something or another. It made them look like they really were a ragtag pair of friends.

Watching them from behind, Sir Kay grew quiet and pensive.

Because I was too caught up thinking about Luna...I might've been blinded and focused only on how suspicious and strong Rintarou was. I might not have been looking at him as a real person.

"Rintarou Magami... Um, please accept my sincere apologies."

He stopped on his heels at Sir Kay's unexpected remorse.

"To make an honest confession, I'm still terrified of you. Though it may be a slow process, I'll try to understand you more from here on out. That's what I thought seeing you just now. It'll be difficult to rid myself of this fear, but...I'll devote myself to it."

"..."

"My lord...I place her care in your hands. I'm sure in the battle ahead of us...Luna will need your strength. Probably more than mine, so—"

Grumbling, he suddenly interjected, "Hey, Sir Kay...you can't be thinking of leaving me alone to rein in King Airhead? Don't be ridiculous. Give me a break."

"Whaddaya mean by King Airhead?! King Airhead?! That's super-disrespectful?!" protested Luna, puffing up to object.

Ignoring her, Rintarou turned quickly to Sir Kay. Right then, just in that tiny moment, his expression was free from his usual insolence and narcissism.

He looked somewhat peeved and just the tiniest bit bashful... Suitable for a boy of his age.

"You're right. We both do need to support her," offered the Jack.

"Right. But well...it doesn't look like you'll ever be useful in the battlefield, Sir Kay."

"Uh, guh?! Y-y-you..."

"Hey, Rintarou! That's so rude! Sir Kay's amazing, too, you know!" she defended in a burst of anger. "For example! Uh... ummm... Huh? Sir Kay's amazing because..."

"Please stop, Luna... My heart just might break." Her eyes teared up as she saw Luna struggling to come up with an example.

"R-right! I live by myself, but she budgets my money and makes food and cleans and does the laundry, and she's supergood at all that! Oh, and can't forget the cosplay—"

"LUNAAAAAAAAAAAAAAAAAAAAAAAAAAAAAAAAAAAAAA!"

Their conversation was lively.

The three of them left behind the school building in the night.

*   *   *

Meanwhile, certain other events were transpiring between some skyscrapers in the darkness of an alleyway.

"Haaah…hah…hah…" Running for her life, Felicia struggled to breathe as she supported herself against a wall.

"Are you unwell, my liege?"

"No, I'm fine…but…" Felicia smiled so as to not cause Sir Gawain any more grief, but her pale face didn't have its normal vigor or self-confidence. "We're…complete failures…"

Their plan for the night was to make Luna drop out. They'd used *Netherworld Transformation* in order *not* to involve any outsiders. They were supposed to drag only Luna in by herself to settle things.

But they'd failed.

Rintarou Magami—to think he was an existence so beyond their expectations.

He fit the role of a Joker perfectly: someone who completely threw off calculations on the board.

"But…how did that Mr. Magami enter the netherworld?"

She knew several other people were in the school building that night, thanks to *Detection*, and naturally, she also knew the troublesome boy was by her side.

That was why she'd specifically pulled *only Luna* into the netherworld to eliminate him as a variable…or so she'd thought.

Of course, he probably could have forced himself in, using one method or another. But by then, she would have settled things with Luna.

After defeating and constraining her, she would've retrieved Luna's Round Fragment and Excalibur to destroy them—and decisively remove all qualifications for her to be a King.

"This was a big mistake, even for me. I didn't think he would've been pulled into the netherworld...," she reflected, feeling her confidence in her magical skills break into smithereens. "If this keeps up, Luna will... That girl will end up in the hands of that man..."

"My liege, it's no use regretting something that's already come to pass. Going forward—," he encouraged her as she sank into the depths of despair.

"Good grief, you lost again? I'm disappointed in you, Lord Felicia Ferald."

Tap, tap, tap... The sinister sound of footsteps and a foreboding presence approached them from the back of the alleyway.

From the inky darkness, a solitary figure appeared.

"L-Lord Gloria...?!" The back of Felicia's spine was electrified, raising her hairs.

It was Felicia's temporary ally—Lord Gloria, infamously known as the strongest candidate in this King Arthur Succession Battle.

A veil of darkness cloaked his figure. But even across that black abyss, Felicia could instinctually feel he was smiling coldly.

"But well, I guess you could say your failure was...exactly as I hoped."

"As you hoped...?" she yelped. "Wh-what do you mean by that?" She couldn't hide her trepidation.

But Lord Gloria was endlessly cold as he informed her: "I might not seem like it, but I'm incredibly cautious. I needed to ascertain just how strong that Rintarou Magami was. You did a splendid job of pulling that out of him."

"Wha—?!"

"I see; so he's a dual wielder with several types of magic under his belt. And that *Fomorian Transformation*... I have quite a bit of interest in him."

"Did you...use me as a pawn...? Y-you couldn't have?!

Did *you* use some trick to make sure Mr. Magami entered that netherworld...?!"

"Heh-heh-heh..." Lord Gloria's deep and faint cackle was bone-chilling.

"Because of you, I've gotten a good idea of who he is. Rintarou Magami...can't be considered an enemy, in regards to my Jack and me. Well, he's reasonably strong, but it's simply *out of the question.*"

Lord Gloria probably used some sort of technique to observe them. But even after seeing that inhuman power with his own eyes, he was still composed and unruffled.

"—?!" Like an icy knife slicing through her spinal cord, a chill flooded through her body.

"Know your enemy, know yourself, and you shall win a hundred battles. It's a well-put phrase. Thanks to that, I can kill that fool without worry...heh-heh-heh..."

At that moment, he slipped something out.

From the dense shadows, Lord Gloria pulled out an ominous long sword—his Excalibur.

"I am the true successor to King Arthur. I am the true King who will rule over the whole world. I am its monarch. What I require is absolute victory. I will kill all other candidates... Yes, that's the only way, isn't it? Collect the four treasures? Ha! I'll take my sweet time once I kill all the other candidates... Isn't that right?"

"P-please wait...?! Please! J-just not Luna...," she yelled, as though entreating him, and took one step forward— In that moment...

"Stop! Felicia!" In a gust of wind, Sir Gawain instantly readied his sword and stood in front of Felicia.

There was the earsplitting sound of an impact. The knight was blasted by a blow from the long sword and violently hit the side of the skyscraper, causing the concrete wall to crumble.

He was at the end of his rope and lost consciousness.

"S-Sir Gawain?!"

"Oh dear, as we'd expect from him. The paragon of a knight bravely offers up his body to protect his King."

What had tore into Sir Gawain was a single stroke from Lord Gloria's sword, aiming directly at Felicia's neck.

"Well, absolute loyalty to the King once caused the Round Table to collapse… Isn't that such an ironic tale?"

The battered knight couldn't move, groaning in pain and coughing up blood, unable to stand.

Faced with Lord Gloria's Excalibur, Sir Gawain was practically a child.

"Wha…?! Lord Gloria… Did you just…? Did you just really try to kill me?!" Felicia howled, shuddering. "What's the meaning of this?! We were supposed to be a united front until the four treasures began—"

"Ha, you serve no use to me now. Your value's in that old elven blood of yours and your magic… But you see, I've finally finished preparing a magical rite to steal that from you and make it mine… Once that happens, my victory is even more set in stone."

"Guh… That's what you've been scheming all along?! You made an alliance with me…in order to steal my power…?! You tricked me…?!"

"Isn't that the case for both of us? You think I didn't notice?" He guffawed, seeing through her intentions from the beginning, and his shoulders shook in glee. "You saw me as a threat from the very start. If you didn't do something about me, there would've been so many more casualties in this battle. So you needed to eliminate me from the start…in order to protect your precious friend. But I was too strong. You just couldn't compare to me."

"That's—?!"

"So in the public eye, you pretend to form an alliance with me, but under the surface, you planned to cooperate with the other candidates...and eventually assassinate me the moment I lowered my guard. That's what you were plotting, right? You were hoping to get Luna to drop out, knowing she'd be too weak to take me on and die if we battled head-to-head. That was your plan, wasn't it?"

"Th-that's..."

"It's fine; you can stop this farce. Felicia...you're dropping out right here." Lord Gloria pulled out a jewel amulet on a chain from his pocket.

Etched onto the jewel was XII. It was a Round Fragment.

"Twelfth seat of the round table, heed my call."

When he recited the spell, a flash of lightning went off above his head, and a magic circle momentarily allowed a Gate to materialize out of thin air.

A Jack leaped out from that Gate.

CHAPTER 4

𝔗𝔥𝔢 𝔏𝔢𝔞𝔡𝔦𝔫𝔤 ℌ𝔞𝔫𝔡

I frequently have this one dream.

It's a far-off, nostalgic dream of a time before this one.

"Hey, Arthur, what do you think you're doing? ...Are you crazy?"

In the dream, I've just returned to the Camelot castle in the kingdom of Logres, where I approach the throne of a slumbering young boy King—Arthur.

"So you added that King Pellinore to the Round Table?"

"Yeah, I did. Wow. I'm so happy I've found such a trustworthy vassal." He laughs lazily.

I press on him in exasperation. "You idiot! Yeah, sure, he's stupid strong, but nothing good's gonna come from having that boorish warrior serve under you! That secretary of state, Sir Kay, was in tears, saying she was sick to her stomach! Are you trying to stress your sister to death?! If she wasn't around, this kingdom would be under by now! All you've got are thoughtless dumbasses at your Round Table. At the very least, you gotta be more considerate to your sister!"

"Ha-ha-ha-ha... I guess I gave my sister more trouble to deal with..."

"Aren't you at least scared?! You almost got killed by that same King Pellinore just the other day! If I hadn't gotten involved, you wouldn't be sitting here right now—"

"Okay, okay, we cleared up that misunderstanding, so can't we put that all behind us?" Arthur grins innocently. "With the deciding match with King Lot coming up, I need to have a ton of strong vassals, right? Plus, did you know that King Pellinore...is super-funny? He uses brute force to settle everything and then *actually* settles stuff that way."

"So it's because he's funny, huh? You're always like that. That fool will never actually fall in line with you..."

"It's okay... I'm sure it'll all be fine."

"Huh? Where'd you get that confidence from...?"

"Because I've got Sir Kay and you, too, ■■■■." Arthur would always be laid-back, all smiles.

"Tch, ah, well, fine. I'll do something about that pig... Seriously, you know you're an annoying King, right? Why'd I make the mistake choosing to support you?"

Though I seem to be oozing with discontent and dissatisfaction, I'm not actually as upset as I make myself out to be—

—It was that dream of serving Arthur, the boy King.

Ever since I've started forming my own thoughts as a kid, I've had it a lot.

When I became older and my mind matured, I started to understand those were memories of a past life—through instinct rather than logic.

There was no other explanation for them.

I was a child prodigy. In my dream, I could fight with swords, use magic, learn anything—*do* anything. In real life, I was able to achieve everything, just like my dream self. As I watched and mimicked my dream self, the list of things I could do continued to expand and grow in my real life.

I didn't know the reasoning behind it, but my modern self had inherited all the abilities and memories of my past self. In so-called modern times, I'd be classified as one of those popular characters: a reincarnation armed with abilities that cheat the system.

The only problem was I was too good at everything...

"Hey, hey, look, Dad! *I got the highest score on the test today again!*"

"Hey, hey, listen, Mom! *I was number one at gym class today, too!*"

Everyone around me called me a *genius* or a *child prodigy*...at first.

My mom and dad were proud of me—only at the very beginning.

When did it start? When did everyone stop seeing me as *amazing*? When did their looks of admiration and aspiration morph into calling me a socially inept *monster*?

When was the first time...? When did I first notice those looks?

Was it during the national soccer rally, when I overtook everyone to shoot a goal? Or when I competed with Mr. Overachiever, always in the highest bracket in the national exams, and beat him just by cramming overnight? Or when I beat up a gang of fifty delinquents all by myself to protect my classmates?

Was it when I told my mother and father about a mistake in a research paper they'd dedicated half their lives to writing? Was it when I thought up a new theory on the spot that surpassed theirs? Was it when I made my dad angry and my mom cry for some reason?

By the time I noticed, everyone looked at me like I was a *monster*...

...And I was all alone. No one would come near me. I didn't even have parents anymore.

No, wait, I felt like somewhere in there, there was this one weird kid who kept praising me, saying *"Amazing! Amazing!"* and *"I'll make you into my vassal in the future!"* or something...but that was a long time ago. I can't even remember what this kid looked like anymore.

Well, anyway, halfway through my teens, I realized something.

That's just unfortunately the way things are.

Those who don't conform get beaten down. That's how the world is.

In my past life, I was a character with so much power, it would've even surprised me. No one in this world could stand against me, and as indemnification for that, I was in solitude.

In easy mode, in this endlessly boring world, I could only kill time.

I couldn't go all out. I wouldn't go all out. Without any sense of achievement, without joy, without feeling, without something to live for, my life continued in waste.

That's why I had no choice but to act recklessly. I'd be reckless to make this stupid, dull life into something fun. I'll do whatever I want to, however I want to, all alone.

So that was why I decided to take the guidance of a *certain girl* and join this King Arthur Succession Battle.

I thought maybe then this boring-ass life would become slightly more enjoyable.

That was all it was. I really didn't have any lofty principles or even a semblance of a goal when I joined this battle.

But... Maybe, just maybe, I wanted to prove something to myself.

*   *   *

"C'mon, Arthur, let's get out of here! Ha-ha-ha! Seriously, get your head out of the clouds!"

In the dream, I didn't have any of the weariness that I carry now, as I served King Arthur. My past self must have also been feared and loathed: In fact, he might've even had it worse, but he still seemed happy, vibrant, and full of life.

And my dream self was most alive next to King Arthur.

Why was that? What were you so happy about? What's different between you and me?

Was this King called Arthur *that* special to you?

But why in the world were you—was I...?

It could be..., I thought.

I searched for the answer, hoping to find it with the King Arthur Succession Battle...

Slap!

"Hey, Rintarou! Why've you got your head in the clouds?!" screeched Luna cacophonously.

He'd been lost in thought, thinking about his dream last night, one that he hadn't had in a while. But with a start, he was brought back to his senses by her piercing voice and her handheld fan, brought down with a hard whack on the back of his head.

He found himself in the middle of lunch.

In front of his eyes was an assortment of bread that he'd bought with the student council budget the other day.

Just then, a crowd of students from Camelot International came pushing toward the school café, desperately swarming them in order to buy that bread.

Right, now that he thought about it, he was currently working as a salesclerk in that café with Luna. "What the heck am I doing...? What did I come here for again...?"

"Gimme that breaAAAAAAAAAAAD with custard filling?!"

"I—I want that red bean bun! Hand it over!"

"I'll take a hot dog bun!"

"...Welcome. Thank you so much. They all cost one dollar...," he cried, continuing to sell the bread in tears.

"Get yourself together, Rintarou! This lunchtime rush is the lifeblood of our business! You call yourself a salesclerk?!"

"I'm not! I'm absolutely not one!"

"Anyway, just sell, sell, sell! Sell anything and everything you can while we're still in a seller's market! Snatch that money from these impressionable rubes!" Luna yelled in a very revealing maid outfit with a dangerously low back. She was well aware of her own pretty face and unscrupulously used it to its fullest extent...and it had an immense magnetism in attracting customers.

"I'm so done with King Airhead..." He sighed, turning his gaze away from her and glancing to his side.

"Guh... Th-that comes out to three dollars...ugh... D-don't look at me...!"

Of course, Sir Kay was wearing the same exposing maid outfit as Luna. Teary-eyed, she quivered as she made her sales to a large swarm of male students. Lined up in front of her, everyone had their phone out and ready.

This is too sad... He couldn't help but feel sympathy at her pitiful and pathetic state.

But the biggest reason for the unprecedented success of the limited-time café was...

*   *   *

"I did it! I got the super-special-rare Swimsuit Kay card!!"

"I got the super-rare Kay in a Long Sleeve Shirt, Innocently Waking Up card!"

"Damn, seriously?! That's too lucky!"

"Ahh, I want one… I want a rare card! Then I'm gonna just go buy five more pieces of BREAAADDDD!"

""""GET BACK IN LINE!"""""

"Heh… Making her portraits into cards, creating the Sir Kay Trading Card Game (manufactured by the student council)…and attaching limited-edition booster packs to the bread was a smashing success!"

"You think that poorly of a knight of the Round Table?"

Incidentally, the subject in question was emotionless as tears streamed down her face like a waterfall. It seemed she'd given up on everything and stopped thinking.

"Ah-ha-ha-ha-haaa! We're making a killing! I can't stop laughing!"

"I thought it was strange. When you said you wanted to secure a supply chain to stock up on provisions for the long battle ahead and asked me to go look into all the bakeries in the city…why did I seriously think you were actually creating reserves for a hideout?! Dammit, dammit, dammit!"

"Stop, Rintarou! A smile is the lifeblood of a salesclerk! If you look sad, you'll tank our sales!"

"Who do you think is causing me to make this face?! You idiot! Wait, didn't you…sell your Excalibur for money? Why are you trying so hard to raise money when you should be swimming in cash…?"

He'd made a mistake in forming an alliance with her, no doubt—100 percent. Rintarou was wholeheartedly wallowing in regret.

"Oh, you're really putting your heart into this, Rintarou." It was the homeroom teacher, Mr. Kujou, here to buy some bread. "You guys make a surprisingly great team, don't you?"

"Hey...gimme a break, Mr. Kujou." He sighed in annoyance.

But the teacher seemed somewhat reassured, a smile forming on his lips. "It seems I didn't have to butt in. I originally had my head full thinking another problem child joined my class, but... yeah, as long as you're with Luna, I think things should be fine."

"Huuuh...?" he protested, not understanding what Mr. Kujou meant. "Things should be fine? For me? What do you mean by that?"

"Well, based on your background... Er, as your homeroom teacher, I got your records from the higher-ups. It's sort of a black-list. You're pretty well-known in the education scene."

"...Huh?!"

"But it looks like you've had your fair share of trials and trib-ulations. Ah, but don't get the wrong idea. I'm not going to lecture you or counsel you or anything. It's just..."

"It's just...what?"

Mr. Kujou glanced at Luna. "I think you're really meant to be with her. I'm sure this is a good thing for you."

"What...?"

"It'll be good if you stick around Luna, and if she shakes you up. I think that'll solve the issues you've got before long."

"I—I don't get what you're saying... I'm getting pretty fed up with her, actually..."

"Ha-ha, don't say that. I'm sure you'll get it soon." He ordered a croquette sandwich and a small bun with custard filling.

Rintarou received a five-dollar bill from him and handed back the bread, plus change.

"...Thanks for coming."

"Thank you." He left calmly.

He sent him off, watching his teacher leave, as he continued to scrape his mind, deep in thought...

"LUNAAAAAAAAAAAAAAAAAAAAAAAAAAAAAAAA?!"

With Tsugumi Mimori at its head, the members of the Ethics Committee parted the crowd and appeared on the scene in a fluster.

"Oh, Tsugumi! Howdy!"

"Luna! J-j-just how much of an immoral mess do you need to make before you're satisfied?! How dare you sell these indecent cards at school!" she screamed, shaking in anger, as she thrust one of Sir Kay's cards right in front of Luna's eyes.

"Huh? I'm not really selling cards, though?" she responded sarcastically, folding her hands behind her head and playing dumb. "I'm merely doing business in an official capacity for the student council. All I'm selling is bread. That bread just so happens to include trading cards as an extra. You mad?"

"No matter how you look at it, you're selling the cards, and the bread just happens to come with it! Do you really think you can use a technicality to get away with this?"

"Oh, by the way, if they collect all the cards, they'll also get the super-duper-rare card Kay Getting Out of the Bath as a complimentary gift from me to you!"

"That selling strategy is straight from a mobile game! That's literally a crime!"

Rintarou's and Sir Kay's eyes became distant as they listened to Luna and Tsugumi's familiar back-and-forth.

"Guuuuh! Why you?! With all that happened yesterday?! How

aggressive can you be?! I can't stand it anymore! This is gonna put you in handcuffs! Now, everyone, let's dismantle this sketchy booth!"

"""""Yes, ma'am!"""""

The committee members charged all at once.

"Don't mess with us! This is *our* li'l Kay you're talking about— Uh—I mean, our bread! You trying to tell us to go through the afternoon without a proper meal?!"

"Right! Protect, PROTEEEEEEEEEEEEEEEEEEECT!"

"""""AAAAAAAAAAAAAAAAAAAH!"""""

Once again, the student council and committee clashed head-to-head, and as usual, the place invoked a scene from hell. Yeah, it was all storm and stress and pandemonium.

"This again? Seriously, what's wrong with this school?" Rintarou was exasperated.

"Tch…this place is done for!" yelled Luna. "Sir Kay, I'm leaving the fort in your hands! Sell all the leftover bread! You got that?!"

"Wha—? Whaaaaaaaaat?! I-in this chaos?!"

Leaving her knight to deal with this ridiculous, unreasonable mess, Luna grabbed Rintarou's collar and yanked him away. "Look, Rintarou! Don't just stand there! We've got to hurry and skip town!"

"Hey, wait?! Stop… Just where are we go—? AHHHHHHH-HHHHH?!"

With Rintarou's collar in hand, Luna stepped right onto a window frame in the hallway and jumped out of the school building.

It just so happened they were on the third floor.

With that, they slipped out of the school grounds.

First order of business: Luna changed from the maid outfit into her uniform in a convenience store bathroom.

"Seriously, were you *trying* to kill me?! You're seriously, really reckless! Hey!"

"Ah-ha-ha! Don't sweat it!"

The pair walked along a large street in Area Three of Avalonia. Built on top of the man-made island, this international city was divided up into a total of thirteen areas. Area Three was the so-called student town. With Camelot International at its center, the student dormitories, boardinghouses, entertainment venues, restaurants, and parks were gathered in that block.

Unlike Area One, the hub of the city, and Area Two, the epicenter for commercial business, there weren't any state-of-the-art skyscrapers. In fact, this area made one think of an old English townscape in the countryside.

"To top it all off, we left school *and* we're skipping class... At this rate, I'll end up under the radar of that Ethics Committee, too. This is such a pain."

"Too late. You already are! Thanks to last night. Aren't you a man? Don't complain about things after everything's already said and done! You're my vassal, aren't you?!"

"Heeey, hey, hey!" He honestly didn't have any strength to argue anymore.

"Anyway... So what should we do now, Rintarou? It's not like we can just go back to school now and go to class. Hmm..."

"Yeah, you're right. You're completely right...and...that's... all...your...fault!" he reprimanded as sarcastically as possible, but it had no effect on her fearless smile. "Tch... Well, it doesn't matter. I'm gonna change subjects. About the King Arthur Succession Battle... Generally, the battle starts at sunset. In other words, we can't be careless, but we can assume afternoons are safe."

He glanced over at her with those eyes again—the eyes of someone who'd walked along the underside of the world.

"We can't waste a single minute or second if we want to stay in and win in this death match to get his seat... Do you get what I'm trying to say?" he asked cryptically.

"Yeah. You're right. I get it." With the air of a King, she majestically proposed, "Let's go on a date, Rintarou."

"Yeah, exactly. First, we'll gather info on the other Kings. When all's said and done, there's one person I want to find......"

For a while, the internal and external information flowing through his brain passed by each other. Something was not matching up.

He fell silent.

"Hey you, King Airhead? Hellooooo? Were you even listening? How'd you come to that conclusion? Could you explain that to your dumb vassal, King Airhead?" he crooned, standing behind her.

"Ow, ow, ow, ow, ow, ow, ow! That hurts! Ouch, ouch, ouch, ouch, ouch!" she yelped. Sandwiching her forehead between his fists, he dug in with his knuckles. "That hurts?! What do you think you're doing, you idiot?!"

"THAT'S WHAT I WANNA ASK YOU, YA IDIOT!" Rintarou howled, grabbing her lapels as she glared at him with hot tears in her eyes. "Just how did you come to that conclusion?! We don't have time to joke around—"

"Hmph! You don't get it, do you, Rintarou?! You just don't get why we absolutely need to go on a date right now!" she spouted with a smug grin, puffing out her chest and pointing at him. "Listen up, all right? Officially, we've still just met each other to everyone else, right?!"

"I don't give a shit what anybody else thinks, but you do realize we literally just met, right?"

"And! It's not hard to imagine we'll have a gruesome life-or-death battle with the other Kings and Jacks when we look for the four treasures!"

"Oh, so you had the brains to think that far, at least. That's a relief."

"Then! In order to get through this bloody battle, you and I... need to have trust and unity—a bond even stronger than a King and his vassal. It's not an exaggeration to say having this bond is indispensable!"

"...I guess."

"So let's go on a date!"

"...I guess?"

Something was off. He felt like she'd made a sudden jump in logic to get to that conclusion.

"Well! Because I'm the worthy and true King, my transcendent charisma already knows you in your entirety, Rintarou! But! You need to know me a lot better, don't you?! Right?!"

"...To be honest, I've already had more than enough of you."

"In that case! Look, we're going on a date, Rintarou!"

"Whoa?! Hey, don't pull on my arm! Ugh, seriously! How did I get myself into this mess?!"

Just like that, the two spectacularly skipped school and treated themselves to a date on a weekday.

...Geez, it's not like I'm interested in her or anything.

The moment they stepped foot in the establishment, a wave of sounds and light crashed into them and almost washed them away. Crammed in the space were all kinds of games in different sizes, complete with monitors, glass enclosures packed with dolls and plushies, and photo booths, among other things.

They were in the Nine Star. It was a well-known, large arcade in Area Three.

"Heh-heh, I'll show you the ropes, Rintarou, since I'm sure you've never gone out with a girl before. When it comes to dating, an arcade is at the top of the list of places you have to go! If you don't take a girl to one on the first date, you get negative points! That's a little nugget of wisdom for ya!" she advised proudly with a puffed chest.

"Do you even know what a date is?" he retorted. "Normally, wouldn't you go to a café or a movie or a mall or something first? Okay, actually, I guess if you need to kill time, you might go to an arcade."

"Now, Rintarou! I command thee to convert this Benjamin into dollar coins! That's a King's order!"

"Are you a hard-core gamer?! Just how long are you planning on fooling around in here?!"

Seriously, he complained, but for some reason, he still went to exchange the money without much resistance.

"Oh, Luna! Is that you? Girl! Haven't seen you in forever!"

"Heh-heh. This must be a fateful encounter! Let's battle on Gliah! I'll win this time!"

When he heard a voice behind him, Rintarou turned from the coin machine and saw Luna exchanging friendly greetings with flirty boys and gaudy girls—definitely a group of party animals.

"Oh! Sorry, you guys! I'm with someone today! Hee-hee, it's a date! A date! Wow, it's so hard being popular!"

"Ah-ha-ha! Damn, Ryo, rejected!"

"Ugh… Ah, well, guess we'll take a rain check on that battle, then!"

"Luna, where'd you find a guy weird enough to date you, huh?"

"Heh! Why wouldn't he want to snag a beauty like me? There just aren't that many guys who catch my eye!"

This was Luna's day-to-day: She handled everything with ease and let it wash over her.

Seriously, she's always popular, no matter where she goes…

As a heap of dollar coins rattled down from the machine into a cup, he thought to himself.

Now that he was thinking back on it, there was always a large crowd around Luna, even at school. Whether they were her supporters or her enemies, they never stopped coming.

But if you look closely...there's really something charming about her...

At that moment, Luna was in her school uniform, looking polished in it, but she wasn't dressing it up in any particular way.

But for some reason, she wasn't even a shade less vibrant than those girls in front of her, heavily accessorized and up-to-date with the latest trends. If anything, it made her stand out from them in this deluge of light and sound, and she seemed to glow all the more.

Hmph. She certainly never sinks into the crowd, no matter how characterful everyone around her is—just like him.

Rintarou was still lost in thought as he carried the cup brimming with coins and returned to Luna.

"Thank you, my dear vassal, Rintarou! Serving and performing favors are the cornerstones to the bond between a King and her vassal! Therefore, I shall give you a reward! You may also use these coins to play games to your heart's content!"

"I'm not going to even make a joke about this. I'm not, okay?"

Rintarou glanced down at the *ten cents* she'd handed to him with unimpressed eyes.

Are there even any ten-cent machines you can play on in this day and age? ...Sigh.

She happily hooked her arm into his. "Hey, Rintarou! Since we're here, let's play together! That'll definitely be the most fun! You're okay with that, right?!"

"...I guess that's fine." He sulked in resignation and shrugged his shoulders. "But I'll probably win no matter what we play, you know? I don't think it'd be fun for you."

"You idiot! You think it's not fun unless you win? What are you, a kid?"

"Hmph…"

"It's fun just playing together! It's just a game, right? It's not all about whether you win or lose!"

"Really? Why would you do something where you wouldn't win or lose…?"

Then, well, that was that.

"Ah-ha-ha-ha-ha-ha-ha-ha-ha-ha-haaaa! This is nothing, Rintarou!"

"Gnnngh…I—I wouldn't expect any less from you…!"

They amicably faced each other with a fighting game, fiddling with joysticks.

On the monitor, Rintarou's male character in a helmet was losing pretty pathetically.

"Huh? What? Didn't you just say 'I'll probably win no matter what we play?' Bwa-ha-ha! Look where you're at now!"

"Don't mess with me! You had me use the weakest character in the whole game and chose a character with a nine-to-one strength advantage. That's unbelievable!"

"You idiot! History is written by the victors! In games, winning is everything!"

"Dammit. You've changed your tune! Take that! I'm not gonna hold back! I'm going to start using the strongest character, too!"

NGAH, NGAH, NGAH.

"Ahhhhhh?! Hey, you coward!"

KO —Win for Toki.

$$* \quad * \quad *$$

More time passed.

"Ugh, ahhhhhh?! You're seriously gonna steal my life item from me, Luna?!"

Facing the monitor for a shooting game, they aimed their gun controllers side by side, indiscriminately mowing down the zombies closing in on them.

"Just hurry up and kill all the ones near you, Rintarou! I'll get the boss!"

"You're not getting any of them! You're the worst! Move! *You* get the zombies around us!"

"Ahhhhhh?! Why'd you take my vaccine?! Look at my zombification gauge! Seriously?!"

"Hey, don't stop shooting! They're coming! They said the cyborg professor is coming?!"

And even more time passed.

"Look! Come closer over here! You won't fit otherwise!"

"Ahh, this is so lame."

In front of the camera in the photo booth, they were up close and personal—their shoulders touching.

"Ugh, seriously! I said if you don't get closer, you'll get cut off! Look!"

"Whoa?! H-hey…!"

In a surprise attack, Luna intertwined her arms around Rintarou and hugged him. As soon as she did, a subtle fragrance from her body and hair wafted toward him and tickled his nose. Her body was soft and warm, and he couldn't help but stiffen when he felt her pleasant warmth on his arm.

"Yup! Looks good!"

"…Uh, is it? That's nice."

Noticing he was uncharacteristically flustered, he unhappily clucked his tongue as he watched Luna from behind. She happily examined the images they'd taken on the touch screen.

…If she were like this all the time, she'd be like a normal girl.

The fact that her "normal attitude" was considered the usual was such a waste, Rintarou thought absentmindedly.

"Hee-hee-hee…" Using the touch pen, she was bestowing some unspeakable doodles on his face in the photo. "Ah-ha-ha-ha-ha-ha! No way! Rintarou, you've sure gotten handsome!"

"Wh-why you?! In that case, how about I do this to you! Like this! And that!" He stole the touch pen and undauntedly drew on Luna on the screen.

"Wait! How could you do that to a girl's face?! You're the worst! Then I'll—"

"Like I'll let youuuuuuuuuuuuuu!"

They were still in the cramped booth.

As they grappled to steal the pen and draw on each other's face, an unsightly battle raged on.

It went without saying that more time passed.

"I said do this one! Get rid of this tile! That's what my intuition tells me!"

"Hey, you idiot, you don't even know anything about mahjong! I'm the one who's going to decide which one to get rid of!"

They were having a giant fight in front of a strip-mahjong machine.

"Look at the discarded tiles! No matter how you think about it, there's a high chance this one's better, right?!" he pointed out.

"No, it's this one! This one is the one that'll come! That's how the game's flow is going! Rintarou, I bet you're just playing it safe and don't even have a winning hand! That won't do any good for your King!"

"That's definitely the tile she wants! There, we don't have time! Go!" *Clack.*

"Huh?!"

"*Ron! Riichi pinfu tanyao iipeikou dora 4!* Tee-hee, better luck next time. ♥"

On the monitor, the half-naked girl character's expression never changed as she used the tile he discarded to win, revealing all her tiles...meaning Rintarou lost twenty-four thousand points.

"What?! Seriously?!"

"Noooooooo?! What are you doing, really?! We would've gotten Alisa completely naked in one more rouuuuuuuuund! You're stupid, Rintarou, stupid!"

"Gnaaaaah...!"

"It's not over yet! We're not done yet! We'll definitely make Alisa strip! Okay, we're going to hit continue, Rintarou!"

"You're way too into this... Do you really want to make her strip that bad?"

Clink, clink, clink...

And even more...

"No, no, no, nooo! Get it, get it, get it!"

"Get it yourself!"

"Like I said, I want *you* to get it for me!"

"Look..." Rintarou sighed as Luna threw a tantrum next to the glass enclosure of the crane game.

"Just get it! That's a royal order! An order! If you don't follow it, you'll get capital punishment for the crime of—disrespecting me!" she yelled at the top of her lungs as she pointed at some ugly stuffed sheep in the machine.

"What a despot. Listen, Luna. All crane games have settings to adjust the strength of the claw. And I know for a fact they don't want customers to get the things in this crane game yet..."

"Hmph? So you can't do it? You said you could do anything. Hmm, I guess that's all you amounted to, after all. Even though such a cutie is begging you?"

"Guh... Why you..."

"Well, if you say it's impossible, I guess that's it. Ah, wow, I'm so disappointed. Your performance review is doing a nosedive."

"Whaaaaaaat?! Dammit! Fine! I'll do it! Just watch! This thing is a piece of cake, if I'm the one working the crane!"

He didn't even notice her gloating grin as she fooled him, and Rintarou put a whopping amount of coins into the machine.

They were finally finished.

"Ah-ha-ha-ha-ha! That was fun, wasn't it, Rintarou?!"

After they'd played themselves out, they put the game center behind them.

"But losing a hundred dollars kind of hurts, doesn't it?" She giggled and turned around to him as she stuck out her tongue slightly and fooled around.

"Yeah, it does. And for some reason, three hundred dollars disappeared from my wallet. I wonder how that happened?" Plodding behind her, Rintarou had completely dead eyes. "Yeah, I wonder how that happened when I was playing just as much as you?"

"Yeah, I wonder why?" She must've felt guilty, as she was

sweating up a storm, smile twitching. "A-anyway, thanks for this sheep, Rintarou! I've been eyeing it for a while! It's the first offering from my vassal… Hee-hee, I'll treasure it as your King!"

"Yeah, you better. If anything, it's probably worth a dollar, and it took me two hundred times that amount to win it. I'm an idiot, dammit…" Rintarou sighed as his miserable eyes watched Luna happily fiddling with the stuffed animal. He fished for more thanks. He was actually a very petty guy.

The two of them horsed around with each other.

"Okay, so where do you want to go next?" She pulled on his hand innocently like a child.

"Hey, hey! Are we gonna keep going with this date (LOL)? Gimme a break…"

"Well, why not?! We're going to really deepen our friendship today!"

"Oh, that's so weird! I don't know if we've deepened our friend-ship, but I sure feel like we've done a great job digging a deep trench between us."

"Oh! Right! There was one place I've been wanting to go to for a while! C'mon, let's go, Rintarou!"

"You've got to actually listen to people. Wait—like I said, don't pull me—!"

…That was how things kept progressing.

That whole day, Luna dragged Rintarou all over the place, doing anything she pleased.

They went into a café and tried out new pastries, window-shopped for clothes, discussed light novels at Animate, and wandered around the streets without any specific destination in mind…

Luna always had a high-octane smile, bright like the sun in

the middle of the summer. Rintarou always had the expression of a new employee, already exhausted with corporate life.

That ragtag couple continued on their endless date.

After all was said and done, time seemed to go by in a wink.

"I did it! I finally got rid of that nasty brute! Chapter Twelve is won and done!"

"Oh, you did, did you, sire? Good for you."

In the end, they sat side by side on a bench by Sword Lake Beachside Park at the eastern coast of Area Three and kept each other company as they played social games on their phones.

"Heh. The strongest magical knight Twilight Magic User Merlin you lent me supported my win! My KLK (King of Lound Knights) path is starting now!"

"I've been thinking about it, but is this really a date? Like, is it actually a date? Well…I guess it doesn't matter." Rintarou closed his game and stopped thinking about it.

"Your support knights are kind of weird, aren't they? Why are all of them super-high-class five ★ characters with second awakenings and fully maxed-out levels and skills? Do you buy a lot of in-app stuff?"

"Who knows."

"But you haven't got a single friend… Do you actually not have friends in real life?"

"Shuddup. Leave me alone. I just like playing alone," he sharply interjected and looked away from his phone screen at their surroundings.

At some point, the sun had begun to set, illuminating the park beautifully.

The sky was clear and burning crimson. Across the wrought

iron fence, he saw the sea. The horizon devoured the scarlet sun, radiating the sky brilliantly like rolling golden hills. And the waves washed over and out, warping the sun in its reflection, as if a mirage or illusion, and burned itself into his eyes.

"Well, we went hard and played to our heart's content..."

"Yeah." Luna was satisfied, but she asked him in a slightly nervous tone, "Hey, Rintarou. Um...was today fun?"

"Yeah, it was..." After everything, that was probably the truth. Rintarou answered honestly.

"You had a good time? Oh, good! Heh-heh! Making an effort to recognize a vassal's services is just part of a King's job! Make sure you feel grateful for me!" Luna beamed in relief.

"Yeah, yeah!" he replied carelessly with a wry smile.

Then, as if that were their cue, the two of them broke off their conversation.

Up until that point, Rintarou and Luna had continued to talk without interruption, so their silence was a little uncomfortable.

Well, what should I do now? If it's a date, I guess I need to invite her to dinner or something and walk her home?

As he grew a little tired, Rintarou thought of that absentmindedly...

"Say, Rintarou...why did you come here?" she asked suddenly.

When he gazed at the side of her face, Luna's eyes seemed somewhat distant as she looked out beyond the horizon line.

What could she have been looking for at the blinding border of the glittering sky and ocean?

"Rintarou... Why did you join the King Arthur Succession Battle?"

"Well, I told you, didn't I? It seemed like it'd be fun...," he droned.

But she kept pressing him. "Let's say...Rintarou, did you maybe come to meet someone or promise someone something...? Is that why you came here?"

"...?"

At that question, he felt a strange discomfort. Her hypothetical situation seemed a little too specific.

He looked at her face again, gazing at her gentle expression as she looked out at the ocean with nostalgia in her eyes.

"...Not really," he replied honestly. "I don't have any complex reasons beyond that. I really just came here because I was bored. The normal world was suffocating and boring...and I wanted to do something fun."

"I see... Right, yeah." Luna suddenly broke into a serene smile. "Ha-ha. You really are a weird person."

He knew immediately she wasn't smiling because she found his answer amusing. He saw her expression cloud in loneliness the second he answered... At least, that's how he felt.

It looks like I gave her the wrong answer.

But what kind of reply had she expected from him?

He didn't understand the reason behind her question, but he felt guilty about something or another, and it pricked the bottom of his heart, which he pretended not to notice.

"H-hey, what about you?! Why'd you get involved in the King Arthur Succession Battle?"

"...Huh? Haven't I told you already?"

"Nope."

Luna gallantly stood up to face Rintarou. "That's obvious. I want to succeed King Arthur and become the best King ever and have the whole world in my hands and"—she declared with majesty—"brag my face off!"

Rintarou felt the tension drain from his shoulders as the great reveal fell short.

"I wanna become the greatest person in the world and merci-lessly take advantage of people as I please! I wanna enjoy life without working or lifting a finger! So I'm not giving up! I'll become King Arthur!"

"Sh-she...really is worthless..." Facedown, he yanked at his hair, as if to say he's had enough. Now that he thought about it... It probably would've been a lot better to let Luna lose this battle.

"Then once I'm acknowledged as the World's Best King, I'll make a certain person my vassal."

Suddenly, Luna's behavior changed.

Taking notice, he glanced at her dubiously. "...? Your vassal?"

"That's right. There's someone I *have* to make my vassal."

"What does that mean?"

"..."

For a while, she looked over at the ocean in silence.

"Hey, Rintarou, do you know the actual goal of the King Arthur Succession Battle?"

"Yeah, of course I know. It's because of the Catastrophe, right?"

—Pardon this sudden interjection.

This world was divided into two: the real world, home to man-kind, and the illusory world, the realm of gods, fairies, and other apparitions. They were separated by the Curtain of Consciousness.

Rooted in humanity's collective consciousness, this boundary started to form as a by-product of technological and social advance-ment. It became stronger and stronger with each new invention.

Though the real world and the illusory world were originally one and the same, this Curtain of Consciousness forced those from the illusory world to one side of the boundary—causing them to disappear from the real world.

To put it bluntly, everyone started to believe there were no such things as ghosts, which made it come true.

In present day, this impenetrable curtain prevented those in the illusory world from interfering with the real world, and most humans could no longer see them. With that, mankind was freed from the control, terrifying power, and threat of the apparitions. With humans controlling the world, they lived there happily ever after. Or at least, that's what they'd hoped—

"In the near future, that Curtain of Consciousness will collapse," Rintarou stated with a slightly grim expression. "We don't know why. But the three goddesses of fate prophesized that, and they're worshipped by the Dame du Lac. So that's that.

"The ancient gods and fairies will be revived in this real world, which is powerless now that there are no real heroes anymore. With their immense magical powers and abilities, everything will revert back to the time of myths—when the gods dominated humans."

"Right, the Catastrophe. It'll end the human world as we know it." Luna gently pulled her hair into a ponytail.

The cool evening air started to mix in with the wind, making her hair flutter in waves.

"The winner of the King Arthur Succession Battle…his successor will receive the power to conquer the whole world and the duty of facing the Catastrophe.

"When the world eventually faces grave danger, King Arthur will once again be revived to save the world… *Rex quondam, rexque futuras*. That's what he was destined to do."

If anything, the King Arthur Succession Battle was the battle to select our *savior*, the one who'd prevent this Catastrophe.

That's the Dame du Lac's true goal.

The power to rule the world is just tossed in as a freebie—nothing more than a lure.

"As the heir of the Artur house carrying his bloodline, I had to go through all kinds of special training since I was small to prepare to join the King Arthur Succession Battle... At a certain point, they started telling me about the Catastrophe... I became so scared of it."

"..."

"Anyway, I really hated that I needed to fight in the battle...to prevent the Catastrophe. I didn't get why *I* had to do something so terrifying."

"..."

"But the adults around me wouldn't listen to me at all. They said that was the fate of the Arturs and the one true desire of a knight... But I was so, so scared that I'd always hide and go cry alone."

"..."

"But during those times, there was this kid who used to say... 'Don't worry. If you become the world's greatest King, I'll become your vassal,' and 'I'll smash that Cata-something-or-other to smithereens for you once I'm your vassal.'"

Her distant eyes squinted even more, remembering something that'd happened far in the past.

"I was born in Winchester in England. I think this kid's parents came for business, and we just so happened to meet. We spent one summer together... It was probably just one month, but that time together saved me."

"..."

"Oh, an amazing kid who could do anything—a much better candidate for King Arthur than me. When we were together...it kind of felt really safe...like I'd be able to get through anything...

But even more than that, it was super-fun. We spent a month playing till exhaustion, and I still treasure that memory."

"…"

"When we had to part ways, I didn't want to, and I threw a tantrum. I wanted for us to play more, but we made a promise: Someday, when I became the greatest King in the world, that kid would become my vassal… That's what kept me going, even when I was almost crushed to death by pressure." She turned to Rintarou and smirked in amusement. "Well, I've grown a lot since then. There are a lot more things I care about, to the point I believe I need to save the world from the Catastrophe. I want to fight in order to protect those things. But… even now I'm…"

Halting for a moment, she continued, "…It's weird, right? That I'm trying to become King just because of some promise a kid told me?"

"…Not really? …Isn't that fine?" He shrugged. "No matter what your reason is, it's a whole lot better than mine. You should do what you want. Like you do normally, leaving everything as a mess."

"You're right. I'll do what I want—can't break old habits."

"Hmph… Well, I hope you find that peculiar kid who wanted to become your vassal… He must be a real idiot. I'd like to get a look at his face."

"Yeah. I wonder where he is and what he's doing now?" Luna grinned as she looked at him.

"…What?"

"Who knows. Wanna take a wild guess?"

"Tch, you're so weird… Or should I say you misled me with all that talk! All that jabbering about using people to your advantage and ordering them around and not wanting to do anything? How is any of that a real motive?"

"Huh? Well, acting like that would make the World's Best King even more dignified and majestic, right?"

"What kind of kingship is that?" Of course, as usual, he cradled his pounding head.

Bam! At that moment, a blast of noise shook the ground, trembling in its wake, followed by the sound of rustling feathers as birds left behind a grove of trees.

"…Huh? What was that?" Fluttering with surprise, Luna's eyes were wide open.

"Careful, Luna. I sense a faint Aura coming from those trees," he warned.

As a disquieting feeling unexpectedly made its way toward him, his eyes immediately sharpened.

"Call Sir Kay. Someone might have laid some sort of trap… I'm going to go check."

Without hesitation, Rintarou started walking toward the grove.

"Is it farther back?" he asked, surveying the large circle of trees in the beachside park.

Fallen leaves crunched under Rintarou's feet as he followed the faint Aura into the forest. The farther in he went, the brush became thicker and thicker and the stronger the smell of the foliage became.

As the sun set, the area around him became darker as he trudged on.

"Hey, hey, don't you feel kind of excited exploring through the forest? It's kind of like it brings up childhood memories!"

"Geez, I said to wait."

As though her participation was a given, Luna was at his side.

And of course… "L-Luna… Wh-when you said you were on…a date…a *date*… I can't believe you meant this idiot of a boy… We don't even know who he is… And he's the absolute worst… Scum… I can't believe you meant Rintarou Magami…*grumble, grumble…*"

Plodding behind them was Sir Kay (this time in full gear), wearing an expression like she was witnessing doomsday in front of her very eyes.

"Anyway, this is Rintarou Magami we're talking about... He'll lustfully take advantage of your supple, youthful body and use everything he can, playing with your body and heart before he crushes you; then in the end, he'll throw you aside as though you're nothing to him and run off to find another girl... I can't accept this... As (someone who's pretty much) your older sister, I definitely cannot accept this... Anyone but that Rintarou Magami..."

...Wow, these two seriously have no sense of danger... Wait a sec! How much of a lowlife does she think I am?

As he let that meaningless drivel go in one ear and out the other, he kept following the Aura, straying far from the trail and farther and farther into the thick brush...

Eventually, they encountered the figure.

Someone was sitting at the roots of a colossal tree, where they were squatting and leaning weakly against the trunk for support.

That person was— "Sir Gawain?!"

It was Felicia's Jack.

"Oh. Hey! Wait?!" Rintarou shouted.

Without heeding his warning, Luna made a dash to the wounded knight, with Rintarou and Sir Kay sprinting after her.

"Sir Gawain?! Wh-what happened to you?!"

As they got closer, they noticed that he'd sustained horrible injuries all over his body, as if he were some beat-up old rag. Tight around his body, his armor had been slashed open like paper and warped—it didn't even look like armor anymore. There were countless gashes all over his body—stab wounds, open slashes, bruises—making for a bloody, gory mess.

If he wasn't magically summoned from the soul of a great

knight, if he hadn't been incarnated through mana, if he wasn't a Jack—he would've long taken his last breath.

"Wait... What about Felicia? Sir Gawain...where *is* she?!" Luna shrieked.

As a Jack, Sir Gawain should've protected his King, Felicia. In any other circumstance, she should've been right beside him, but there wasn't any trace of her.

"Ugh...I can't believe...th-that I've run into you all in a place like this..." He thrust something out to Luna, dizzy with shock.

They were Felicia's Excalibur and Round Fragment.

"What...? Is this...?" Though she'd taken it from his hands without missing a beat, she looked at him for answers.

"Hey, Gawain. What happened? Speak up," commanded Rintarou, unusually serious.

"Luna Artur...as a longtime friend of my liege, Felicia...I have something to ask of you...please...," he coughed out, starting to explain...

"Oh? Just when I was looking around to retrieve the Excalibur and Round Fragment... It seems I fished out some sweet prey."

Without warning, a voice reached their ears at once.

From the back of the forest, a figure stepped through the fallen leaves and slowly made its way over to them.

Gaining on them one step at a time, it emanated an antagonism and pressure—almost crushing them from above and electrifying their skin, making it crawl.

As they swallowed their breath, a man eventually appeared from the shadows.

Lean and tall, he had a long face with a clever look. His eyes sharply sparkled behind his glasses in a cold, inhuman gaze.

With an Excalibur in a sinister shape, freely emitting a dark

Aura, in his hands—it was proof he was a King in the King Arthur Succession Battle.

It was— "M-Mr. Kujou?!"

Petrified, Luna shuddered in terror, her pupils dilating as she was frozen in place.

Excalibur in hand, the figure—Mr. Kujou—was their homeroom teacher.

They hadn't immediately recognized him. His piercingly icy eyes were miles away from his warm, amicable presence as a teacher, and these two images didn't match up.

"I was wondering where you could've gone, skipping school... I didn't expect to see you here."

"M-Master Kujou?! Y-you were a King?!" cried Sir Kay as their world came crashing down in front of their very eyes.

"I knew it." Rintarou snorted and glanced at Kujou.

"Oh? Rintarou, you knew my true identity?"

"More or less. At lunch, I saw your hands, when I was handing you your change... They're not the hands of an amateur. Those were the hands of a swordsman, with a considerable amount of practice."

"Ha-ha-ha... How perceptive you are, Rintarou."

"You're just careless. You seemed suspicious, so I was gonna look into you...but then Luna suddenly said she wanted to go on a date. Well, you saved me some trouble."

A faint, frosty smirk formed across his lips. "Let me tell you. My real name is Souma Gloria Kujou... I'm the noble son of the Kujou Corporation, which took in the Gloria house, the bloodline of King Arthur. I'm one of the Kings in the King Arthur Succession Battle," declared Mr. Kujou menacingly, his presence becoming as terrifying as a giant.

Shiver. The temperature felt bitterly cold.

—Huh?! Wh-what is this guy?!

It was then that Rintarou realized in his very soul—this Kujou was an unthinkable abomination.

Even with him right in front of my eyes, I can't believe it... This guy Kujou...is just too strong?! I might be a cheater, but this guy's something else! What the hell...is inside him?!

Rintarou broke out into a cold sweat and readied himself.

"Mr. Kujou...what did you do to Felicia?!" she firmly pressed.

"Hmm? Oh, I heard you've been friends with Felicia since you were kids, huh? Don't worry, she's still alive. Well... I'll kill her soon enough."

"—Huh?!"

"But you don't have to worry about that. You'll die right here anyway," he spat, pulling a chain out from his pocket.

It was a Round Fragment, XII.

"'Twelfth seat of the Round Table, heed my call.'"

"The twelfth seat?! You can't mean—" Rintarou's eyes jumped out of his head.

Purple blasts of lightning ran above Kujou's head, calling forward a magical triquetra circle to form and a Gate to materialize.

A Jack descended alongside an aurora borealis. With long, flowing locks and sharp, bladelike eyes, he was chiseled like a Greek sculpture and wrapped in bluish-silver armor. Accompanying him was the dragon-slaying blade, Aroundight.

That Jack was so strikingly handsome, it was hard to believe he belonged to that world.

"Heh...so it was you...?!" In a rare moment, Rintarou froze with nervousness the second he saw him.

"You are... You can't be... No...!" Sir Kay was taken aback, dumbfounded.

Sweating, Rintarou eyed that Jack. "Sir Lancelot du Lac. It goes without saying you're known as the strongest knight of the Round Table…an undeniable beast."

He was Sir Lancelot, the most famous knight in the legend of King Arthur and widely known for his bravery, even in this era. It was said he'd won a fight against two giants the size of mountains at the same time. It was said he'd disguised himself as Sir Kay and won against several dozen pursuers, and then he continued to battle all the capable knights of the Round Table—to an obvious victory.

It was said slaying dragons was his forte.

It was said he'd taken down five hundred experienced knights over the course of three days at a certain battle.

In tournaments, he was always victorious—as long as Sir Tristan and Sir Lamorak didn't enter. He could easily handle Sir Gawain, even with the Sun's Blessing.

With this knight entering the stage, anyone would've frozen in place.

"Hmph. We meet again, you cowardly traitor," Sir Lancelot spat, his hostility skewering Sir Gawain.

"Ugh…S-sir Lancelot…"

"King Arthur's gravest error was appointing a lowly man the likes of you as a knight of the Round Table… Nay, creating a gutless table of incompetent knights—a collection of rabble who could scarcely protect their King—that was his first mistake," he scoffed, readying his weapon. "I will right that very error by my sword. Yes, save for me, the knights of the Round Table are unnecessary to the King. I will kill every incompetent knight in this battle! *That's the reason I am here!*"

His bloodlust grew, the foreboding sensation whipping around them like a tempest, assailing Rintarou, Luna, Sir Gawain, and Sir Kay mercilessly.

"Lord Kujou, my true lord! Command me! Allow me to kill these knights! To destroy your enemies! I will protect you with my sword, my King, and we will pave the way forward with their blood and corpses! Now! Allow me to…massacre the knights and pretenders!"

Everyone stiffened upon seeing his grotesquely twisted rage and blazing hatred.

"Th-this is quite unlike you, Sir Lancelot! What happened to you?! You were filled with more love than anyone else and adored the path of chivalry! Why have you become so cruel?!" Sir Kay yelled in disbelief.

"Guh… It's my fault you changed so much…" Sir Gawain hung his head with regret.

"Sure, Sir Lancelot. To your heart's content. Don't let a single one escape," ordered Mr. Kujou—curt, abrupt, unfaltering, merciless.

"AAAAHHHHHHHHHHHHHHHHHHHHHHHHHHHHHH!" Sir Lancelot roared like a rage-filled beast, dashing toward them.

It was one-sided—and the unilateral battle began.

His speed was far beyond the imagination, more than one would know what to do with. He was lightning, blasting through ground.

"GWAAAAAAAAAAAAAAAAAAAAAAAAAAAAAH!" he shouted, cutting down Sir Gawain with the fervor of a god of thunder, seeking his complete and total annihilation.

"ARHHHHGUUUUUUH!" cried the wounded knight.

But he wasn't finished. Whipping his blade back, he instantly whirled to Sir Kay, striking her down before she could even draw her sword. Leaving the two Jacks in a spray of blood and sinew, Sir Lancelot bounded toward Luna—his sword swinging like a lightning bolt.

As it whizzed toward her with seraphic speed, Luna couldn't even respond at all—

The sound of an impact cut through the air, nearly warping from the force of the swords coming together.

"Rintarou?!"

"Damm—it!"

Above her head, the sword eager to bisect Luna from head to toe was narrowly intervened by Rintarou, meeting Sir Lancelot's weapon with his crossed swords.

He'd already gone into his *Fomorian Transformation*, white hair waving in the wind and his dark power frighteningly cocooning his whole body.

But that still wasn't enough.

"DIIIIIIIIIIIIEEEEEEEEEEEEE!"

Sir Lancelot held the upper hand with an overwhelmingly powerful grip. Rintarou dwarfed in comparison.

When the Jack violently slashed with his sword in a flash, this impact sent Rintarou's body sailing, striking him with the speed of a gale: a slice from above, a backhanded strike, a vertical stroke from the right. The three instantaneous flashes combined in a savage attack.

As Rintarou met each stroke, its power pierced through his body, making his bones and his internal organs grate against each other.

"GWAAAAAAAAAAAAAAAAAAAAAAAAAAAAAAAAAH?!"

Eventually, he was unable to keep guarding against these blows and tumbled through the forest, causing tree after tree to crash down as he slammed against them.

But his body still didn't stop.

"Rintarou?!"

"Ha-ha-ha-ha-ha-ha-haaaaa! I expect nothing less, Sir Lancelot! You're the strongest Jack and worthy of me, the true King Arthur!"

With Luna's screams and Kujou's loud cackle, this uncanny ensemble performed their piece in the deep, dark woods.

"Now, Sir Lancelot... This is a command from your King. Kill that impostor. This world only needs one King—me... No room for any others. Kill her now."

"—As you wish."

With soul-crushingly murderous intent, he projected this bloodthirsty desire to Luna, all alone, causing her to hallucinate in absolute terror, assaulted by images of the grim reaper. Had she been a normal person, she would've sunk into the pits of despair and been in a stupor or shook from fear and cried while begging for her life or been broken—

"...Hmm?" Mr. Kujou's eyebrows knit together.

Luna was unexpectedly majestic, crossing her arms together and smiling daringly.

"What's wrong, Luna? Did the despair go straight to your head?" he jeered with a smirk.

"Hmph! Like my Rintarou would be beaten so easily! He'd never let this end this quickly!" she spat, full of confidence—

"Huh...?" That's when Mr. Kujou noticed something.

The air around them started to loosen, warp, and worm around: the trees, Luna's silhouette, and everything else blurred, as though their eyes couldn't focus.

"What...is this?" He grimaced, glaring at this obvious abnormality.

"Ugh...I somehow made it in time." From the shadow of a tree, Rintarou appeared, safe and sound, no wounds in sight.

"I see... So this was *your* doing." Outdone, Mr. Kujou's mouth warped with sarcasm. "Just now, you used *Silhouette* to trick Sir Lancelot into beating an illusion... In that time, you set up *Netherworld Transformation* and cut us off from the real world."

"Correct. While you're getting lost in the netherworld, we'll take our time withdrawing to safety." Rintarou grinned next to Luna. "Wow, seriously, it's so fun here. Sure, my past life had people stronger than me, but looks like that's the case on this side of the world, too... Thanks, Kujou. I haven't been bored at all thanks to you."

"Oh?"

"You're strong. If we competed head-to-head, I don't think I'd win. But...I'm the one who always wins in the end. You just wait and see for now."

"Hmm? It doesn't seem like you're desperate to say the final word. Ha-ha-ha, it seems you really *do* believe you can do that... even after you saw how much stronger I am. Ha-ha-ha... I have quite an interest in you, Rintarou Magami..."

In response, Rintarou smiled shamelessly, while Mr. Kujou's face warped with delight.

As this went on, his teacher became fainter and fainter. Meanwhile, from Kujou's point of view, his pupil was disappearing into the warped air...

"The greatest obstacle to my rule isn't another King... It may actually be you."

"What an honor. Go to hell."

Mr. Kujou gave them some parting words. "Now then...it's about time. Luna Artur, let me tell you this: Felicia Ferald's life will end at midnight."

"?!"

"...If you value her life, you'll need to come...to the penthouse of Central City Park Hotel...in Area Two."

That was the tallest building in the city.

"I've rented out the entire floor... I'll be there with the girl. I won't run or hide... Mwa-ha-ha, we'll massacre you all there."

Clash!

A clear, metallic sound rang out as the warped space righted itself.

For a split second, the air became blindingly white and hot—and then Mr. Kujou and Sir Lancelot disappeared, temporarily locked away into the netherworld Rintarou had prepared with some improvisation.

"Felicia..." With a pained expression, Luna gripped Felicia's Excalibur and Round Fragment.

On the verge of death, Sir Kay and Sir Gawain were collapsed facedown.

No one said anything. They couldn't say anything.

Under these grim circumstances, Rintarou opened his mouth. "...We're withdrawing, Luna. With a netherworld as simple as that one, it'll only contain them for a minute. They'll come back right away. We're returning to square one for now..."

He dispassionately urged Luna to plan her next move.

CHAPTER 5

𝔓𝔞𝔯𝔱𝔦𝔫𝔤 𝔚𝔞𝔶𝔰

After getting away from the beachside park, they gathered at an abandoned house in Area Three. Their group illegally trespassed and slipped into a room that might've originally been a parlor room or something at some point. It was deserted now, holding nothing but a few empty wooden crates gathered quietly in a corner.

Based on the dustiness of the room, it seemed a long time had passed since its former owner lived there. And through the window, they could see the sun had mostly set—darkness penetrated their surroundings, painting over everything.

But Rintarou invoked a faint sphere of light with his *Firefly Light* magic and drove it away.

"Everything we did...Lord Luna...was to keep you safe from the hands of that Kujou," confessed Sir Gawain, gradually opening up to tell his side of the story as Rintarou started to heal his wounds—not out of his own volition but Luna's explicit orders.

"Souma Gloria Kujou...has the strongest knight of the Round Table, Sir Lancelot, at his service. It's said his power rivals those of heroes from King Arthur's time. Without a doubt, he's the leading contender in this King Arthur Succession Battle... At the same time, he's a radical, aiming to massacre all the other Kings."

"Hmm? What an insidious, awful villain... He makes me look cute and adorable in comparison," joked Rintarou, pretending to be clueless in this serious situation.

"Any battle against Lord Kujou will end us as a death match. My liege Felicia realized many Kings would fall prey to him, until he was dealt with...so she publicly joined forces with him, while desperately thinking of a way to beat him.

"We wanted to find his weakness and then make true alliances with other Kings. And we didn't want to involve you in this perilous battle, so we were desperate to make you forfeit at an early stage."

Luna's lips slightly contorted, and nostalgia filled her voice. "Right. Felicia and I were friends in primary school. We used to play a lot together, but...our families had bad blood between them, since our households were both competing for succession. At some point, we grew apart, but...huh...Felicia still thinks of me as a friend."

Sir Gawain continued his explanation. He told them about how Kujou had been using Felicia; about how he'd intervened in the fight between her and Luna; about the day before, when Kujo had turned his back on her, attacking her and Sir Gawain; about various events that had transpired without anyone's knowledge. Just as he was about to finish—

"Luna Artur, I must put my shame aside and ask a favor of you," he appealed, placing a sword at Luna's feet and falling to his knees. His head swung low. "I cannot...win against Kujou and Sir Lancelot alone. But I still wish to save Felicia. Please lend me your strength... Just look at me now."

"No way. You're kidding. Why'd we help an enemy?" Rintarou

curtly rejected him, calling to him as he sulkily lay on top of the empty crates. "Heh... In the first place. Gawain... You don't even care about Felicia, do you? You just want to beat Lancelot, huh? Like you did *that time*."

"—?!" He had no response for Rintarou's contemptuous observation.

"Rintarou! How dare you talk that way to a knight who's devoted himself to his lord?!" Sir Kay stood up in arms.

"Shut it, Sir Kay... There's a dark side to this guy's heart," he spat out. "Back during the era of King Arthur...this guy and that beloved knight Sir Lancelot were best friends...right?"

"Um, yeah, that's right. From my perspective, Sir Gawain and Sir Lancelot were..."

"But this guy was uncontrollably jealous of Lancelot. I mean, he didn't even amount to anything without the Sun's Blessing. And even then, he was still under Lancelot's feet." He glared at Sir Gawain, head hung low in silence. "Then, Gawain, you persuaded your little brother Agravain to *fake* an adulterous affair between Lancelot and Arthur's bride Guinevere...didn't you?" he accused without any heat in his voice, but his anger started to seep through.

"What?! How idiotic?! Is that true?! Sir Gawain!" Sir Kay blurted, looking at the knight in shock and disbelief...as he wordlessly accepted the accusation.

"That scandal started the battle between Arthur and Lancelot, breaking the Round Table up into two sides. To the very end, you claimed allegiance to Arthur, pretending to fight the good fight against Lancelot. Even when Arthur tried to end the war, you wouldn't listen. You even used Gareth's and Gaheris's deaths as an excuse to keep fighting for revenge. This guy simply had to win against Lancelot one way or another." Rintarou gritted his teeth as he cut away at Sir Gawain. "The rest is history. During this pointless quagmire, that idiot Mordred was inciting a rebellion in his home country...and then we had Camlann Hill. And the glorious Round Table was put to its end, just like that."

"..."

"But it's generally accepted that Lancelot caused the fall of the Round Table, and you were the picture-perfect symbol of loyalty, following Arthur until the end... If you ask me, it's the opposite—the polar opposite.

"You're the one who destroyed his Round Table.

"Lancelot was more loyal to Arthur than anyone, sacredly upholding the code of chivalry...only to be betrayed by his best friend in the end. He was innocent, but he took the fall for a shameful adultery, so he was treated as the mastermind behind the fall. He couldn't protect Arthur or even see him on his deathbed... Even old Lancy would snap at that."

"...I can't believe you know that much, Rintarou Magami..." With a dry, self-deprecating smile, he didn't deny any of Rintarou's claims. "I don't know who you are. I don't know how this dark side of history... But...it's true. Everything you said is more or less the truth," he choked out, groaning over his own words.

"Sir Gawain...?! I-it couldn't be... You..." Sir Kay balked.

"Hmph, look, you see that?" he concluded, turning to Luna with a faint smile, as if to say everything fell into place. "For old time's sake, this guy's using his loyalty as a front to take advtange of Luna, just because he wants to beat Lancelot. It's not for Felicia's sake—it's for his own ego."

Or at the least, that's what he thought—

"That's the only part you're mistaken about...," refuted the knight, who'd been quietly accepting responsibility for every other accusation.

"Whaddaya say?"

"It's true I wanted to become a great knight like my uncle…like King Arthur. I was envious of Sir Lancelot for being the closest to him, and I strived to surpass him. But I was the scummiest of them all. I still don't know why I justify two wrongs as a right… Even after my death, I still regret what I'd done. That's why… That's the reason why I ask this of you!" he belted out, looking up at Rintarou earnestly. "*This time,* I wish to be a true knight, acting out of loyalty for his King! I wish to become the true knight I couldn't be when I was alive! As a knight, I wish to save my liege in this modern era—I wish to save Felicia! Even though I'm nothing but a fraud… *this* wish is real!"

For a moment, Rintarou was taken aback by Sir Gawain's fervent appeal…

"Heh… That's probably a lie, too." He chuckled, laughing it off as he came to. He shrugged. "Luna, you should just leave this guy. We'll have our own backs and think of a plan to hunt Kujou."

He plastered on the fakest smile. "First, we'll abandon Felicia, of course. Won't be wise to face Kujou's group head-on. Then our best bet is to turn his attention on the other Kings—to ultimately kill someone who's stronger than us. In that case, we gotta think about when we're gonna intervene and seize the moment—timing's everything. Now we've got a reason to make contact with the other Kings."

"…"

"Ahhh! Trying to figure out how to beat these strong guys has suddenly gotten me all fired up! I'm definitely glad I joined this—," he announced gleefully when he noticed Luna was looking intently at the knight's bowed head. "…Hey, Luna. You can't possibly be thinking…that you want to actually take this guy at his word and go save Felicia right now…right? Like, you better not be thinking anything ridiculous like that. Got it?"

For a while, Luna closed her eyes, clearing away the bottom of her heart as she quietly absorbed herself in thought. "Yes, I am… I plan on saving Felicia," she boldly declared, grinning from ear to ear. "Oh, but Sir Gawain has nothing to do with this. I'm going to save her because I want to."

Rintarou was dumbfounded. "That's suicide. The way Kujou is right now, there isn't even a one-in-a-million chance of winning against him. Plus, we don't even have a home field advantage. If we want to fight, we'd need to plan out the location and prepare. And first of all, Felicia's an enemy, isn't she? Why do you want to save an enemy?"

"I still want to save her," she asserted flatly with a brisk and dignified smile. "I want to save Felicia. What's a King, if she can't even save a dear friend, right in front of her?"

"—What?!"

"Because I definitely do love Felicia."

Because I definitely do love everyone.

Luna's words released an unspeakable wrath within Rintarou.

"ARE YOU FREAKING SERIOUS?!" he cursed, shoulders squared as he hounded Luna, yanking her forward by her lapels. "You wanna know what happens when you believe in anybody and everybody and offer them all a helping hand? Camlann Hill, that's what! You want that to happen all over again?!" he asked cryptically.

"…Rintarou?" she implored, blinking.

Without minding Luna, Rintarou raged on—something broke open the floodgates.

"That guy…that Arthur! He loved everyone indiscriminately, and they all idolized him! I warned him so many times that'd be the end of him, but he kept fighting in order to protect everyone! And all that resulted in was Camlann Hill!"

Yeah, Camlann Hill—the place of King Arthur's final battle. The death of the legend. The end of a dream.

The mighty King fought for the sake of the country and his people, and this final battle was…not a battle against his enemies but ironically against those he loved.

"King Lot, King Pellinore, Balin, Guinevere, Gawain and his brothers, Lancelot and his followers, Lamorak, Morgause, Morgan, Mordred…! I prophesized they'd be the ones to cause the fall of the Round Table! If he'd simply abandoned any of them, that wouldn't have happened! But like an idiot, Arthur wanted to share a piece of the Round Table with him! He was a kid—he never grew up, not even at the very end! To be blunt, he was unfit to be King!"

Then Rintarou looked up at the ceiling as a regretful look crossed his face.

"But the one I hate the most is myself! I couldn't be by that kid's side at the very end! I was tricked by the Dame du Lac, and I couldn't do anything except watch, sealed in a rock. I watched as Arthur, his beloved Round Table, and the entire kingdom were mercilessly destroyed!

"Can you imagine?! Can you imagine his grief and sorrow as he saw everything he loved callously broken at Camlann Hill before his very own eyes?!

"I—I could only watch as the cold wind blew!

"I didn't care that he was just a kid! But if only! If only I'd been by his side like I should have been and taken the reins! Then this whole thing…wouldn't have…happened…!"

After yelling with all his might, it seemed Rintarou had released some of his pent-up energy.

"…Grow up, Luna. That's what you have to do to become

King," he griped, breathing jaggedly as he let go of her lapels. "This situation is too different from the little scuffle we had last night at school. Give up on Felicia. Listen to me and follow my lead. If you do that, I'll make sure you're King. It's time for us to lay low."

Luna looked straight at Rintarou Magami.

"...The world is so strange...," she muttered, as though enlightened. "I more or less knew already, but...I guess you proved me right. Rintarou Magami...you used to be *Merlin*, right?"

Merlin. In the legend of King Arthur, there was no one who didn't know that name, alongside King Arthur and Sir Lancelot.

He was the child of a human and a so-called demon—a Fomorian.

He was the world's oldest and strongest wizard and a peerless warrior at the same time. He was Balin le Savage's travel companion. With Sir Kay, Sir Bedivere, and Sir Lucan, he was at King Arthur's side, ever since the King raised his flag, and served as Arthur's counsel.

However, Merlin was pitiful in the end. He was tricked by the Dame du Lac, who feared his power and sealed him away in a stone... Halfway through King Arthur's rule, he walked right out of the legend.

"Yeah, that was my past life. I don't know the logic behind it, but in the past, I was the one called Merlin... I have his memories. It feels like someone else's, though."

"Rintarou..."

"But, well, because that was my past life, my current life's been really terrible in a lotta ways. I was a monster among a flock of sheep. Everyone shunned me, feared me, and there was no place for me anywhere. Nothing good has ever happened in my past life or my current life."

"..."

"But when I joined forces with you, I felt, just a little, that with you…this hell of a boring world might get a little better. So, Luna. Give up on Felicia. Listen to me. I'll make sure you become King. So…" He extended his hand to Luna.

But she didn't take it… Instead, she shook her head.

"Sorry, Rintarou."

"Is that how it is…?" Disappointment and grief registered immediately on his face. "Guess in the end, you're gonna be a fool, just like Arthur, huh? How idiotic. I'll never know why my past self was so happy to serve under King Airhead… I still don't understand, dammit. Guess everything's been ruined."

"…Hey, please, Rintarou." This time, Luna gently reached her hand out to him. "This is an order. Give me your life."

"What?!"

"I feel like…as long as I have you, I can do anything or go as far as I want. I feel like I could win any battle—as long as I have you. So please come with me and—"

At first, Luna's speech could have been misinterpreted as arrogant, selfish, and narcissistic, but one look at her gaze proved otherwise. Her eyes illuminated her faith and confidence in him. For some reason, it made anyone who listened to her experience an impulse to do as she asked.

"Heh… Like I'd join you in a suicide mission," he maintained. Rintarou turned his back to her and waved her off. "If you ask me to think of ways to win, I'll think up plenty of tactics for you. If you tell me you want to run from Kujou, I'll use everything in my power to help you get away. If you ask me to make an alliance with the other Kings, you can count on me to lead the negotiations. But…I won't join you to commit suicide for no reason."

"…"

"Luna. You know you're heading to the jaws of death by

ignoring my counsel. As of now, I renounce you as King. Hmph, this is where we part ways," Rintarou spat relentlessly.

For a while, Luna was speechless, words stuck in the back of her throat...until she sadly smiled. "I see. Well, I guess that's that. Don't worry, Rintarou. This is just me being stubborn. You're not wrong about anything... None of it's your fault."

"..."

"Sorry, I definitely...wasn't capable of having you as my vassal. If I'd been a better King..."

"..." Rintarou listened for a while quietly, sticking to his words. "See ya. Have a good life, Your Highness...no, *Luna*."

Turning his back on her entreating look, Rintarou left the abandoned house alone.

"I misjudged him...that Rintarou Magami."

It was after they'd parted ways. As they headed to Kujou's lair, walking down the streets, Sir Kay was indignant.

"I thought that boy was scum. I couldn't fathom his motives, but...but I thought he would be your ally until the end, Luna, through anything... That's what I believed, at least."

"..."

"So he was actually that wizard Merlin. I see, now that it's been said, I understand. He still has the same patronizing attitude, arrogance, and audacity." She recalled the scoundrel of a wizard's uninhibited smirk. "Merlin was also generally a good-for-nothing guy, but...he wouldn't have abandoned his King, no matter the reason. But what's in the past is in the past, after all...Merlin and Rintarou are wholly different people."

"Don't blame him too much, Sir Kay," Luna pleaded, trying to pacify her. "Merlin is in the past. Right now, he's Rintarou, and he doesn't have anything to do with this battle. He was just lending me his strength—kind of like a volunteer. In the first place, strategically speaking, everything he said was completely right... If anything, I'm the one who's wrong. It can't be helped that the prodigy used up all his patience with me, dumb as I am."

"B-but..."

"I think maybe, just like Rintarou said, if I'd listened to him and abandoned Felicia here...he would've made a plan to beat Mr. Kujou. But in exchange, Felicia would've died..."

She was still full of faith... That's exactly why Sir Kay was silent as she looked at her profile. As they walked, sadness and loneliness followed them.

"But, oh well... It strikes home. Rintarou... If only I had you, I..."

With unrequited yearning, she looked far out into the sky. Even after he'd curtly abandoned her, Luna was still attached to him.

"Luna...why do you have so much faith in Rintarou Magami?" she asked, thinking her behavior odd.

"Who knows? Well...I guess I really am just a girl at heart?"

"...Huh? What does that mean...?"

"It's nothing. It's in the past," she lamented with a certain nostalgia.

"I'm really incredibly sorry...Luna," apologized Sir Gawain with regret in his voice as he followed them from behind. "My liege's...Felicia's wish was not to bring you into this. Everything was to keep you out of Kujou's evil grasp. But in order to save Felicia, I've involved you in this mess. In the end...I'm just an egotistic, worthless knight."

"..."

"Ha-ha, what a joke—saying I wanted to become a true knight in this era. It seems nothing's changed about me, even after I've died once or twice. I'm still..."

"Don't worry about it, Sir Gawain." Luna grinned as she turned just her face to him. "Let me make myself clear: I'm saving Felicia because I want to. If you were to follow her will and leave me behind...well then, I would've had to punch the life outa you in order to go save her."

"..."

"A knight needs to put his King first, right? Even if it's against the King's wishes... Isn't it a true knight that puts their body and loyalty on the line for their King? I think that knights are surprisingly egoistic and selfish."

For a while, Sir Gawain was silent.

"Luna... I'll entrust my sword to you temporarily. My liege is Felicia Ferald and her alone. But just for now, I will swear my loyalty as a knight to you, her savior. I pledge my body and sword to you. Please use my life...as you please."

"Sir Gawain..."

"Thank you, Luna. Your words have become my salvation. I'm sure you might've been a great King to follow in King Arthur's footsteps—after Felicia."

"Oh, come on! At least say I'm number one! You don't even have to mean it!"

It was the calm before the storm. Their tepid conversation went on as they all continued to walk.

Before long, they reached Area Two and its hub of the business buildings.

It was the most developed area in the city, the most refined block.

The roads were set in a rigid grid shape and properly maintained. The line of skyscrapers reaching high into a canopy were state-of-the-art designs of the near future. At night, the streets were illuminated by lights shining brilliantly like glittering chandeliers. With these glowing lights, cutting through the deep curtain of night, this grand scene opened before them a large panoramic view.

They parted through the passersby, becoming fewer and fewer as they continued onward. Everyone was armed with a sword or a suit of armor, but no one was suspicious of the group. That's because they'd used *Sleight* in order to blend in.

By the time these events unfolded, it'd been two hours since they'd left the shack.

Closer and closer, they walked toward a giant skyscraper towering over the rest of them, reaching into the heavens. Lit up majestically was Avalonia Central City Park Hotel.

It was the most expensive five-star hotel in the city.

"Whoa...," Luna uttered when she stepped into the entrance hall from the front door, her eyes fluttering.

There to welcome her were innumerable dazzling lights in a luxurious chandelier, plush sofas for guests, an immaculate table, the artful suits of armor...all kinds of priceless fixtures.

Hypervigilant of Kujou's trap, the group planned to head to the top floor using the emergency stairwell. Using *Sleight* and *Open Lock* in order to not be noticed by the front-desk workers, they sneaked into the stairwell and bounded up the floors. Even though both the emergency stairs and elevator were enclosed spaces, the stairs still seemed better than the elevators—in case Kujou had set a trap.

Clink, clank, clunk... In the dim stairway, their shoes echoed crisply as they made their way up. From the windows of the landings, they saw the cityscape slowly became lower and more distant. If the situation had been different, they probably would've enjoyed this stunning scene.

Clink, clank, clunk... Their footsteps reverberated through the stairwell as they continued forward earnestly. They came across not a single one of the traps they'd prepared for…even at the very end.

Eventually, they stood in front of the door to the top floor.

"…Let's go." Luna nodded at Sir Kay and Sir Gawain behind her. She held her breath as she pushed open the door.

As soon as she did, Luna's eyes burned with the vivid crimson light of the blazing setting sun.

"Huh?! Wh-what is this place?! Isn't this supposed to be the top floor…?" Her eyes had adjusted to the darkness, so she narrowed them, in a daze over the scenery that spread before her.

It was wilderness—a range of gently rolling *hills*, reaching to the limits of the horizon. And even though the sun had long since set, it was still sunny—dusk.

It was a scene of intense destruction: the burning, sinking scarlet sun, the scorched earth that covered the hills to infinity, and the smoldering fires that scattered around. There were swords and arrows in the ground and flags torn asunder, standing erect almost like countless gravestones. Under them, knights, horses, and soldiers alike had collapsed into piles of corpses.

They turned around to find the door and stairway they'd come from was nowhere to be found. The three of them could only stand in the middle of this destruction in shock.

"…Th-this is…," observed Sir Kay in disbelief. She was in a daze. "I can't believe it… This is *Camlann Hill*…?! But how…?!"

"Hmm? It's just a little joke."

They heard a voice come from a hilltop.

"Of course, this isn't the real Camlann Hill. It's a replica I've reproduced with *Netherworld Transformation*. If we're going to fight to our heart's content without bothering anyone while denying you a chance to escape, then doing that in a netherworld is the best, but…just any old netherworld would be dull, don't you think?" reasoned Kujou, looking down calmly upon them. "After all, a King will die here today. If that's the case, it'd be most fitting to do it *here*, right? What do you think, Luna?"

Camlann Hill—the ruin of the dreams King Arthur and his knights tried to protect. He had fought against the traitor Sir Mordred in his last battle here, where King Arthur and nearly all the knights of the Round Table had met their end.

The destruction and devastation had been so intense and gruesome that Camlann Hill had been put into a boundary of its own—as the resting place of the Round Table. It was separated by the Curtain of Consciousness on the other side, in the Illusory World, and it was the site where all the knights' souls would go to peacefully rest.

It didn't matter whether the knights died before or after the battle of Camlann. After all, the concept of time was meaningless to souls anyway. On top of that, Camlann Hill was the emblem of destruction to all the knights of the Round Table. It was where they all realized it as their end, and the place overflowed with their tears.

Gathered at Camlann Hill, all the souls of the knights now rested their wings under this scene of destruction, waiting quietly and watching over it.

They waited for the return of the King—for the time when their lost glory would be resurrected.

"How dare you!" Sir Kay explored in fury. "Kujou! Are you insulting our deaths and way of life?! This place…this scene isn't something you can just play around with!"

"Don't put on airs, Sir Kay. You're a measly little knight—don't raise your voice at me, the one true King. How unpleasant."

Humiliated, she fumed in silence.

"Felicia!"

Next to Kujou was undeniably Felicia.

She'd been chained to a cross on top of the hill—crucified.

At the center of the cross was a magic circle with a large Aura passing through the patterns and letters floating around it. They seemed to be in the middle of some sort of magical ceremony.

"Felicia! Are you okay?!"

"Guh...Luna... I knew it... You did end up coming here...," croaked Felicia. Tears formed at the corners of her half-conscious eyes. "I—I...didn't want to involve you... I...wanted to protect... you..."

"...M-Mr. Kujou! What did you do to her?!" she fumed, ignited by fury.

"What? I'm simply using a ceremony to steal the elven blood and magical knowledge from her body." Kujou shrugged his shoulders, nonchalantly wondering why she'd even brought it up. "Well, to be precise, I'm going to destroy her soul to take that power... So naturally, she'll have to die. But isn't she fulfilling her most cherished desire, if her powers are supporting the true King?"

"Y-you're so...! I won't forgive you...!" Fed up with their conversation, Luna drew her weapon.

At the same time, Sir Kay and Sir Gawain also unsheathed their swords and readied themselves.

"Don't be hasty. We have plenty of time until this ceremony is over... Not that it means anything, since you're going to die here anyway."

Kujou gripped his Round Fragment.

Lightning ran through the air after leaping from the Gate that had materialized and summoned—

"We meet again, sham King and knights..."

—Sir Lancelot, the strongest knight of the Round Table, who now stood before them.

"I will not use my mark of a King, my Excalibur, on bottom-feeders like yourselves... It'd be a disgrace upon me for using it on you."

"Do not worry, my lord... There will be no need for you to use it. I, Lancelot du lac, will make sure to defeat these scum with bloody festivity and grandeur."

"Heh, you're as reliable as always. I expected nothing less of you, Sir Lancelot...my faithful knight. There's no greater knight than you. I have no use for any other rabble. I only need you, the strongest, by my side as the one true King..."

"I am grateful for your praise! I will devote my life and all to you, Lord Kujou!"

As Lancelot's entire body shook with delight—an overwhelming wave of hatred, bloodlust, and spite crashed into Luna's group.

"Guh..."

Despair gripped Luna. It wasn't through logic that she understood her imminent defeat, but through her soul. As she desperately swam through the raging waters of anguish, the sword in her hands seemed weaker and weaker.

And the spot by her side was empty—lonely.

Sir Kay and Sir Gawain couldn't fill this feeling of absolute hopelessness gnawing away at her heart.

If only Rintarou were there. If only she had her Excalibur.

But...at that moment, it wouldn't do any good to beg for the impossible.

"Let's go, Sir Kay...Sir Gawain...!" she shouted, as though to rebuke her wasting heart and wave aside her feeling.

"Y-yes!"

"…Understood."

Sir Kay and Sir Gawain prepared for the battle.

"Oh? Come to think of it… Where did that Rintarou Magami go?" Kujou finally noticed with raised eyebrows.

"…"

"Nothing, huh…? Well, I get the gist of what happened," he jeered. "He's incredibly smart and shrewd… So much so that I even want to keep him under my palm. He wouldn't come with you to this reckless battle, so you parted ways… That's about right, isn't it?"

"…Shut up."

"Ha-ha-ha-ha! You can't even control a single vassal! A poor excuse for a King!" he guffawed, his laughter echoing and ringing all throughout the hills.

To silence him, Luna charged. "HYAAAAAAAAAAAAAAA!"

She violently burned through the mana in her entire body and ran at him like a gale. She was using *Mana Acceleration* in rapid succession, causing her Aura to manifest and emit a harsh glow, scattering from her whole body as she headed toward Kujou on the hill, closing the distance between them all at once.

"You shall not pass!" Sir Lancelot aimed for her and ran down the hill like a gale.

The two of them clashed head-on and struggled—or not. There was no way Luna could challenge him. In an instant, she was pushed down the hill step-by-step as she grappled and swung her sword.

"Guh—it's too heavy?!"

Her soles etched a deep rut as she was forced down the hill. She couldn't stop. She couldn't stop her descent at all.

Sir Lancelot's charge forward was like a steam engine. He couldn't be stopped.

"STOP NOOOOOOOOOOOW!"

It was then that Sir Kay came at Sir Lancelot from the right.

"SIR LANCELOOOOOOT!"

Sir Gawain came from the left.

Like quick-witted beasts, they flew up the hill at him from both sides and slashed at him at the same time.

However—

"Feh, a lukewarm attempt!" He flipped around violently like a tornado.

"AHHH?!"

"GUUUUUUUUUUUH?!"

With a single blow, Luna, Sir Kay, and Sir Gawain were instantaneously blown away by the power of the sword. They bounced off the slopes of the rolling hills and clumsily rolled down.

"Guh!" Luna pierced her sword into the hill to halt her movements.

When she raised her head, Sir Lancelot stood far ahead like an impenetrable wall. Her knees were about to give out from intimidation.

Kujou and Felicia seemed as far away as the stars.

"H-he's strong...! As expected of Sir Lancelot...!"

"Oh my. Is that all you've got in you?" Kujou sneered, far ahead, next to Felicia on her cross. He smiled faintly as he sat down, looking at them with mirth.

"...Of course not!" Using her sword as a cane, she stood herself up with sharp determination and sheer will. "HAAAAAAAAAA-AAAAAAAH!"

Once again, she ran up the hill, aiming for the very top.

And of course, Sir Lancelot came at her like a hurricane.

She couldn't see any way she could win.

Only her stubbornness kept her going in this fight of despair. The battle had just begun.

CHAPTER 6

Luna's Sword of Steel

It was around the time Luna's party had started their death match.

"…Ah, well."

The night descended after he'd separated from Luna's party, and muttering to himself, Rintarou sat on a bench at a deserted bus stop.

Maybe because it was outside the city, but there wasn't a single car running along the road in front of him. There were a lot of empty lots, and many miles lay between each house. Even the lights were far away—it was a lonely place that made people keenly aware of their solitude.

"Seriously, what a foolish bunch. Why fight when they know they're gonna lose?" he spat, sincerely unable to understand her reasoning.

There was no one around to hear his monologue.

"Ugh, boooring. So lame. Is the succession battle already over for me…? Just when I thought it was getting interesting. Ah, well." He forcibly made himself think of something else and considered his next move. "This time, I'll find a slightly smarter King to butter up… Argh, dammit, I should've gotten more intel on Kings other than Luna from *that girl*…"

It was *that girl* who'd invited Rintarou to join the King Arthur Succession Battle.

With her entire body concealed under a hood and long robe, she'd claimed to be a member of the Dame du Lac… But he didn't even need to put any more thought into it—she'd been insanely suspicious all along.

He still couldn't understand her ulterior motives, but she'd appeared before him a month prior when he'd been skipping school and wandering around the world at large. That's when she'd told him about the King Arthur Succession Battle and offered him data on the Kings he could curry favor with.

It seemed she had all the data on the Kings—from their lineage and powers to their Excaliburs and Jacks.

First on her list was Luna. The moment she told him she was the weakest contender, Rintarou didn't hesitate to pick her, dismissing all other Kings and not bothering to hear what their powers were.

Why didn't he gather intel on the others? The only possible answer: This whole thing was nothing more than a game to kill time. In fact, whenever he found a game he liked, Rintarou wasn't the type to depend on online game-play guides, choosing instead to solve things by his own hand.

"I didn't think I'd be on the job market again." But, well, complaining didn't help him. "Ugh, ah, can't be helped. I guess I'll look for a new King tomorrow…"

He came to a clear-cut conclusion.

He decided he'd completely forget about Luna, cut her out.

…That's what he wanted to do.

So why?

" …"

Why? Why did her sad smile keep flickering in his mind? She'd flashed it when they parted ways, and it'd been uncharacteristic of her usual carefree self.

Hey, what's wrong with you, Rintarou Magami? Why are you getting all clingy and attached to her?

He scratched at his head.

Luna Artur... I chose her because it'd be the hardest to win this game with her, which made it the most fun... That's all there was, right?

Since they'd parted ways, his thoughts were ambling, meandering, and wandering through the back alleys of his mind.

Right... Because it'd be fun. That's the guiding principle behind all my actions. Because my everyday life in this normal world is too damn boring... I joined this battle to make it more interesting. I joined Luna's faction for the same reason. That's all it is. Nothing more.

To make his life more interesting, he'd abandoned Luna and looked for another King. End of the discussion.

Then why—? Just thinking about leaving her makes me—

As he continued to be lost in thought, the third bus came to stop in front of Rintarou...opening its doors...and eventually driving away.

Time continued to pass. He continued to waste it.

Rintarou couldn't move at all.

Dammit...! In the back of his mind, he cursed at himself.

"...Huh? Rintarou? What's wrong?" suddenly called a voice behind him, causing him to raise his head.

It was...a face he recognized.

"You look terrible. Did something happen? Weren't you with Luna?"

"Nayuki?"

In her school uniform, Nayuki Fuyuse stood behind him. He hadn't sensed her approaching nor did he receive any advance warning. Maybe she'd been riding on the bus just earlier or something.

"It's nothing. It's about Luna... I'm over with how reckless she is," he confided as ambiguously as possible and turned away, knowing he couldn't tell her the truth.

She sat next to Rintarou in her prim and proper way. "Ah-ha-ha...I don't know what happened... But am I right to guess you got in a fight with Luna?"

"Well...pretty much."

It was so abridged that all the important parts were cut away, but breaking it down in principle and theory, well, it got to the point to be honest.

"It's like she doesn't even listen to what anyone says ever," he criticized, letting irritation coat his words, as Nayuki smiled wryly. "I gave her tons of options, thinking about what would be best for her, but she chose the one road she absolutely shouldn't take. I might have only met her two days ago, but I'm already fed up."

"What does that mean? Could you give me more details?"

"......" Of course, Rintarou chose to remain silent.

After some time passed between them, she didn't seem annoyed in the slightest and chuckled gently. "...It's okay; I understand. It's something you can't talk about... I won't pry any further."

"It'd be great if you didn't. To be honest, making up some story is the last thing I'd want to do," he said with his usual arrogance.

Even as she faced this, Nayuki remained kind and gentle. "So... what are you going to do now, Rintarou?"

"What am I going to do? Well, I don't have a reason to be at school anymore... For now, I'm gonna quit."

It wasn't like Luna would be at school the next day anyway. They'd either find her corpse somewhere or think she was missing.

Before long, he'd be treated as the prime suspect, and the mallet would undoubtedly come down on his head since he'd been with her the whole day. That seemed like a sorry mess.

Absentminded, Rintarou continued thinking about that.

"I...personally kind of wanted you to stick by her side," Nayuki began cryptically.

"Huh? Why? I just said I tired of being around her—"

"Rintarou. You were amazing yesterday. You answered all of Mr. Sudou's problems so easily. Ha-ha... Luna... She was just covering for you, right? In reality, you solved them all yourself, didn't you?" She suddenly changed topics.

For a moment, he was bewildered, unable to follow along...but replied in his normal sarcastic tone. "...Well, yeah? I was born different from you plebeians so—"

"It must be so uncomfortable...having to stuff your real self into something you're not," she pointed out, to which he was simply at a loss for words. "Rintarou, aren't you actually super-lonely? You act like a tough guy, but I think you don't like being rejected by people. That's why you hide your true self. Because you don't want to be hated. Because you don't want to be rejected.

"But all that must be...so hard and difficult and boring..."

His mind brought forth images of his parents, turning their backs on him as they went on a work trip somewhere—never to come home.

"Rintarou. Did you know? When you introduced yourself in front of everyone on your first day...you seemed really bored. After that, you were so disinterested in everyone who came to talk to you. It was like you didn't expect anything from us... At least, that's what I gathered from your expression."

"N-no, that's not...," he shamefully tried to refute.

"But you know what?! These past two days, you seemed like

you were having the time of your life...getting dragged around by Luna. Especially when you were selling that bread with her!"

"What—?" Rintarou suddenly felt like someone had hit him upside the head. "Huh?! Looked like I was having fun?! You've got to be joking?!"

"I'm not. With Luna, you seemed like you were alive...like, I was even a little jealous."

"...Nayuki?"

"Weren't you having fun with her? You were with her all day today, too, weren't you?"

He thought back to earlier that day: spending the entire day with Luna, being dragged around, going on a date, being yanked around some more.

Even after everything, she never treated me like some monster. She was the first one to treat me like a normal person.

Sure, at the very end, she'd dragged him around, doing as she pleased...but if asked whether he had fun or not...even he wasn't a child who'd say no for the sake of being stubborn.

Yanking his hair, Rintarou stood. "But—! That doesn't matter! I'm done with her! Our ragtag friendship is over! I don't have time to humor her! I've only got one reason for doing anything—that's to make this stupid life more interesting...to make it actually enjoyable!"

Huh? Oh no. He'd realized something. *I was desperate to change my super-dull life.*

But maybe I already have—

In that case, why am I here?

Why aren't I by her side?

He stood stock-still in shock.

"Didn't Luna say she wanted to become the best King in the world?" she asked.

"..."

"I don't really get why she wants to be a King, but...it seems like she's serious."

"..."

"To tell you the truth, before your first day...there was a certain corrupt corporation forcefully trying to buy out the school by using some pretty dirty schemes... I think they wanted to make a forward operating base as they mined the energy source or something. We're a private school, so the negotiations went unexpectedly smoothly. The teachers also tried to prevent this from happening, but even though they did what they could, the other guys clearly had the upper hand..."

"They tried to buy the school?"

"Anyway, the school was on the brink of closing its doors for good. We all were set to disperse and transfer to other schools... But it was our beloved alma mater. And we were sad... In the end, Luna was the one who protected it."

"Huh? She protected it? How did she go up against a corporation? How'd she get the money together?"

"She apparently had some sort of really valuable antique item."

"An antique?"

"Yeah... It was like some precious sword or something, so valuable it was almost priceless."

"...A sword?!" He hurled himself upright and looked at her incredulously. "I-is that true?!"

Based on their current circumstances, the sword in the story had to be Luna's Excalibur—without a doubt. She'd said something scummy like she'd sold it for money, but was that what actually happened?

"Y-yeah... She sold it to the corporation and stopped the purchase. She didn't tell anyone, so there aren't many people at school who know."

What?

"I think she said...'How can I be a king if I can't protect a place that's important to me?'"

Yeah, I see. Rintarou realized something.

She was a genuine, authentic, honest-to-goodness idiot.

This was the real deal. She'd allowed her lifeblood, the Excalibur, to slip out of her hands without even thinking of the future or the consequences and recklessly rushed into things.

But she'd take her idiocy and channeled all her power into her beliefs with utter sincerity, even when her life was on the line... That was how she ruled.

It wasn't that she couldn't leave her friends behind or abandon them: She didn't operate on pseudo-kindness or a naive sense of justice. Nothing she did was fake or based on pretense; she actually believed this was the correct way to rule as a King... If she lost her grip on that, Luna would've died—in a lot of ways.

Abandon Felicia. Rintarou had barked for her sake.

But that was the same as telling her to die.

How idiotic... Stop, dammit! Are you that big of an idiot...? This is just too stupid... I can't just leave you alone...!

He held his head in agony.

"Rintarou...I don't know why Luna is so fixated on being a King, but it seems to be really important to her. She's always like that. She acts more like a King than anyone... Sometimes I think she's been too hard on herself, but..."

"..."

"Rintarou, please. Please could you stay by her side? Luna seemed genuinely happy when you were with her in a way I've never seen before."

Time ticked on.

Questioning how he felt, Rintarou looked up at the sky for answers.

But the sky didn't share any insight. He had to come up with the answer himself.

"Huh? Rintarou? What's wrong? Weren't you waiting for the bus?"

"...I remembered I had to take care of something," he muttered, starting to walk away from the bus stop.

"Something urgent?"

"...Right, seems like it. I'm almost as much of an idiot as she is." He laughed dryly with a touch of self-derision.

"...Go at it. Don't lose hope, Rintarou. I'm rooting for you from the bottom of my heart. Always...for a long time... That's how I atone," she whispered, as if she saw through him. Her voice seemed to press gently against his back.

"...?"

Why was it?

It hadn't been very long since he'd met Nayuki. But he suddenly felt like he'd known her...since long ago.

"...Oh, right. By the way," he began, flipping around to face her in an attempt to cast aside that strange feeling. "Could you tell me the name of the corrupt corporation that tried to buy the school? Also their address? I have some business to attend to over there..."

He cracked his fingers and smirked diabolically as he asked.

....

This is a story from my childhood, when I was a teeny-tiny little kid.

In those days, I was receiving special training as a knight, learning magic and sword fighting as a daughter born to the English house of Artur.

One day, I'd have to inevitably fight in the King Arthur Succession Battle.

And then—I'd succeed King Arthur and save this world from the Catastrophe.

All throughout my childhood, my parents and extended family always drove that home. But I couldn't handle the pressure: I'd end up shaking and in tears when no one else was looking.

I didn't want this. I wanted to run away. I didn't want to become a King.

I was scared. I couldn't help but be in fear.

Why did *I* have to do something this terrifying?

I was still young when people told me I'd fight for strangers, save the world, and become the ideal King—it didn't click. I didn't feel like doing that at all.

But that day, during my unremarkably colorless childhood…I met him.

"<Hey, you. Why are you crying?>"

I was alone, crying in a deserted park, when someone suddenly called out to me in fluent English. I snapped my head up in surprise.

Looking down at me was a Japanese boy around the same age.

"<Whatever—come on. I'm bored. Let's play together.>"

He forcefully pulled me by my hand and started running.

"B-but…"

"I'm guessing something bad happened, right? Just forget about everything. It doesn't matter. Forget it, and let's do something fun together instead!"

On that day, for the very first time, I skipped out on my lessons on how to become a great King. Caught up in playing with him, I forgot all about home until the sun went down.

We hung out the next day and the day following and the day after that…running through the hills and fields, exploring an abandoned house, climbing up trees, pretending to be knights, catching bugs, going fishing… We even played old board games and popular card games.

Every day, I skipped training and snuck out to spend my time with him. We were like two puppies innocently messing around, playing from dawn till dusk.

Naturally, I got in trouble with everyone at home and received scolding after scolding, but…I didn't care about it at all. It was more important to spend time with him.

He was scheduled to be in England for a month, because his parents were working or something. He was absolutely amazing.

I'd gone through all kinds of special training to become King in the future. When it came to sports, studies, and even playing, I had confidence that I wouldn't lose to any ordinary child my age. But…that boy was more competitive when it came to everything.

No matter what I did, he could do it better than me—every time.

"Ha-haaa, you're still not even close."

He was arrogant, pushy, and self-important. He did anything he wanted, oblivious to those around him, but…he was a precious friend of mine, especially when I'd been all alone.

He never exhibited any restraint, and he was always relentless when we were together.

But with every meeting comes a parting.

Time passes by when you're having fun, and the day he'd return to Japan came all too quickly.

No, no, no! I wanna be with you longer! I wanna play!

I don't want you to leave!

As I was splayed out and throwing a big fit, the boy scratched his cheek in thought.

"Okay, okay! Uhhh, I don't really get it, but…you're gonna become a King someday, right?"

"Yeah…*hiccup*…"

"And…you kept saying you'd make me your vassal all month long, every chance you got, right? And you were real insistent about it, too."

"Yeah. But you never became my vassal…*sniffle*…"

"…I'll become one."

"Huh?"

"Someday, when you become the best King in the world."

"…R-really?"

"Yeah, it's a promise. But you have to become a King that's worthy of me, okay? You have to become a really great King or I won't become your vassal, you got that?!"

I don't think he understood anything.

The world was divided into the Real World and the Illusory World.

I belonged in the Illusory World and he to the Real World.

The boy wouldn't have known what the King Arthur Succession Battle was, even if I told him. He'd made that promise casually, going along with it as though this were a game of make-believe. He probably was trying to show off for me, since I was being such a brat.

Regardless…that innocent, empty lip service of a promise… made me happier than anything.

It became my source of hope as I quivered in terror of the battle to come. It saved me.

"Yeah…when that happens…I'll make you my vassal, *Rintarou!*"

"Ha, just leave it to me! I promise! Someday, when you've become the greatest King in the world, I'll dash right in like a hero! Just you wait!"

*　　*　　*

....

"Ugh…!"

Running down her spine, the pain shot through Luna's body, sharply bringing her wandering attention from her distant memories to the present.

It seemed, for a moment, she'd gone unconscious.

"Oh my, what's wrong, Luna? Is that all you've got?" taunted Kujou, looking down at her with complete composure from the top of the charred hill. A frosty smirk faintly played across his lips.

"Ugh…guh…" Her consciousness still hazy, Luna checked her condition one bit at a time.

To say the least, she was in a terrible state.

The gashes, slashes, bruises, and lacerations all over her body… were invariably deep. She was riddled with wounds, making for a bloody, gory mess.

It was a miracle she was still alive.

Eating away through her body was a burning sensation, as though swarms of poisonous snakes were biting her all over.

On the other hand, Sir Lancelot was completely unharmed.

He hadn't broken out into sweat at all, not a single change to his breathing. As always, he had the air of a fierce god, placing an immense pressure on his surroundings, and he stood imposingly between Luna and Kujou.

"Now then…it's about time for you to understand. Just look around." Kujou jerked his chin.

Some ways away from Luna, next to a singed rock, was Sir Gawain, and Sir Kay lay at the base of the hill.

Like her, they were in a pitiful state, lying weakly on the ground.

"This is it. This is the difference between a winner and a

215

loser... You understand, don't you, Luna? This is the difference between you and me... You've *lost*."

The battle had long ago been decided.

In a loud swoop, he spread his arms in victory. "Now then, get on your knees in front of the King and beg for my forgiveness. Crawl along the ground and lick my shoes. You may apologize for dreaming of taking the throne, as unfit as you are. If you do that, I might use you as a servant...because I'm *such* a generous King."

"Ha-ha-ha-ha...that has to be a joke, ack...ack...!" Luna coughed, hacking up blood. With her sword stabbed in the ground, she leaned on it to squeeze out all the strength in her body and soul to stand up.

Then, not complying with any of his words...Luna readied her sword once more, as though possessed. But she already couldn't support the weight of the sword, and its tip shook visibly. On the verge of death, it took everything she had to continue standing...but her eyes burned like the flash of a blue flame and were not dead yet.

"This doesn't please me." Kujou clucked his tongue in annoyance. "I showed you how much I overpower you, and you still dare to oppose me? You should be fearful of someone as grand as I. You should feel the need to prostrate yourself before me."

"Like I would...ever do that... I'm...a King...," she spat, swiping the blood off the edge of her mouth with a macabre smile.

A blue vein stuck out on his forehead. "How dare you lie that you're King, you lowlife...!"

It seemed her words had incurred his wrath.

"Oh, well...I thought I'd let you live and use you to negotiate with that troublesome Rintarou Magami boy, but I was wrong to even consider giving you mercy. Retire, Sir Lancelot."

"As you wish..."

Kujou had Sir Lancelot withdraw and slowly went down the hill toward Luna.

In his hand was his diabolical Excalibur, pulled out from within the shadows.

"Before you depart for the afterlife, this is a little parting gift from me to you. My Excalibur is known as the Military Conquest Steel Sword... It defeated the former Roman Empire, and it's the manifestation of King Arthur's raids... the most fitting sword for me, the King who stands at the apex of everything."

It glinted, releasing a sinister light.

"This sword's ability is to 'Display power even greater than the strongest opponent in the battlefield.' ...You get it? Do you understand how invincible I am? In effect, no one can defeat me."

"...Wh-what the hell...?! That's so unfair..."

"But unfortunately, there won't be an opportunity for me to fully display the powers of this sword during the King Arthur Succession Battle...since no King is stronger than me."

Approaching her with calm, rhythmical steps, he came to a halt in front of Luna.

Luna was just barely standing...and couldn't move at all.

"Guh... Lu...na...!" strained Sir Kay, beaten to a pulp.

She and Sir Gawain couldn't move, either.

"Stop...please...Lord Gloria...just not her..."

On top of the hill, hung by chains on the crucifix, Felicia couldn't raise a finger.

There was nothing more they could do.

"You've understood it now, haven't you, Luna? This overwhelming and absolute power... This is what a King is."

Those were his parting words.

He aimed the jagged blade straight at the base of her neck.

"...Ugh!" Finally accepting what was to come, Luna closed her eyes.

Well...I guess I did what I could. It's too bad this is it...but I think I was a King until the very end... Well, I guess if I have any regrets...

Sorry, Sir Kay...I was such a stubborn King. Sorry, Felicia...I couldn't save you...

Rintarou, it seems like you don't remember anything, but...I really didn't think you'd come running in for me the night before... We went our separate ways, but...I'm so happy we got to see each other again...

With some strange satisfaction, she smiled very slightly.

If there's anything I wished for, it was to be able to fight until the end with you... I really did want to make you my vassal for real...but that'd be asking for too much... Yeah, it might have been temporary... but I was really glad...that I could fight with you...

With full intent to cleave into her head, Kujou slowly brought down the long sword.

"Die."

Good-bye...

Mercilessly, Kujou's blade swung, ripping through the air.

CLAAAAAAANG!

With the sound of breaking glass, a large rift opened in the space.

From it, something shot down like a black flash of lightning, aimed at Kujou.

"LUNAAAAAAAAAAAAAAAAAAAAAAAAAAAAAAAAAAA!"

CLANG!

In an instant, the scorched hills echoed with metallic screeches.

"What?!" In shock, Kujou lifted his long sword promptly above his head and took the defensive, as his weapon creaked and vibrated under pressure.

"Ha… You bastard! What do you think you're doing to my King?"

Like a meteor blasting in the sky, Rintarou crashed into Kujou's long sword with his weapon.

"AHHHHHHHHHHHHHHHHHHHHHHHHHHHHHHH-HHHHH!"

His other sword flashed from the side.

Tracing an arc toward Kujou's torso, that sturdy sword caused him to promptly jump away. At the same time, the sound of something being destroyed rang out far behind him.

When Kujou instinctively turned around, there was *another Rintarou* using his sword at the top of the hill to interrupt the magic ceremony and destroy the cross where Felicia was tied up. Upon release and being thrown on the ground, she was bewildered, eyes jumping out of her head.

"Was that a *Silhouette*…?!" Kujou asked. The other Rintarou grinned at him and dissipated into thin air.

"Sorry I'm late…," the real Rintarou said curtly as he stood in front of Luna, whose only reaction was to blink. He readied his two swords.

"Rintarou?! How…?!" she yelled. "Weren't you fed up with me…?!"

He ignored her and thrust his left sword into a stone next to them.

But the sword in the stone wasn't his usual cane sword.

It was a more majestic, precious sword—a bastard sword, emanating a peculiar brilliance neither gold nor silver, forged from a mysterious metal. With a hilt in the shape of a pink water lily, an azure phosphorescence radiated from the upright blade, inspiring awe.

It was a sword that inspired all to bow before it. It was—

"My Excalibur?! How...?! Why is it here...?!"

"Hmph... You made me go through all that trouble. Don't let that thing out of your sight ever again."

His words didn't even register in her ears as she approached the sword with great hesitation. Slowly, very gently, she reached her hand to the hilt.

Oh, she looks like him... She looks just like him...

With Luna in front of him, Rintarou was overcome with his memories in his former life as Merlin.

He could vividly recall the scene, the beginning of King Arthur's journey.

There was Merlin, Sir Kay, and Ector.

Then, as everyone watched, Arthur reached his hand toward the hilt of the sword in the stone.

This image of King Arthur overlaid over Luna, together—

—she pulled Excalibur out and lifted it above her head.

As though overjoyed to return to its true owner's hands, that Excalibur started to glitter in heroic delight.

"...You gotta have that sword if you're gonna be a King," Rintarou quipped, shrugging his shoulders while watching Luna look at her raised sword with great emotion.

Then he turned his attention. "Yo, Mr. Kujou. How've you been?"

"Oh...so you've finally come, Rintarou Magami."

"The headliner has always got to come late. That's what fires up the crowd, isn't it?" He readied his two swords to finish their conversation...

"Oh, Rintarou. I had something I wanted to discuss with you."

"I don't have anything to talk to you about. You really did a number on my King... I don't really know why, but I'm pretty ticked off...at both you and me!"

Rintarou didn't hesitate as he invoked his *Fomorian Transformation*. A repulsive Aura overflowed from his body.

"Ha-ha-ha... You're supposed to listen to your elders," Kujou warned, coolly brushing him off as he made a proposal. "Rintarou Magami, how about you join me?"

"Whaddaya say?" His eyebrows knit together.

"I actually think quite highly of you. I know your true identity, more or less. If I was to guess...you were the great wizard who served King Arthur. You were Merlin, right? Am I wrong?"

Bull's-eye. Rintarou froze for a moment.

"It seems you haven't completely regained the power from your past life... But you're fit to become my vassal. I mean, Merlin was always looking for the rightful King to rule the world, wasn't he? Look here. What you desire is right in front of your eyes."

"..."

"I'll make you a promise. When I rule the entire world in my hands, I'll let you do whatever you want. Under my control, you alone will live with complete freedom, doing whatever you please. You'll have the license to do anything. How's that sound? I think we'd make a dream team, don't you?"

It was a tempting proposal. After all, Kujou was the strongest King, attended by the strongest Jack. If they joined forces, victory was certain.

"Hmph…no way, you idiot." Rintarou refused to give in to this temptation.

"Hmm. Can I ask why?"

"'Course. If I stuck around you…it wouldn't be any fun for me!"

"I see… Well, that's too bad. It is what it is. Sir Lancelot…"

"…As you wish." Sir Lancelot once again bound toward Rintarou and blocked him.

"I've lost interest in you, Rintarou Magami. I can't have you troubling me any more… You'll die by Sir Lancelot's sword."

Sir Lancelot made the atmosphere itself feel oppressive, pushing down on them like a roaring storm on a rough ocean. It swallowed Rintarou up without mercy and apprehended him.

Guh… So the monster has arrived…!

In a cold sweat, he squared off with the strongest man of the Round Table.

Dammit, as usual, going at him directly means there's no chance of winning…! Seriously, why'd I come here without taking any countermeasures?! Whatever! I just need to fight or die trying!

He was shocked at the extent of his own stupidity but readied himself to fight this grim battle.

"Rintarou!" Luna yelled, holding her Excalibur up in the air. "Let me tell you what my Excalibur symbolizes!"

"Huh?!"

"It's hard to use it by myself, but with you right now, I know I can! I offer my life to you! So please…give your life to me!"

Rintarou was quiet, calmly in thought.

Yeah, he was well aware and sorry to say it, but Luna's Excalibur was a *useless* sword.

First of all, to activate the sword, there was an imposing prerequisite.

That requirement was trust. There needed to be absolute trust between a King and a vassal.

But Rintarou couldn't have any faith in someone besides himself, and he didn't think Luna could trust him even one bit.

At least, that was what he used to think... He wouldn't have dreamed of depending on her Excalibur.

But now—

For some reason—

"Yeah, I'll take your life and give you mine!"

"Thank you! You're my best vassal!"

As they grinned at each other, he stepped in front of her.

Then Luna sheathed her Excalibur and...closed her eyes for some reason.

"...Huh?" Kujou was on guard after seeing Luna's suspicious behavior.

"..."

But nothing happened.

Time crawled by.

"...What are you planning to do? How about you hurry up and use Royal Road?"

"Ha-ha, don't get hasty, chief." Rintarou turned his fearless smile on Kujou, who seemed dubious. "Now then, how about we square off in this final battle!"

With that, he kicked off and ran up the hill like the wind.

"AHHHHHHHHHHHHHHHHHHHHHHHHHHHHHHHHH!"

Roaring, he dashed straight at Kujou.

"Hah... I don't get it. It doesn't matter. Stomp them out, Sir Lancelot."

"As you wish."

At that instant, a violent wind wrapped around the knight, spiraling and whirling, and Sir Lancelot hurled himself onto Rintarou.

Dammit, will I be able to hold out against this...until Luna declares what her sword symbolizes?!

Truth be told, the *Fomorian Transformation* put a large strain on his body. His soul may have come from Merlin, but his body was that of a normal modern-day person. When Rintarou held the transformation for too long, it would burn out, and even if that wasn't the case, Sir Lancelot was uncompromisingly strong.

Rintarou desperately prepared himself to meet swords with his foe.

"Huh?!" In an instant, Sir Lancelot's movements dulled.

"LANCELOOOOOOOOOOOOOOOOOOOOOOOOOOOOOOT!"

A burst of grating metal. An overflowing force. Flickering sparks.

Sir Gawain's sword had come flying in from the side, crossing Sir Lancelot's.

"HAAAAAAAAAAAAAAAAAAAAAAAH!" Sir Kay sharply swung at him from the other side.

"Tch—" Taken off guard by the surprise attack, the Jack jumped back.

Upon closer inspection, a warm, glittering wind cocooned gently around the two knights, healing their wounds under the temperate wind.

"Felicia, is this all you?!"

It was the *Spring Wind of Abundance*, fairy magic. As long as they were in that glittering, healing wind, their wounds would continue to heal—helping them recover, even as they sustained new injuries. It was an extremely powerful form of fairy magic that could easily change the tide of battle.

"Rintarou Magami!"

Called by his name, he looked at the top of the hill.

Felicia lifted her Excalibur and invoked Royal Road. Sir Gawain must have thrown it over to her. The sword dazzlingly brightened the dark battlefield and slowed Sir Lancelot's movements down very slightly.

The Sun's Blessing was revived in Sir Gawain as he was bathed in that light.

"I don't know what you're trying to do, but we'll do something to hold Sir Lancelot back! You go for Lord Gloria!" Felicia yelled, sprinting down the hill toward Sir Lancelot.

Sir Gawain, Sir Kay, and Felicia surrounded the knight to incessantly lay into him all at once.

"You might have taken us all out the other day, but this time, we won't go down so easily!"

"Hmph!" the Jack responded, nonchalantly blocking the whirlwind of their three swords.

It was a three-on-one fight. Sir Lancelot's movements were dulled by Felicia's Excalibur, and Sir Gawain's power was amplified by the Sun's Blessing. They put their lives on the line and leaned on the support of *Spring Wind of Abundance* as they fought.

However, even when they used all their strength—

"AHHHHHHHHHHHHHHHHHHHHHHHHHHHHHHHHH?!"

"YAAAH?!"

"GWAAAAAAAAAAAAH?!"

Faced with Aroundight, allowed to run amok like a demon, the three of them were blasted into the air.

Even after combining their powers, they were still defeated and scattered by Sir Lancelot, the strongest knight of the Round Table.

However—

"Th-this isn't over…!"

"Guuuh!"

They were protected by the *Spring Wind of Abundance*, holding onto some semblance of life as they continued to hound Sir Lancelot over and over again.

Truth be told, they were barely managing to buy some time.

They could probably only maintain it for a few minutes at most.

"—All right! Let's go! come on!" Rintarou readied his swords and closed in on his target.

"I can't believe I have to use my Excalibur against the likes of you...," Kujou lamented, sympathizing with his humiliated sword, as his face warped in annoyance. "Why not? Pay close attention—Royal Road, Excalibur, the Military Conquest Steel Sword! Bow before my power!"

At that moment, darkness shot out of his sword and swallowed Kujou whole, accompanied by a seething crimson Aura. His power inflated and grew, becoming more powerful than Rintarou's *Fomorian Transformation*.

"What?! Why, you—Just what did you do?!"

"Ha-ha-ha-ha-ha-ha-ha-ha-ha! No matter what tricks you pull out, you'll never win against me! That's how this sword works!"

Gaining momentum as he charged forward, Rintarou's sword slammed into the lackadaisical swing of Kujou's long sword, meeting with so much force that the impact broke through the hill, smashing it into pieces and roiling the earth itself.

"GAAAAAAAAAAAAAAAAAAAAAAAAAAH?!" Rintarou was blasted away and bounced off the ground...

"Rintarou Magami...Luna Artur...! You're nothing more than pebbles rolling along on the side of the road en route to my ascension to the throne... Suffer by my HAAAAAAAAAAAAAAAAAAAAAND!"

Without a moment to spare, Kujou thrust toward Rintarou, walking over one step at a time to his target, as spires of earth thrust up toward the skies in his wake.

"AHHHHHHHHHHHHHHHHHHHHHHHHHHHHHHHHH!" Rintarou roared, determined not to lose, as he assaulted his all-powerful enemy.

"Die! Die like a worm!" Kujou sped toward him.

"Daaaaaaaaamn it!!" He streaked toward Kujou.

Straight on, their swords pounded into each other: Kujou's sword bit into his dual blades. The air warped around them as it was forcibly pushed back by their blows.

Kujou's blade flew sideways in a horizontal cut, only to be caught by his opponent's two swords.

He launched another attack from overhead, which Rintarou used his right-hand sword to parry.

Then Kujou launched a series of strikes that struck from alternating sides. The blade swung so dangerously close to Rintarou that he barely managed to deflect it with his left sword.

Blow after blow, each impact throbbed at Rintarou's core as he clawed his way past these attacks while inching backward.

"There's no EEEEEEEEEEND!"

Kujou swung downward with all his might.

"Tch—" Rintarou dodged to the side.

The hill split into two under Kujou's virtually infinite strength. It was hard to believe it'd been whole only moments before.

Dammit, is he crazy...?! This guy's insane!!

Forced to be on the defensive, Rintarou scowled at the sharp, frosty pain that ran up and down his spine, soaking his face in cold sweat.

Run. You'll definitely die. Fighting head-on here is reckless. This is a bad idea.

Rintarou's soul and logic were screeching at him, threatening to pull his brain apart.

But—

Rintarou took a quick glance at Luna behind him.

She still had her eyes defenselessly closed...and he watched as she focused on breathing.

That's weird...just by knowing I'm with her... A surge of matchless power bubbled up from deep within him... *Makes things fun!* In the middle of the hellish battle, Rintarou grinned boldly.

"AHHHHHHHHHHHHHHHHHHHHHHHHHHHHHHHHHH-HHHHHHHHHHHHHHHHHHH!" Repelling a swing from Kujou's blade, he immediately drove his right sword toward his enemy.

"Ngh—" Kujou wavered, unable to respond instantly to this lightning-fast move, forcing him to withdraw. "Rintarou Magami... Have you gotten stronger?! You've exceeded me?! Impossible...?!" Flinging his eyes open, he was suspended in place for a moment, before bouncing back to raise his sword. "But I have my Military Conquest Steel Sword!"

Once again, he activated his Royal Road, bleeding a vibrant crimson Aura like a severed jugular and increasing in strength all the while. *Does he have no limits?*

"It's useless! No matter what kind of power you use, my power will always exceed it!"

"Oh, is that right?! Good for you!" Rintarou's body blurred as he moved side to side, switching from the left, to the right, to the left again—traversing Kujou's blind spots.

By using only his abilities from the *Fomorian Transformation*, he could maneuver at a speed that far exceeded a human's.

"DAAAAAAAAAAAAAAAAAAAH!" Disappearing into the mist, he leaped upward, coming down hard with a shower of powerful blows on the top of Kujou's head.

BAM!

But Rintarou's attack was stopped short by his opponent's raised sword, lazily countering him. "You see?! It's useless—useless!" He closed in the distance between them as Rintarou regained his composure and stance.

With that, he thrust his long sword violently at Rintarou. It made a sound like a gun firing. *BANG!*

"Just bow before me!"

He made a feral jab at Rintarou. *BANG!*

"I am the true King!"

Again, vehemently. *BANG!*

"You little shit! Trying to thwart my rule? This merits death!"

Again, tempestuously. *BANG!*

"Because of that, you'll die HEEEEEEEERREEEEEEEEEEE!" *BANG! BANG! BANG!*

Their swords viciously danced and sang a bloodcurdling medley into the heavens, burning distantly under the sinking sun.

Kujou raised his long sword and thrust and thrust and thrust—

Forced onto the defensive again, Rintarou barely managed to match the flurry of long sword attacks as a violent storm seemed to whirl from it. Each blow grated against his body, sending pain shooting through his bones and organs. Blood started to trickle from the corner of his mouth, and he felt his consciousness going hazy.

"Heh..."

That still didn't wipe his ghastly smile from his face.

Even though he was cornered—

—Rintarou seemed like he was having fun.

...Thank you, Rintarou... Thank you, everyone.

Away from the battlefield, Luna was deep in thought as her eyes remained vulnerably closed. In the meditative darkness, she could feel the mortal combat occurring nearby, the sensation prickling and crawling over her skin.

With her sword in her sheath, she stood blindly in front of her enemies. This was basically suicide. Absolute terror chafed away at Luna's soul.

Rintarou, Felicia, Sir Kay, and Sir Gawain—everyone's souls were being ground down as they continued to fight. She could sense this—almost painfully so. She wanted to open her eyes right now, driven by the impulse to help everyone.

At any moment, the tables could turn, causing someone to lose their precious life—it was all she could imagine, the thought threatening to drive her mad. It made her want to cry.

But she wouldn't help them. She couldn't.

That would betray the trust of the people who were fighting for her.

Because she believed in everyone—because she believed in Rintarou, she couldn't interfere. Though that decision tore at her heart, she resisted the mounting impulse to help that was pressing hard against her back and kept her eyes closed, steadying her breath. She just continued waiting for the time to come.

...She continued to wait.

...And wait...

...

...And then it seemed time stretched out into an eternity...

That was when: *ba-dump*. The Excalibur in her hands mysteriously started to pulse under her grip.

Zwoosh.

"What...was that...?!" Kujou whispered, suddenly feeling a chill run along his spine.

Up until that moment, he'd been callously inflicting wounds on Rintarou.

That sensation he felt was dread.

When he dared to look for the source, he saw that Luna still had her sword in its sheath with her eyes closed.

But then why?

Why did he feel such horror from seeing that little girl?

As the true King, why did he fear her?

"Guh! Sir Lancelooooooooooot!" Kujou yelled, forcibly brushing aside Rintarou, who was tenaciously persisting with a side strike. "Kill Luna! KIIIIIIIIIIIILL LUNAAAAAAAAAAAA!"

"HAAAAAAAAAAAAAAAAAAAAA!" Felicia's sword came.

"AHHHHHHHHHHHHHHHHH!" Sir Gawain's sword came.

"YAAAAAAAAAAAAAAAAAAAAHH!" Sir Kay's sword came.

It didn't matter how many times they were knocked down, blown away, battered, or grievously wounded. They persistently nipped at Sir Lancelot's ankles as they did their best to hinder him.

They weren't aiming to defeat him. They were fighting simply to delay him.

Sir Lancelot still didn't have a single scratch on him—his opponenets were the ones who were in ruins. But they squeezed out every bit of life to keep up the defense. When faced with the three, fighting with their lives on the line, even Sir Lancelot couldn't overcome them. His hands were tied.

"Dammit! How could these nobodies do this to my Jack...?!" Kujou clicked his tongue slightly and lifted his weapon over his head.

GONG!

Rintarou's two swords deflected them as he pounced on Kujou like a bird of prey. "It's time to pay your due, Mr. Kujou! I'm going to tell you just one thing!"

"GUUUH?!" The swords hammered in; their wielders stared at each other at close range.

"Basically, you're… not worthy of being King!" Rintarou yelled in triumph—

FWOOSH!

The Excalibur Luna had in its sheath unleashed a blinding light, even brighter than Felicia's. It shined with an intense white heat upon the fake Camlann Hill.

"What is that sword…?!" Kujou yelled out, gripped with inexplicable alarm and panic at this sight. As he swung down his sword to drive away his foe, he vaulted away from Luna. "It doesn't matter what power you use—MILITARY CONQUEST STEEEEEEEEEEEEEL!"

Once again, Kujou used Royal Road.

With that, he'd have no problem facing her—no matter how much power she summoned.

He'd certainly become stronger than her.

"Wha…at?!" he sputtered. Kujou was at a loss.

His Excalibur had done nothing.

"Why?! Why won't it respond?! She's obviously strong! Just look at it?! My power should always be stronger than that… So why?!"

"Ha-ha! Your sword's power relies on your opponent's strength to increase your own power!" Rintarou preached as though reciting a requiem. "But it's based directly on the opponent you're facing! If the power comes from something else…for example, if it comes directly from a sword, then your Excalibur can't do anything!"

"Grh…?!" he stammered.

That was when Luna opened her eyes and declared: "Royal Road!"

"That mountain of a giant was a most terrifying and formidable opponent.

"As it grasped its large club and brought it down upon King Arthur, his crown fell upon the ground.

"'You cannot continue to fight so recklessly, Your Highness,' said Merlin.

"'You are surely tired from battling for days on end. Leave this to Sir Kay and Sir Bedivere, so you may at least steady your breath.

"'Sir Kay and Sir Bedivere are knights who have devoted their lives to you, and you must believe in them.

"'Entrust your life to them, and they shall entrust theirs to you.

"'This bond of the Round Table is...your true power as king.

"'A devil or two is nothing before a king.'

"King Arthur thought that for the best, and he momentarily withdrew from the front lines to leave the giant to Sir Kay and Sir Bedivere.

"Then—"

John Sheep,
LAST ROUND ARTHUR, FIFTH VOLUME, FIFTH CHAPTER

"MY EXCALIBUR, THE STEEL SWORD OF CAMARADE-RIIIIIIIIIIIIIIIIIIIIIIIIIIIIIE!" Luna blared, drawing her sword with both hands as she swung it over her head.

In that moment, an awful light erupted from it, soaring upward as if to strike the heavens, like a titanic light threatening to cut down a giant's head from the clouds in a single stroke.

"Wh-what is that?!" Kujou shouted, forgetting to run away and becoming motionless.

"That's Luna's Excalibur... In the past, King Arthur went on a journey to slay a giant at Mont Saint-Michel and entrusted the battle to his knights so he could rest. Then, he cut down the giant in a single stroke... That sword is a symbol of that anecdote, an embodiment of the bond and trust between a King and vassal," said Rintarou.

"Wha...?!"

"That sword's power is pretty simple: 'Close your eyes and remain exposed *in front of an enemy*. Remain defenseless for a fixed amount of time, so the grand power of the sword can be released.'"

"What *is* that sword...? That sword..."

"I get what you want to say. It's impossible to use it on your own 'cause it takes the King out of the battle temporarily. Which makes it a useless, shitty sword, right?"

It was probably the most difficult Excalibur to use.

Luna's Excalibur couldn't compare to the Radiant Steel Sword of Glory, useful in practically any situation, particularly when battling with a group. It also couldn't compare to the Military Conquest Steel Sword, capable of providing matchless power in single combat.

When the Dame du Lac claimed it was the weakest sword, there was no point in refuting that. It was fatal to sheathe your sword and close your eyes in front of the enemy, leaving yourself defenseless.

It went without saying that numbers were important in combat. To temporarily pull out the King, the core of any group's power, went beyond common sense. And in the first place, the only time anyone would want to rely on a one-hit wonder was when they were already at an overwhelming disadvantage.

For these reasons, using this Royal Road meant that the group was risking their lives. On top of that, the King needed followers who'd actually leave their lives in the King's hands.

For example, they'd need to offer up their lives in the same way Sir Kay, Felicia, Sir Gawain, and Rintarou were fighting and believing in Luna now.

If they could fulfill those imposing conditions, they'd be able to use Royal Road exactly once. When it came to the *power* of this single stroke—Luna's was the strongest among all the Excaliburs.

"It was the weakest sword, an unusable sword—an unneeded sword. That's what I'd thought…," Rintarou emphasized, shrugging, as Kujou backed away, stumbling over his feet. "But in her hands, it might be the strongest sword there is."

"AHHHHHHHHHHHHHHHHHHHHHHHHHHHHHHHHHHH!"

Luna brought down her blade and its monolithic light that reached the heavens.

"Th-that's impossible!"

The whole thing came down, like the Tower of Babel collapsing down directly on Kujou. An aurora rained down from the sky, burying his vision under it as it fell.

He couldn't escape. He couldn't avoid it.

Where would he have even run in the first place?

"—AHHHHHHHHHHHHHHHHHHHHHHHHHHHHHHHHHHH!"

Kujou wailed shamefully as this destructive mallet came down on him from the heavens and cornered him.

"Impossible?! How can this be happening to me?! I was supposed to rule the entire wooooooooooooooooooooooooooooorld?!"

The light gushed forward, completely engulfing Kujou, swallowing him whole.

Everything was tragically charred, hot and white—

And the fake Camlann Hill was severed in two, disappearing along the end of that mystical light.

Heading to the New Battle

Here they were at an undisclosed location, following the death match.

"Hee-hee… They really got you there, didn't they, Mr. Kujou?"

"…You… Hmph, what do you want?"

A girl concealed in a jet-black robe smiled gleefully down on him as he rubbed Recovery Salve all over his scarred body. His face contorted in annoyance.

"Oh, looks like someone woke up on the wrong side of the bed. Show a little more gratitude. If I wasn't around, you and Sir Lancelot would've been turned into charcoal by Luna's hand by now. Why don't you give me more praise for using my magic to save you at the last minute?"

"Tch…" His reply emptily echoed in the room—what seemed to be a storage room—dim, dusty, and piled with stuff in the corners.

"…" Sir Lancelot quietly stood along the stone wall with his arms crossed.

They were somewhere in the international city of Avalonia. To be precise, this space was in this girl's netherworld.

"So what are you gonna do now, Mr. Kujou?"

"I'll concentrate on healing these wounds for a while and be on the lookout. Luna Artur and Rintarou Magami... They're a quite dangerous faction. I can't believe it, but I see them as the biggest obstacle now. I think it'd be wise to wait until the situation changes..."

"Oh? That's quite a craven plan for you."

"Hmph... Say what you want. It's not kingly to rush into things. Sometimes, exploring every avenue and method of escape are what make a great King."

"Well, I don't really mind. Please keep up your strength for the battle to come, Mr. Kujou." She smiled blankly.

"Hmph... Let's leave it at that." He changed subjects as he turned an icy glare at her. "How about you tell me some more details? What's your goal here? Why are you helping us...? Won't you tell me?" He let his eyes wash over her, taking stock of her. "*Tsugumi Mimori*...or should I say *Morgan le Fay*? Like that Rintarou Magami, you, too, are a reincarnation of a hero from the era of King Arthur...the oldest and most wicked sorceress in the world."

Morgan—a young student at Camelot International—Tsugumi Mimori showed him a penetratingly glacial smile from her spot in the shadows.

"Oh? Why, it's because I want you to win."

"That's strange. Then why did you make contact with Rintarou under my nose and pull him into this King Arthur Succession Battle?"

"Oh dear, so you did notice? Ha-ha-ha, I wonder why. Well... it's true. I'm the one who contacted and invited him to this international city."

"Hmph. Just when I think you're going to pretend to work with me and betray me... It wasn't as though you couldn't have assassinated me in my sleep when you brought in Rintarou Magami. Instead, you've been helping me even more than before, as though you really do want me to win this battle. What are you really plotting?"

"Who knows? I wonder what it could be?"

"…Whatever. That was the type of woman Morgan was, even in the legends of King Arthur. Anyway, you'll be useful to me no matter what happens. Keeping a treasonous snake like you tamed is my duty as a King." He snorted unpleasantly.

Tsugumi—Morgan—laughed at him in a peculiar way.

At long last, the King Arthur Succession Battle had started at the blessing of the Dame du Lac.

The battle to select the King to save the world…had been infiltrated by a sorceress, bringing chaos and confusion into the mix.

But at that moment, not a single one of them had a way of knowing that.

"Ahh…it's finally over."

"Yeah…"

A yawn slipped out of Rintarou's open mouth as Luna nodded.

They were at Sword Lake Beachside Park, surveying the sea beneath them and looking over the dark waters on the verge of dawn from their bench.

They were covered in lacerations, and their clothes were rags—so beat up that if anyone saw them, their eyes would leap out of their head, wondering what in the world had happened.

Thanks to Luna's Excalibur, the top floor of that Central City Park Hotel had been completely blown away and flattened out. After everything had ended, they'd run away as fast as they could. But the area around the hotel was probably in pandemonium at this very moment.

When they checked their phones, there were a smattering of rumors: mysterious gas explosion or terrorist attack by an undisclosed country.

They knew they'd done something terrible to the hotel, but the Dame du Lac would massage out the smaller details using some method or another.

Because Kujou reserved the entire top floor, no one had been injured, which was the only silver lining to this whole ordeal.

"Seriously, that was an absurd thing to do... You've got to use some discretion...," he grumbled.

"Wh-what?! I didn't have the time for that!" she defended herself, sullen. "Oh..."

She noticed something.

The sun peeked its face over the horizon, slowly starting to cut through the shadows.

It was the sunrise.

This long night was finally ending.

The two of them simply watched dawn break side by side.

"Um, so...," she started with some hesitation. "Thank you, Rintarou."

"What?"

"For coming back to me... You really are my best vassal, Rintarou!"

"You really are my best vassal, Merlin!"

Her face and words overlaid with someone nostalgic from far away and long ago.

It was the face of his precious friend, whom he'd vowed he would be with until everything finished—even though, in the very end, he hadn't been there for him.

"…"

For a while, Rintarou looked intently at her from the corner of his eyes.

"I think I understand just a little now why…in my past life…I served that Arthur," he whispered.

"Huh?"

He stood up and looked down at Luna. "Hmph, don't get any wrong ideas, you idiot! I haven't accepted you, King Airhead, as my King, okay?"

"Whaaaaaat?! Why not?!"

"I just wouldn't be able to sleep right if I abandoned you, since you're so similar to him! Well, I'll watch over you for a while. You better be thankful to Arthur!"

"Wh-what are you talking about?!"

"Well, make sure you put all you've got into it. You better become a great King who'll make me want to actually serve you. You know, a King like Arthur, overflowing with charm. If you do that…"

She suddenly started to get a little annoyed. "Wh-what?! All you ever talk about is Arthur this and Arthur that?! You idiot, Rintarou! Why are you making me jealous of my ancestor?!"

"Huh? Jealous? What does that mean…?"

"Uggggggggh! What is this?! I can't believe my biggest rival is my ancestor—and a guy, at that! The future is bleak!"

"Ummm…?"

"Plus, you don't remember anything at all! Normally, someone would remember at a time like this, wouldn't they?! How dense are you?! This is a crime! You're disrespectful!"

"Sorry, I've got no clue what you're talking about…"

They were going through their usual boisterous exchange.

"…Really now… You two are way too relaxed." Sir Kay, just

returning from the hotel after gathering information, placed herself below the two.

"Oh, how was it, Sir Kay?"

"Master Kujou is missing. Of course, it's reasonable to assume that he'd vanish without a trace, seeing when we were thrown out of the netherworld and thanks to the Excalibur."

"Right...so Mr. Kujou is out," said Luna.

"Those Dame du Lac are probably scratching their heads, wondering how this happened right about now," sneered Rintarou.

Kujou was dead. Even after hearing that, their expressions didn't change in the slightest.

It wasn't as though they would.

That was how things went in their world, right from the start.

"Though we've managed to defeat him, the battle has just begun... You cannot let this victory get to your head, Luna."

"Yes, indeed! You've always gotten careless and conceited right away, even when we were young!" maintained Felicia.

"Yes, don't do anything to hold back my liege!"

In that moment, Rintarou moved like a blur—and he latched onto their faces as they stood behind Sir Kay.

"Hey! Why are you guys here like you're. One. Of. Us?! We're supposed to be enemies!!"

"Ow—ouch, ouch, ouch, that hurts!"

"AHHHHHH! You're crushing my heaaaaad!"

They scampered back in a fluster as they shook off Rintarou's death grip.

"Oh, I see? Did you come to settle this? The sun's just come up and Gawain's powers are at their highest, so you thought this'd be a good opportunity? All right. In that case, I'll clean you up..."

The pitch-black Aura ripped out of Rintarou, drawing out his *Fomorian Transformation* and his sword.

"S-stop! Stop it! Please wait!"

"Y-yeah, Rintarou Magami! Until we reach the final stage of the succession battle, aren't we a united front and one in the same?! So put away your sword?! Please?!"

The pair said things he didn't understand, but he settled down, unimpressed.

"Hey, Luna? You didn't...?"

"Ah-ha-ha! Actually, I haven't told you yet, have I, Rintarou?!" She thrust out her chest as he stared at her with scorn.

"A-anyway, we forced a terrible King, Lord Gloria, to drop out, but if there are other Kings like that, the succession battle won't go smoothly, right?!" negotiated Felicia.

"W-we believe we should join forces for some time! Then, when the succession battle reaches its final stage, we shall have the battle to end all battles! Isn't that right?!" pleaded Sir Gawain.

"Ha-ha! Don't you need our power in the coming battles, too?!"

They spoke with great pride.

"Nope. We don't need you." He shot them down, expressionless and his sword still at the ready. "Why can't we just settle this right here and now?"

"Eeeeeeeeek?! Wait, please put away your swoooooord?!"

"W-wait, Rintarou Magami?! Just let us speak, and you'll understand! First, let's talk! Okay?!"

They trembled with tears in their eyes as they withdrew.

"Oh, come on, Rintarou. Don't say that," Luna placated.

"...Okay, okay, I get it. That's just the kind of person you are, I guess."

With that, Rintarou reluctantly put his swords away and ended his *Fomorian Transformation*.

"Seriously, I knew it from the start... All right, you guys, let's have a truce and an alliance for a while. But we're the ones who make the political decisions in this relationship. You're gonna follow Luna's direction, mkay?"

"Oh-ho-ho-ho-ho! If you really want to have an alliance with us, then I suppose we'll simply have to ally with you! Oh, well, I guess *it's our only choice*! Oh, it's such a crime to be beautiful!"

"Hey, Rintarou Magami! Just because my King is cute and beautiful, if you dare lay a hand on her, I, Sir Gawain, a knight among knights, shall never forgive you!"

"On second thought, I think I really should take care of you guys right now. Stay right there."

""EEEEEEEEEEEEEEEEEEEEEEEEEEK?!""

Facing his sword, Felicia and her knight screamed and hugged each other.

"Actually, Gawain, dear? Did you forget that I was Merlin? As Merlin, I've got a little something to say to you for your major role in breaking apart the Round Table. Actually, I've got a mountain of things I'd like to discuss…"

"H-help meeeeeeeeeeeeeeeeeeeeeeeeeeeeeeeeeeeeeee?!"

A dark Aura seeped out from Rintarou as he limply held his swords in each of his hands while slowly approaching Sir Gawain and Felicia, scrambling to their feet to run away. "Seriously, those guys always get carried away…"

"Ah-ha-ha-ha-ha!"

Not going after them, Rintarou simply watched them scamper away from behind as he put his swords away in exasperation.

Luna giggled with glee. Sir Kay was spent and sighed.

"Oh my, I wonder what's going to happen now…"

"It'll be fine, Sir Kay. I'm sure it'll all turn out okay," she assured, even as Sir Kay was uneasy. "Rintarou's here… Everyone's here, so…I'm sure it'll be okay."

"It'd be great if it turned out that way…"

"Hmph…" Rintarou seemed slightly embarrassed as he snorted and took in the glittering sunrise on the horizon.

This breathtaking scene seemed to hint at a promising future.

But the battle had just begun, and the future ahead would be difficult one…

"Well, I think things are gonna be kinda fun from here on out."

Without even noticing it himself, Rintarou was beaming.

AFTERWORD

Hello, I'm Taro Hitsuji.

This time, my newest novel *Last Round Arthurs* has gone to print.

I have endless gratitude for those involved in the editing and publication process and those who picked up this book. Thank you all very much!

"Mr. Hitsuji, Mr. Hitsuji, won't you write a new book with the legend of King Arthur as its theme?"

This book came to be because of my editor's words.

Honestly, at the same time, I was thinking *He's trying to give me a pretty ambitious killer pass!* (LOL)

I mean, the world is already saturated with manga and games about King Arthur. I thought I wouldn't change anything, even if I did a book now...

As I started to dismiss it, my editor gave me an even more insane killer pass.

"It's fine. You just have to make King Arthur a useless bum."

W-w-wait just a second?! That won't work! No matter what I do, King Arthur could never be useless!

This is basically the image the world has of King Arthur, right?

1. A knight king, noble and fair with dauntless courage, and

2. An ideal, just king who constantly fought for his people and for peace, and

3. A tragic king, filled with regret and broken dreams—unable to ever reach his lofty goals.

Because these are the expected characteristics of King Arthur, if you took them away, he wouldn't be King Arthur anymore. In other words, King Arthur and a good-for-nothing simply don't go together... At least, that's what I'd thought at the time.

Well, anyway. I began by trying to get together some resources and materials on the legends, so I ordered Thomas Malory's *The Legends of King Arthur*. (It was superexpensive!)

At its start, the legends weren't any more than rumors and stories passed down from knights in various parts of England, but the decisive edition that compiled everything together into one story was this Thomas Malory's *The Legends of King Arthur* (also called *Le Morte Darthur*).

In other words, the book should be called the original origin story for all the various King Arthur legends.

I pored over the book, but my first impression was...*What is this even?* *sweats nervously*

It turns out the original King Arthur was scum (LOL). He'd violate and impregnate passing women or plan a surprise attack on an enemy from behind if they were too strong to beat (and he'd still lose). And in order to deal with his unwanted child, Mordred, who was prophesized to kill him, he kills all the children born in the same year (and even after all that trouble, Mordred still survives). If an enemy country tried to make him obey their rules, he'd be all like *Shut up! You obey me, you idiot!* He'd start an *invasion* (never mind building up defenses) more out of anger than justice...and the stories went on and on.

I mean, he was a completely different offbeat king compared to his image as the just-knight king.

And when you think about it, that's obvious. During his time, strength was justice, winning was the will of God, might was right... That was just how things were. There was just no way our modern concepts of justice would've existed back then. Even the concept of chivalry didn't come to existence until way later.

At the same time, I saw how the current "fair knight king of justice" King Arthur was nothing more than a figment of someone's imagination. We've projected our own—or rather, all our ideals to this image of King Arthur, blowing him out of proportion as a cult hero.

There are just as many legends of King Arthur as there are authors.

In that case, I knew I could write my ideal legend—for myself, by myself!

This new book *Last Round Arthurs* has Thomas Malory's *The Legends of King Arthur* as its base with the addition of many extreme interpretations, made by yours truly. Set on the stage of a modern society divided between the real world and illusory world, this new legend of King Arthur started to reveal itself to me bit by bit. Though it has the same roots as the existing legends, it branches into something completely different.

I've already made a mess in the first volume. For example, by making that one famous knight an underdog and that other famous knight innocent...

Of course, I always have mainstream appeal and clichés in mind! The heretical main character is Rintarou Magami, and the scum King Arthur is played by the heroine Luna. Knowing they're both quite the characters, I plan to make this series a fast-paced, refreshing, fun story with them at center. Even if it follows the same approach as the *Akashic Records*, I think I've created a story with a different flavor and approach to an old favorite.

And the illustrator Haimura really breathed life into the world of *Last Round Arthurs*. Thanks so very much, Haimura!

I also want to thank my managing editor! Now that I think back on it, we had more arguments and staticky back-and-forth than usual over this novel, but the reason I can share this novel with the world is, of course, all thanks to you!

I hope you enjoy this new King Arthur legend that came to be because of all the people backing it up.

Taro Hitsuji

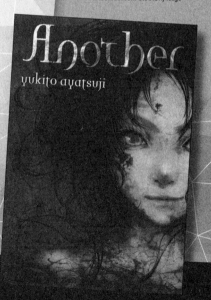